MW01124278

STAY CONNECTED

Join the exclusive group where all the cool kids hang out... Olivia's secret club for cool ladies! Consider this your formal invitation to a world of hot guys, fun people, and your fellow book lovers. Olivia hangs out in this group all the time. She made the group specifically for readers like you to come together and share their lives and interests, especially regarding the hot guys from her novels.

Check it out! Everyone in there is amazing, and you'll fit right in.

https://www.facebook.com/groups/LilaJeanOliviaAsh/

Sign up for email alerts of new releases AND an exclusive bonus novella from the Nighthelm Guardian series, *City of the Rebel Runes*, the prequel to *City of Sleeping Gods* only available to subscribers.

https://wispvine.com/newsletter/olivia-ash-email-signup/

Enjoying the series? Awesome! Help others discover the Dragon Dojo Brotherhood by leaving a review at Amazon.

http://mybook.to/DDB1

FATE OF DRAGONS

Book Two of the Dragon Dojo Brotherhood

OLIVIA ASH

BOOK DESCRIPTION

DRAGON DOJO BROTHERHOOD BOOK TWO:
FATE OF DRAGONS

A dangerous and cruel dragon shifter is holding my sister hostage.

And I am going to *kill* him. With my bare hands, if I have to.

He wants to trade—Irena's life, for mine.

For my freedom. For the ancient and deadly dragon magic I fused with when his cronies kicked me into a pit to die.

I came back from the dead, and I brought the fury of hell with me. Now, they're running scared—as they should. All of them, except this guy.

As the cherry on this toxic pie, my mentor is hunting me, too. She's using every skill she ever taught me to track me down and lock me away.

My mentor trained me to obey her, and she's pissed that I won't bow down to her anymore. Determined to drain my magic, Zurie wants to reprogram my brain with enough drugs to make me an obedient little assassin again.

It won't happen. And the poor fool who hurts my sister—well, he's in for an early grave.

CONTENTS

CHAPTER ONE

T he hunt is *on*.

I crouch in the thick underbrush, my eyes narrowing slightly as I zero in on my prey.

Tucker Chase presses his back against a tree thirty feet away, peering around it with a grim expression as he searches for me. My eyes rove over his hard body, across his pecs as they press against his black military-issue shirt. The fabric strains against his thick biceps, the color of the threads almost a perfect match for the dark stubble on his strong jaw.

Those green eyes of his briefly flit toward my hiding place, but he scans past me instantly.

Good. He doesn't see me.

I look for the black flag tied to his belt, and sure enough, it hangs over the many pockets he usually keeps stocked with an assortment of firearms and knives.

My gorgeous weapons expert doesn't know he's about to lose our little game.

He sneaks into the shadows of the forest, and I have to admit I'm impressed. We've been working on his stealth, trying to hone his ability to slip silently through the night, and he's getting *much* better.

Tucker accidentally sets his foot on a twig, but he notices it this time and hesitates before the stick cracks beneath his shoe. Gently, he lifts his foot and steps aside to a clear patch of dirt before continuing.

I smile with pride.

Still, he's technically my prey right now, and I'm not about to let him—or any of my men—win.

What can I say? I'm a sore loser.

I sprint through the forest, silent as a ghost, and I'm on him in seconds. Before he can even turn around, I kick out his knees and tackle him to the ground.

We fall, rolling through the dirt, and I pin him to the forest floor with one arm against his chest. My legs hook around his, rendering him immobile while I wrap my hand around his flag.

His eyebrows shoot up in surprise, and before he can say a thing, I tug the flag off his belt.

Our eyes lock. I smirk in victory and rip his flag in half with my teeth, winking as I shoot him a dashing smile.

"Death," he moans melodramatically. "The cold spear of Hades sails through my heart!" With one hand on his brow, he arches his back like a bad actor trying to land a leading role. "For I am betrayed by the woman I love! She has scorned me, ripped my soul in twain!"

I chuckle and stand, stashing the torn flag in my back pocket as a victory token. "Drama queen."

"Betrayed," he moans again, eyes shut as he really loses himself in his tragic little death scene.

I laugh. "You're such an idiot."

"You love it." He grins and blows me a kiss.

Chuckling, I jog off into the forest to find my next mark.

Since Jace wouldn't play our game, only Drew and Levi are left for me to find.

If I'm being honest with myself, there's no chance I'll

find Levi. My only hope with him is wait for him to attack and tug off his flag before he can get mine.

Levi's just too good—even for me, and I still don't know how a feral dragon got to be so stealthy. He could be in the trees above me and I wouldn't even know.

Suspicious, I peek up into the branches, the hair on my neck standing on end as I wonder where he is.

Nope, nothing.

Surrounded by silence, I press my back against a trunk and listen. Eyes closed, I let my other senses take over as I search for Drew instead.

The quiet rustle of leaves catches my attention—about twenty feet to my left, a large man with a slow and confident gait walks through the forest toward me.

Drew.

Gotcha.

I dip around the tree to remain unseen and climb a nearby oak, perching on a thick lower limb as I wait for him to walk under me. Though I might be able to take him down like I did Tucker, I highly doubt it.

Drew is built like a tank, and tanks don't go down easy.

As expected, the dragon shifter walks below me, his eyes scanning the tree where I was moments ago. As a dragon, he can probably sense me in a vague way—they all seem able to do that.

I frown, hoping that little ability of theirs fades over time.

Below me, Drew pauses, frowning, his brown hair and beard perfectly framing his strong face. Shoulders back, his broad chest is wide and solid. From his biceps to his neck to his thighs, he's pretty much pure muscle.

And the way he walks—he moves like a king.

I wish I knew more about him, but he's like a file full of juicy intel I can't access. This man is brimming with secrets, and I know I'll never coax them all out of him.

Without a sound, I leap, angling my shoulder so that I can hit the space between his shoulder blades and take him down.

Ideally.

Instead of taking him to the ground, I smack against his solid body. The full force of all my strength only throws him slightly off balance.

Ugh.

It didn't work.

With a huff of annoyance, I roll across the leaves and slide, jumping to my feet as he turns to face me.

It's infuriating. Even with my enhanced strength from the dragon magic bubbling in my body, I can't *touch* this guy.

With a cocky smirk, he charges me.

His shoulder hits mine, and he takes me down. I've never faced an adversary like Drew, and I have to confess, I'm grateful he's on my side because almost nothing I do fazes him.

He pins me to the earth, his hands on my wrists as he straddles me. All the while, that smirk of his remains on his face, equal parts tantalizing and maddening.

"You're supposed to tackle your opponent," he says with a dark chuckle. "Not bounce off of them."

"Har, freaking *har*." I hook my leg around his and, much to my delight, manage to flip him onto his back.

I chuckle in victory, but my moment doesn't last long.

Using nothing but brute force, he pushes against my shoulders and lifts me effortlessly into the air.

Dang it, I hate how *strong* he is. It's like fighting a gorilla who specializes in witty one-liners.

With a few deft twists of his powerful body, he pins me beneath him again. This time, he spreads my legs with his knees.

Though it's probably to keep me from hooking my leg around him again, it also sends shivers of warmth and delight up my thighs. I can feel a rush of heat burning along my neck, up to my cheeks, as his strong body presses against mine, nothing but muscle and dominance and control.

"You're blushing," he says with a wicked little grin. "It's cute."

"Shut *up*." I wriggle my wrist free of his hand and reach for the flag dangling at his waist, but he angles his body out of the way. I'm a second too late as he tilts his hips, teasing me with the flag that's just out of my reach.

A roar cuts through the forest above us, and Levi dives seconds later. Drew rolls out of the way as Levi's claws narrowly miss the flag at his waist, but I suspect Levi doesn't care about winning. He was just giving me an unfair assist.

He's such a sweetheart. But this is a game, and there's only one winner.

His black flag is tied around his neck, a dark ribbon shivering in the wind as he soars. He tilts his head back as he breaks through the canopy again, winking as he breaks through the leaves.

"Cheater," Drew says under his breath, shooting me a knowing glance.

I shrug, brushing off my shirt. "I have no idea what you're talking about."

"Uh huh." Drew charges me again, and this time, I roll out of the way before he can take me down. Relying on my own brute strength won't work against a man like him, so I have to be clever.

"You can move faster than that, can't you?" I chuckle, teasing him, goading him into making a mistake.

But I wonder if Drew even *makes* mistakes.

He charges again, all focused power and muscle this time, and I once more duck out of the way. This time, however, he grabs my belt. My hips are pulled toward him as he slides to a stop, his fingers hooked through my belt loops. He tugs me toward him, my heels leaving skid marks in the dirt as I writhe in his grip.

The downside of sparring with my men is that I don't *really* want to hurt them. If I'm being honest, I'm holding back a little bit.

Okay, I'm holding back a *lot.*

If it weren't Drew, I would raise my hands and try to summon the deadly magic deep within me, the white light that has already claimed lives by burning my victims to dust. Even though I can't control it yet, it sparks in moments of need, moments like this when my opponent has the upper hand.

But this is Drew. I'm not going to hurt *him*.

He pulls me to him, pressing my hips against his, and flurries of desire flutter through my navel as he holds me close.

Grinning down at me, he reaches his other hand ever so slightly under my shirt, running this thumb across my skin as he slowly reaches for the flag at my belt.

But I'm faster.

I yank his off seconds before he reaches mine, and he closes his eyes in defeat. With a sigh, he leans his forehead against mine and chuckles, abandoning his hunt for my flag.

Instead, he wraps his hands around my waist. The movement sends ribbons of need through my core, and it's getting harder to ignore them.

To ignore my desire for *him*.

A surge of heat races down my thighs as I watch his face, momentarily lost in those dark eyes. They briefly flash gold—the color of his dragon's eyes—and I wonder if he's fighting his own flurries of longing.

But our game isn't over yet.

"You going to let go?" I ask playfully, trying to ignore the fact that it would be almost impossible to wriggle out of his incredibly strong grip.

"If I must." He releases me and takes a step back, looking off into the forest as he tries to regain his self-control.

Levi breaks through the canopy like a missile through the air, his claws outstretched as he aims for the flag at my waist.

I stuff Drew's flag in my pocket and dive out of the way as he sails past. He lands, the ground shaking beneath him, kicking up dust and soil as he slides to a stop. He turns to face me, tail flicking gleefully as he looks for another chance to spring, totally immersed in the game now that it's just him and me.

He's a sweetheart, sure, but he's no pushover. Levi's one of the best fighters I've ever seen—and considering I was raised in an assassin's guild, that's really saying something.

As Levi and I circle each other, Tucker jogs up and leans against a tree to watch the show.

But someone else is behind him.

"Are you all *still* out here?" Jace asks with an air of annoyance as he jogs up to us. "Rory, you need to train to control your magic, not run around the woods."

I groan, the thrill of my sparring match with Levi dissolving in a rush.

Ugh. No fair.

I gesture to Levi. "I was about to win!"

Levi snorts in exasperation, and I know that look he's giving me. *You wish,* it says.

I'm a bit surprised that I didn't feel Jace getting closer— with our strange connection, I can feel him almost all of the time. It's just… fuzzy. I know he's nearby, but not *where*—or how close.

I guess I'm starting to unconsciously tune it out, and that worries me.

I do *not* want to be surprised by Jace Goodwin.

"Come on." Jace nods to the towering black spires of the embassy behind him. "I finished a new training arena for you where no one will notice your power surges."

I rub my neck. On one hand, I'm grateful—Jace is doing

everything he can to ensure I'm safe and that no one knows the true depths of my abilities.

On the other hand, he's a total buzzkill.

"But *Mom,* we're *playing!*" Tucker says in a mocking tone, adding a bit of childish whine just to get under Jace's skin.

It works.

"Can it, Tucker," the dojo master snaps. "Rory needs to master this magic, or it's going to control *her.*"

"It's fine, guys," I say to keep the peace.

After all, Jace is right.

Not that I would *tell* him that, but still.

Levi snorts, a huff of frigid air escaping the ice dragon's nose as he brushes his wing tenderly against my back. I flash him a reassuring smile, and he takes off into the canopy, breaking through the overhanging branches and showering us with leaves as he flies off to do his dragonish thing.

He's been heading off into the forest more often, lately, and I'm not sure what he does when he's gone. He always comes back, though, and that's all that matters to me.

"Fine," Drew says, his deep voice booming. "Well, since

the buzzkill needs you, I'll go for a run." The fire dragon brushes past me. Though he doesn't touch me, he still somehow manages to set my body ablaze with desire as he comes close. He briefly looks down at me as he leaves, and that playful smirk of his tells me everything I need to know.

He knows *exactly* what he does to me. To my body. He knows how he makes me sizzle with need.

Ass.

Tucker winks at me and jogs off toward the castle without another word. He knows I'll be sleeping in his bed tonight, and that's apparently enough for him to not make a scene in front of Jace.

I chuckle. These men are ridiculous. Possessive. Dominating. A little grumpy.

I love it.

When it's just me and Jace in the field, his frown disappears. He watches me for a moment, his arms crossed, his face impossible to read as he looks me over.

"Yes?" I ask, a little exasperated by his reserved expression.

"Nothing," he says softly. "Let's get started." With that, he walks toward the embassy, no doubt expecting me to simply follow.

I sigh. Obviously, he still isn't okay with the fact that I grew up as a Spectre, raised from birth to kill dragons like him. It's not like I had a choice, but the hatred most dragons feel for Spectres is too strong to ignore.

I get it. I see why he's having trouble with this, even if I'm different. Even if I defied my mentor—the Ghost—to keep him alive.

And I suspect if it weren't for the mate-bond connection between us, he might not ignore his hatred.

Though I'm not sure where Jace and I stand, I have to admit I respect him, both as a man and a fighter. He and Drew came for me, both of them risking so much more than their lives to keep me safe—their titles, their reputations, the respect of their peers.

They attacked fellow dragons for me, after all. Even though the dragons we fought were the Vaer—the most hated dragon family in the world—there are still strict dragon laws to protect them.

It doesn't matter if the Vaer technically lured me into a trap. There are still more protections for *them* than for *me.*

Or anyone who *helps* me.

As I trudge through the forest, I sigh and stick my hands in my pockets. A happy little sliver of delight snakes through me at the thought of the rescue, of how all four of my men rode into battle at my side.

These guys are making me soft, yeah, but I kind of like it. I would raze cities to protect them.

My team. My family.

My men.

CHAPTER TWO

I n an isolated patch of the embassy's forest, Jace sits on a boulder as he watches me practice.

He lounges like an emperor, an elbow propped on one knee as he watches in silence, observing my every move, no doubt piecing together clues he's picked up in our time together now that he knows what I am.

What I was born to be.

An assassin, through and through.

I try to ignore him. To tune him out. To focus on the brilliant nature around us, on the mist rising out of the ravine barely twenty feet away.

The location he chose overlooks the cliffs surrounding the embassy, with just enough tree cover to mask any magical mishaps as I learn to control the wild power within me.

Well, *most* mishaps, anyway.

In the distance, visible through gaps in the canopy, the towering black spires of the dojo cut through the clouds. Thankfully, it's far enough away in the very real chance things go awry during our training.

After all, the first time we trained together, I destroyed half the wall of his *regular* training facility.

"Focus," Jace demands, his voice tense and deep.

I glare at him, annoyed. "I'm *trying.*"

Perhaps I should have simply nodded and played along, but he's pissing me off. He's not really helping, just shouting obscure commands.

Frankly, I expected more direction from one of the best magical masters of our time.

In response to my curt little reply, I expect anger. Aggravation. Terse banter, maybe.

Instead, he softens, his shoulders relaxing as he looks me over. "I know, but you need to try *harder.*"

I frown.

"Here." He stands and walks behind me, and small sparks of energy blister across my skin as he nears.

This connection we have—I'll never understand it. The way my body aches for him, longs to be near him, craves him completely. Sparks of energy and light fizzle within me at the thought of being near him, and my thoughts always trail to the idea of laying on my back, wrapping my legs around him as he—

Rory, damn it, I chide myself. *Focus.*

As he stands behind me, my traitorous body reactively leans into his hard chest, and a blister of desire bubbles through me at his touch.

Tenderly, he sets his hands on my arms. With his mouth at my ear, he leans his head against mine, and it's all I can do not to melt into him.

Damn it all, I'm a fierce warrior, not a schoolgirl.

This mate-bond of ours makes me putty in his hands, and I hate it. I hate not having control.

I tense, ready to break away, to ask what the hell he thinks he's doing.

"Trust me," he says quietly, as if anticipating my irritation. "Just try this."

I groan in frustration, furious with my treasonous body and the inability to control myself around him.

"Listen for the pulse of your magic," he says quietly, in a voice that's almost hypnotic. "Reach for it. Touch it."

"That doesn't make sense."

"Just close your eyes," he says, a little annoyed this time. "*Try*, damn it."

With a huff, I indulge him and press my eyes shut, waiting for any indication that he's not just blowing hot air out his ass.

At first, there's nothing but the howl of the wind as it kicks up the mist in the ravine. The clatter of leaves in the trees above me. His breath as it tickles my neck. The warmth of his arms pressed against mine.

The way he envelops me, the way my spine curves toward him instinctively, as if he's my home.

I almost break away. It's too much. My impulse is to push away from the controlling thunderbird. To never indulge him, to never give in, to never let him know what he does to me. He wants to lock me away in a tower, hoard me like a treasure and never let me live for fear I might die.

But then, soft as a whisper, I feel it.

A trembling little pulse.

Weak.

Quiet.

But it's there.

It hums in my core, in the center of my body, a dull echo of my heartbeat. It flickers in and out, stronger and weaker, totally inconsistent and out of control.

I *feel* it.

"Good," Jace says, somehow picking up on my new clarity. "Focus on that and nothing else."

That's a little tough when his lips are virtually pressed against my ear, but fine. I'll try.

I frown, brow furrowed as I focus, listening to the little blip of energy deep within me. "What is this?"

"Focus," he says without answering.

Good lord, he's almost as infuriating as Drew.

With my surging annoyance, the pulse grows stronger. It flickers and burns, filling me, and the telltale signs of an episode begin to spark and fizzle along my fingers.

"Wait, no—" I drop my focus, worried now about the magic burning through my blood, but Jace never moves a muscle.

"It's okay," he calmly says. His voice is soothing. He runs his hands up my arms, holding my shoulders tight, pressing me against his body.

It works.

The magic begins to fade. As he soothes my worry, the sparks retreat.

"How did you..." I stare at my hands, losing my train of thought.

He presses his jaw against the side of my head, tender and sweet. "You're more powerful than a thunderbird, but our magic is similar."

Before I can help myself, I smile, grateful for his knowledge. Even though I hate to admit it, I've been too hard on him. He mastered thunderbird magic—if there's one person alive who can help me master my own powers, it's Jace.

I don't really know whether or not to be grateful for *that,* though. He's handsome, strong, and an amazing fighter, but he's still an infuriating control freak.

"Try again," he commands, the tenderness dissolving from his voice.

Ah, there's the Jace I know.

I indulge him yet again, and as I tap into the pulse once

more, it grows. This time, it's a slower build, and though I feel it burn along my fingers again, it doesn't feel out of control this time.

I open my eyes to find white light dancing over my hands and up my arms. It sings and shimmers, beautiful and blinding.

As the tension builds in my arms, I think about all the weapons I've had, about how much easier a knife is to wield—and how much more power this light possesses.

Briefly, the light takes the shape of a knife. It's fleeting, gone in a flash, but I know without a doubt what I saw.

And it makes me wonder just what this power can do. What my limits really are.

It seems like, perhaps, there might not be any. Or if there are, they far exceed anything I could possibly conceive of.

"Your magic is tied to your emotions," Jace says, interrupting my thoughts. "To control it, you must first control yourself."

"Thanks, sensei." I roll my eyes.

Jesus. Talk about a cliché.

"I mean it," he says with a soft chuckle. "Your power surges in moments of need, when you have no other options. You let *it* control *you*. It's because you don't consider your magic a weapon—not really. You haven't been able to control it, so you don't consider it until you have no other option."

"Well, yeah, but—"

"So," he interrupts, "you need to practice with it, touch it every moment you can, any time you can. Make it a habit to check in with it, to be mindful of it, to be aware of what it's doing at any given moment. Connect with it, cherish it, breathe into it."

"You want me to build a relationship with my magic?" I ask dryly. "Like it's a person?"

"You can say that, sure." He shrugs and runs his hands down my arms, wrapping his fingers around my wrists.

"But—"

"It wants what you want, and vice versa." He nuzzles the side of my head in an uncharacteristically tender motion. "You fuel each other."

As his warm body contours to the curve of my back, I can't help but wonder if he's still talking about the magic—or about us.

"Think about what makes you happy," he says, his voice low and gravely.

I close my eyes, and that's easy. Before I found this magic, it would have been hard to say what gave me joy. The vague idea of freedom, maybe. Time alone. My sister Irena—and that's about it.

But now, I have Tucker. Drew. Levi. Even Jace. They make my heart sing, filling me with joy I sometimes doubt I deserve.

True happiness.

I'm beginning to trust them, to trust someone other than my mentor. Though that ignites a flicker of doubt within me, it's easy to squash.

They've proven themselves to me time and time again.

As I think about my men, my magic gets stronger. I smile as I connect with it, feeling solid, feeling unstoppable, feeling like nothing in the world could hurt me —not when I have a light like this within me.

My thoughts turn to Mason, to killing him, to ending the fight with a man who tried to kill me repeatedly. Of feeling the rush of victory as his body fell to the ground. Of knowing he's gone—forever.

With that, the light within me gets even stronger.

"Good," Jace says in my ear. "Keep going."

My thoughts turn to Irena, to the childhood we made the most of, to the bond we share.

It's not long, however, before those thoughts turn sour. Before I remember she's locked away in some Vaer stronghold, getting sicker by the day.

I frown, and the light within me weakens.

It's infuriating to simply sit and wait for Jace and Drew to work their contacts, to get information for me—but I have no other recourse. Short of breaking into Jace's command center again, I'm out of options. Zurie and Diesel aren't going to help me. None of the Knights or Spectres would dare give me intel, and none of the dragon families really like me all that much either.

I'm used to being on my own—but I'm also used to having a lead. And right now, I have nothing.

"Rory, stop," Jace says, a twinge of concern in his voice. "Whatever you're thinking about—"

But I can't.

I can't stop.

Zurie is after me, and she wants to reprogram this independence out of my head. She wants to load me up on hallucinogens and who knows what else, throw me in the dungeons below her home, and *reset* me. *Fix* me. Make me her obedient little slave again.

She'll kill my men, kill Irena, kill everyone and everything I love if that's what it takes.

And I won't let her.

I refuse.

Deep within me, the magic boils. It pops and surges as I
lose myself in my thoughts, bubbling over as I lose
control.

Jace's grip tightens on my forearms. "Rory, wait—"

But it's too late.

A blast of white light rips from my hands, soaring into
the ravine, carving a deep hole in the edge of the cliff as
the rock takes the brunt of my magic.

I fall to my knees, and Jace is there in an instant. My
vision blurs, but he holds me tight, holds me to him.
His arm around my chest keeps me from falling to the
dirt.

My world spins. I feel like I'm moving, but I don't
know what's the sky and what's the ground.

It takes a moment for me to regain my composure, and
when I do, I look up to find Jace watching me with a
worried expression on his face. I'm lying in his arms, my
head against his chest as he leans against the boulder.

He runs his fingers through my hair, and as much as I hate to admit it, the soothing sensation of his touch feels amazing. Every stroke sends a flurry of delight through me, making me feel protected. Secure.

Safe.

"That was good," he says with a smile.

I laugh. "That was *shit*."

He chuckles. "I mean, it wasn't *great...*"

"Thanks. Good pep talk."

"You're getting it." He sits up, helping me do the same, and I groggily take in my surroundings.

I'm sitting on the dirt, the hole in the mountain behind me still smoking a little. It gives me a glimpse into the ravine below, like someone took a massive hole-punch to the edge of the rocky cliff.

"You know, you've got to stop destroying my embassy." He grins. "You need to leave me something to lead, after all."

I shake my head at the stupid joke, but I can't suppress a smile. "Sorry."

We sit in silence, and for a moment, everything between us is fine. Good, even. He manages to not piss me off for a solid five minutes, and I think that's a record.

"Rory," he says, his smile fading.

Ah, crap.

Here it comes.

"Yeah?"

"The mate-bond never lies." He sighs, draping one arm over his propped knee as he stares off into the forest. "Whatever you were before we met, you aren't evil."

"Gee, thanks," I say dryly.

"I see the way you look at Drew," he adds, voice getting darker. He frowns, and he won't look at me. "At Tucker."

"And?" I lean back on my hands, daring him to finish that thought.

He really, *really* shouldn't.

"A mated dragon never shares." He glares at me, barely holding back his possessive anger, and I can practically see the sparks coming out of his ears. "Since we aren't fully mated yet, I can't control what you do, but—"

"You will never control what I do," I interrupt, giving him a cold glare.

Driving the point home.

He scowls.

"Get that through your thick skull," I demand. It comes out a little harsher than I intended, but I've about had it with this guy. I'm drawn to him, my body betrays me every time we're close, and yet I can't stand his possessive nature.

It's one thing to want to protect someone you care about. But Jace—damn it, he just takes it to the next level.

I maintain eye contact, never once breaking our gaze. He glares with the fury of a sun, and that withering scowl has probably sent more than one recruit scampering away in fear.

But he doesn't scare *me*.

"Rory, the mate-bond is serious. It's unbreakable. It's a vow of—"

"Oh, shove it." I stand, entirely done with this conversation. "I may not know the ins and outs of how the mate-bond works, Jace, but I know enough to get the gist. It's not that you don't share, it's that you don't *want* to. You want to control me, lock me away, keep me safe and other misguided nonsense." I laugh at the very idea. "You don't trust my ability to take care of myself. You know what I am, what I was trained to be, what I've *done,* and you still don't think I'm capable of holding my own in a fight." My nose wrinkles in exasperation as I sink into my anger. "I mean, the *nerve.*"

"It's not—"

"And *furthermore,*" I say, interrupting whatever little tirade he was about to launch into. "You don't seem to care about *my* ways. Have you stopped to think about *that?*"

"I—uh," he stutters, entirely caught off guard.

"Shocker." I roll my eyes. "You make all these infuriating demands of me, but have you ever paused to think about *my* culture? Even once? I'm not a one-man kind of girl. I may not be Zurie's little puppet anymore, but that doesn't change the fact I was raised with Spectres. That's my normal. My culture. A Spectre doesn't take just one partner."

"Don't *say* that here." He looks around, clearly concerned of being overheard.

That's cute and all, but I scoped this place out the second we got here, and except for my brief episode, I've been paying close attention. The nearest guard is a sky scout, and he loops around every twenty minutes. We're in the clear.

This is yet another reason he pisses me off—he doesn't understand what I can do. He's seen me in action, and yet he can't fathom the idea that I took my first kill when I was twelve.

I'm not a goddamn damsel.

I cross my arms, furious. "You don't share, but I *do.* You expect me to just adapt and live like you? You don't even *ask.* You don't *care.* I may be at war with the Ghost, but that doesn't change how I was raised."

"Rory, look," he says with a deep and frustrated sigh. "We want different things. I get it. And maybe with time we'll figure this out, but for now I just need you to be careful. Okay?"

It takes all I have to not shake him by the collar. What the hell does he *think* I've been doing? Taking candy from strange white vans? Inviting my enemies over for tea?

"The bosses know you're here." He runs his hand through his hair. "All of them."

I frown, my fury temporarily dissolving with the shock of the news. "*All* of them? How did they find out? Was it Guy?"

Jace grimaces at the traitors name. "No, I doubt it was

Guy. I suspect the Vaer Boss had something to do with it after our attack on Mason's stronghold."

Ah. A bit of petty revenge. I groan in frustration.

He looks me over. "You're safe here, for now, but I can't say how much longer that will be the case. It's an act of war to attack an embassy, but some people are willing to go to war over you." He looks at me with a strange, almost ominous expression, and the deeper meaning is blatantly clear.

The mate-bond is *intense*, even if we don't entirely get along. If someone came for me, Jace would send his army after them—and probably rip out my attacker's throat himself.

"Jace," I say quietly, trying to diffuse the tension. "You know almost nothing about me."

"And vice versa." He crosses his arms and leans against a nearby tree, that intense gaze of his never waning. "But the mate-bond never lies."

"So you keep saying." I rub my face, irritated with his riddles.

"My dragon chose you, Rory." He relaxes a bit, sighing as his expression softens. "Whatever happens between us, there's no one else for me."

I scoff.

Jesus. No pressure.

I open my mouth to retort, but the rustle of leaves in the distance catches my attention. Someone is running toward us, breathing hard and heavy, and I snap my jaw closed. No one but Jace needs to hear what I was about to say, so I swallow the thought for now.

"Look, let's just—let's drop it." He groans and rubs his jaw, apparently oblivious to the scout running toward us. "There's more urgent issues to worry about."

"Like the Bosses?"

I have to admit, I'm grateful for the change of topic.

He nods. "They're planning a gathering and want to meet you."

"Want to size me up, you mean."

"Well, yeah." He shrugs. "You should still go."

I laugh. "Why the hell would I do that? Irena is still out there, and—"

"Rory," he says softly, disarming me with a deeply concerned expression. "This is your one chance to make a strong impression on them. You—"

"Jace!" the guard shouts, a short way off now.

I have to hand it to the soldier headed for us. He's fast.

Jace snaps his head toward the voice, his tender expression dissolving into the familiar mask he wears around the soldiers and students of the dojo.

Around me, he can be soft and endearing—but around everyone else, he's the playful bad boy I met in the courtyard when I first came to the embassy.

I don't know if I'll ever figure this guy out. Not really.

"Promise me you'll go," Jace says quietly, shifting his attention briefly toward me as the guard nears.

I cross my arms, unconvinced. "I'll think about it."

He briefly smiles in gratitude, and I wonder if he expected me to simply ignore him.

Wouldn't be the first time. Or the last, for that matter.

"Jace!" the guard says again, gasping for air as he finally breaks into the clearing. "It's urgent. We need you back at the dojo right away."

"Fine. Come on, you," Jace says with a smirk and a nod to me. "You'll probably eavesdrop anyway."

I chuckle and jog after them. Maybe I was wrong—perhaps he's starting to understand me after all.

CHAPTER THREE

When we enter Jace's war room, I can tell something is desperately wrong.

Four of Jace's lieutenants stand at the far end of a long, slender table that fills most of the room. They're silent and pale, arms crossed as they stare at the floor. The windows to our left let in sunlight, casting thin rays across a large pine box on the table. It's maybe four feet wide and two feet tall.

Red liquid leaks from the corner of the pale wooden timbers, and I can already guess at what's inside.

A flush of nausea burns the back of my throat, but I maintain my composure.

Jace, however, does not.

"Report," he snaps, his voice tense as he walks toward his soldiers, briefly scanning the crate.

I follow, but he gestures for me to remain by the door. I suppress an irritated groan and oblige him—mostly for his benefit, since I don't *really* want to undermine him in front of his soldiers.

Even if he *is* annoying as hell sometimes.

"She—the *box* arrived this morning," one of the soldiers says, his voice breaking.

My annoyed smirk falters as the full weight of what he just said hits me.

Oh, *shit.*

A flare of adrenaline shoots through me, and my heart stutters briefly as I study the man's face. He won't look at anyone. All the color is gone from his skin, and he stares at the floor as if he can't fully process what's happening around him right now.

"She?" Jace frowns, shoulders tensed, and turns his attention toward the box. He lifts the lid, and to distract myself from the horror of this entire situation, I study his face intently.

His gaze sweeps over the contents, and he instantly grimaces. Dropping the lid, he rubs his eyes as if he can scrub the stain of what he just saw from his mind. He turns away from the box and leans his arms against the wall, staring out the window.

"*Fuck*," he says softly.

The soldier who first spoke rubs his jaw. "She—when she didn't come back from her rounds—I just didn't—"

"Rodgers, take the week off." Jace says quietly. "The month, if you have to. Grieve. You are barred from missions until I clear you." The dojo master turns toward his lieutenant, and though I can't see Jace's expression, it seems to shatter the last shred of the soldier's resilience.

Rodgers nods, barely holding back tears, and leaves without another word. As he brushes by me, I don't entirely know what to do. I choose to give him space, to not stare at the tears slowly streaking down his cheeks.

This man—he loved her. That much is easy to tell.

In the past, death like this wouldn't have touched me. We've received threats like this in Zurie's house half a dozen times—heads and appendages of Spectres usually sent directly to Zurie. If the woman cared at all, she never showed a hint of emotion, nor did she allow me or Irena to do so.

Any emotion, any remorse, was met with fierce punishment.

But here—Jace—this is real leadership. Compassion. Rodgers clearly had a close connection with this dead shifter, and for all his asshole behavior, Jace can still show his people kindness.

With Rodgers gone, Jace balls his hands into tight fists. "She was one of the best we had, damn it." Slowly, the dojo master begins to pace up and down the room, his fingers brushing the stubble along his jaw as he loses himself in thought. With each passing second, his sorrow corrodes into fury.

Finally, he looks at the remaining three soldiers with the full weight of his anger. His voice is low. Dangerous. Deadly. "Who sent this?"

"It came with this note." One of the soldiers lifts a piece of paper, previously hidden by the box, off the table. "We don't know who's behind this, but it's clear it was sent as a warning."

Jace snatches the note and scans it, and as he does, his eyes briefly flit toward me. He tries to hide the subtle movement, but he can't.

Not from me.

Just like that, this all clicks into place. I look at the box, and based on its size and shape, I know in my heart what's in there.

A dragon's head, and by the sound of it, it belonged to a damn good soldier. One of the female shifters Jace had in his rank, and clearly one he respected. A small part of me envies the female shifters he trusts to risk their lives, and I wonder why he doesn't give me the same freedom.

But this isn't about me and him—this is about the jackass who dared kill one of Jace's soldiers.

Whoever did this was trying to send a message—to me.

Those who protect you will die.

I grit my teeth, my own fury slowly boiling within me as I grasp the reality of this situation.

I can't believe it. I can't *believe* someone would be able to pull a stunt like this off—to send a dragon's head in a crate as a warning takes immense effort and resources.

And they didn't even sign the card.

The door behind me is thrown open so hard it slams against the wall. I pivot to find Drew in the doorway, his stoic frown burned into his face. His eyes dart over the room, from Jace to the box to the soldiers, and finally to me. Without another word, he shuts the door, joining us.

"This is for officials only," Jace snaps, folding the paper away and stowing it in his pocket. "Get the hell out."

Drew doesn't even reply. He merely lifts one annoyed eyebrow and gives Jace a scathing expression that can only mean *shut up and let me help you, idiot.*

"Damn it, Drew," Jace grimaces, clearly thrown off his game after looking in the box. "I don't have the energy for this right now. For you. Just get out."

"No." Drew walks toward the crate, clearly about to look in, but I set a hand on his arm to stop him.

It's reflexive. Impulsive. I don't even think about it, and a warm sensation pools within me as we touch. This dragon shifter lights a fire in me, and sometimes I hate the way he makes me burn with desire.

As quickly as I reached for him, I let go—but it's clear he felt it, too.

The touch disarms him, too. He pauses, watching me, clearly caught off guard by the subtle and almost intimate gesture. And, to my surprise, he indulges me by remaining at my side.

Jace notices all of this, and it just pisses him off more. He opens his mouth to tear Drew a new asshole, but I don't have the patience for their feud.

I want revenge, and I shove my emotions deep, deep down so that my mind is sharp and focused.

"There's no clue?" I ask the soldiers at the far end of the room. My voice is hard, emotionless. Ready for war. "Nothing at all? Where was it found?"

"Along the southeast border." One of the soldiers sighs. "They destroyed our devices monitoring that area. The only footage is of two masked men taking bats to the cameras."

I frown. "There has to be something else. Did they walk? Take a car? I need details."

Better yet, I need to see it for myself, but maybe I can have a peek later.

The soldier shakes his head. "They walked from off-screen, but they didn't have the crate with them in-frame. I suspect they had intel on where our cameras were, and that more soldiers drove up after the cameras were out."

I know who's behind *that*.

"Damn it, Durand." I bite my lip, losing myself momentarily in thought as I debate who else could be behind this.

I have *quite* a few enemies, after all.

"This sounds like something the Knights would do." Jace leans against the wall, staring at the box, his eyes shifting out of focus. "It's brutal, classless, and garish. Right up their alley."

I shake my head. "It's the Vaer."

Every man in the room tilts his head toward me, a question on each face at my utter certainty.

"With all due respect, Miss Quinn," one of the soldiers says. "How could you be so certain?"

"There are so many people after you," another soldier says, leaning his fists on the table as he studies me. "To be so certain it's the Vaer…"

I briefly glare at Jace, annoyed as hell that so many in this dojo seem to know intimate details about my life and the dangers I face. I wonder how many of his soldiers have read the file they have on me—the one Tucker and I discovered during our little adventure into the dojo's command center.

"The list is endless," Jace says with a nod. "Rebel dragon clans from nearly every family. The Knights. There's even talk of a faction *within* the Knights who want to overthrow their General for being too *soft* on dragons." Jace frowns and shakes his head, and I suppress a shudder.

Tucker's father is anything but soft, and even with a lifetime in the Spectres to draw from, I can't imagine someone crazier than him.

"Don't forget the Spectres," one of the soldiers says.

Drew, Jace, and I share a fleeting glance, but we don't say anything. At least that's one thing his soldiers *don't* know about me.

I know they must all be wondering if this is Zurie, but it's not her style. It's a common tactic among assassins, and she's called it out before as nothing more than a tacky attempt at causing fear.

It's beneath her.

Just her mere presence inspires terror. Obedience. Outright panic. She doesn't need to cut off anyone's head for *that*.

"The Knights don't have the physical power or skill to decapitate a dragon," I point out. "Not without causing a scene. Whoever did this was swift and brutal. Another dragon."

Yet again, the men in the room stare at me, but they know I'm right.

I mean, yes, *I* could do this, but even a Spectre with my skills would draw attention. An accomplished dragon shifter like this woman would have put up one hell of a fight, and that's not something even Zurie could have done solo.

I'm fairly certain she doesn't want to let the other Spectres know their future Ghost is having a little rebellion at the moment. She wants to capture me, and she wants to do it as quietly as possible.

Without a doubt, this is the Vaer. All the clues—and my intuition—point to them. And by coming after Jace's people, the Vaer just made themselves fair game.

Before, it was just Mason, just one asshole with a vendetta and a sadistic streak. Now, I might have the entire Vaer family after me. Their army. Their generals. They're trying to get to me, to trip me up.

And, damn it all, it *worked*.

I frown, chewing my lip, unfamiliar with feeling so soft, so affectionate toward others. It's always just been me, Irena, and Zurie.

But now, I have a family, a group of men I'm becoming fiercely protective over, and everything I've ever known is changing.

I lean against the wall, lost in thought as Drew and Jace dive into an argument about where to station additional security. For whatever reason, they can't seem to agree on anything at all.

After a while, I just tune them out.

Zurie wants to take this beautiful magic from me, take my men, take this new freedom, take *everything*. The Knights want me dead. The dragon Bosses all want me for different reasons, none of them good. The Vaer want me most of all, and I'm beginning to suspect it's for reasons not even Mason knew. Whatever they have in store for me, it's probably a fate worse than death.

With Irena down for the count, the only four people I can trust are in this dojo, and now people are hunting them as well.

It's almost too much.

I'm not used to… *feeling*.

But I can say one thing for sure.

Whoever sent this box, I will personally rip out their spine for *daring* to threaten me and the men I'm quickly beginning to adore.

CHAPTER FOUR

I sit on my rooftop, on the tower with the best view of the embassy's lands, and all I can wonder is where she died.

This shifter—the one in the box. Where she was killed. Where she was found. Where the rest of her is.

I shudder at the horrible idea that this woman was overtaken and killed just to send a message to me. In the scheme of things, she was innocent, and it burns my blood to think of how she must have died.

I hope it was painless, at least. Swift. That the Vaer showed even an ounce of mercy.

It's unlikely.

A dozen dragons sit along the wall below, each warily

tilting their head toward me now and then. They think I don't notice, but I do. They think I don't see their eyes narrowed in suspicion and resentment, the way some of them snort black smoke in their barely-contained anger.

They must blame me for their lost friend. For the danger I've brought to this dojo just by existing, just by being here.

I can't really blame them.

I rub my eyes in frustration. I came up here to think, to be alone, not to be judged.

Half-heartedly, I wonder if I should leave. I don't want to put anyone else in danger, and I'm fine on my own. I don't need a fortress to protect me.

Tucker and Levi would come. Drew, too, probably. And Jace—I sigh. Who the hell knows what Jace would do.

Lock me in a tower, probably.

I'm running low on tech. I have barely any voids left in my bag. My special ammo is gone, but I can replace it with some generic bullets from Jace's storeroom as long as they're a high enough caliber. My override device will probably break in a few more uses, as I tend to shatter the fragile little things by the twentieth or so time.

Sure, I have a bit more tech, but my supplies are running low. It doesn't help that someone stole a few of my voids not long after I got here—I still don't know who managed to pull *that* off.

I frown. I should probably talk to Tucker about it, actually. If anyone had access and knowledge of them, it would be him.

And with the entire Spectre organization fully equipped and after me, heading into the wilderness with so few resources would be a bad idea.

Movement by the window below that leads up onto my patch of roof catches my attention, and I tilt my head enough to see who's about to join me. Two strong hands grip the edge, and seconds later, Drew pulls himself effortlessly onto the dark shingles.

Yet again.

Doesn't he realize this is *my* place to think?

Without a word or even a glance in my direction, he nears. His strides are slow and smooth, utterly at home two hundred feet in the air. Without so much as a nod in my direction, he sits beside me, propping up a knee and leaning an elbow on it casually. He scans the horizon without ever acknowledging my existence.

I sigh in frustration. "I'm really not in the mood to be teased."

He chuckles. "Can't I just keep you company?"

"I don't think you know how."

With a laugh, he lays down on the roof tiles and tucks his hands behind his head, staring up into the sky. "Why are you so certain it's the Vaer?"

"This isn't Zurie's style." I shrug, surveying the world around us as we speak, keeping an eye out for anyone who could overhear. The dragons below are out of earshot, and there are no cameras or mics up on this roof. I've checked.

We're clear until the next scout circles by, but that won't be for another ten minutes.

"What if Irena woke up?" He peeks through one eye to gauge my reaction.

I'm tempted to hit him hard in the stomach for the sheer audacity to ask such a question, but I refrain. "She would just knock on the door."

"She's still a Spectre. If—"

"Do you have a brother?" I ask, interrupting.

He frowns. "Yeah."

"Just one?"

"Just one."

"Older?"

"Yes," he says hesitantly.

"Would you kill for him?" I lock eyes with the mysterious Drew, ready to drive my point home.

Drew frowns and leans up on his elbows, his eyes darting across my face as he tries to guess where I'm going with this. "I have, yes."

"To keep him safe?" I don't let an ounce of emotion show on my face. "To save him from himself, if you had to?"

This time, Drew doesn't answer. He goes silent, that stern expression on his face as he waits for me to make my point.

"Irena and I are all each other have." I drape one arm over my knee and stare off into the sunset. "I would kill for her. I *have*. And she would kill for me. It doesn't matter what I am, or what she is, or what mistakes either of us makes. Blood is thicker than regret, and we would burn cities to the ground if that's what it took to save each other."

I wait, watching the dragon shifter, studying his face as

he takes it all in. Eventually, his expression softens, and he nods. "Point taken."

"So, no," I finish anyway. Even though he's made it clear he understands, I want to make my stance on this absolutely clear. "Even if she somehow woke up and escaped without us knowing, it's not possibly Irena."

"Could be the Knights." He shrugs. "They have firepower."

"Yeah, but not the finesse." I let out a humorless chuckle. "We would have noticed. They would have made a big scene out of it. They always do."

"True."

"That leaves the Vaer."

"The rebel dragon factions—"

"About that," I interject. "Who are they? What do they want?"

Drew rubs his jaw. "They all want different things, mostly to overthrow the current Boss. Every dragon family has had their own rebel faction pretty much throughout time. Where there's power, there will always be opposition."

He stares off into the sunset, and it takes me a moment to realize he just let his guard down.

It was so subtle, so understated that I almost missed it.

This man has always carried himself with authority, and I've known he had access to intel most could only dream of. But the way he just spoke—he accidentally revealed an intimate understanding of what it means to run a dragon family.

Somehow, Drew knows the ins and outs of daily management, of wielding power, of putting dragons in their place.

I'm speechless.

It doesn't really make sense, either—he's not a dragon Boss. I know their names, and no one named Drew has ever come up in a mission profile.

For a moment, I simply stare at him. When I don't respond, he turns to me and seems to realize his mistake. He frowns, but neither of us say anything.

Every time I talk to him, I'm reminded of how little I know about his past. About his abilities. About his life. I have no idea who this man even *is*, and I need to be careful.

Though he came for me when Tucker and I attacked the Vaer stronghold, I honestly don't know if he can be trusted.

But I want to. I want to trust him. The way he listens,

the way he gives me space—he knows what I can do, and he respects it.

He respects *me*.

Deep down, I want to tell him about the pit. Ask about the magic there, about the voices I heard in the mist. I want to tell him everything and see what answers he has, but a little flicker of doubt holds me back.

It's hard to tell if this is my intuition telling me to trust him, or if I'm just lonely. Irena and I usually work through our problems together, and it's been rough to do this mostly solo. After all, Tucker can't usually go two minutes without cracking a joke or trying to take off my shirt.

In the silence, Drew leans toward me. Every one of his movements is so subtle, so smooth. Confident. Sure of himself.

He radiates muscle and power, and it's clear every motion has a purpose. Every tilt of his head, every frown, every expression is meant to serve him in some way, to get a desired effect.

Usually, I suspect his goal is to intimidate others. He just does it naturally.

But as he leans toward me, his rock-hard chest getting

closer by the second, this motion feels intimate. Like there's so much he wants to say, to do, and he can't.

He looks... *tortured*.

His eyes drop briefly to my lips, and he sighs in frustration. He pauses, looking at the roof tile, avoiding my gaze completely.

It's strange to see such a powerful and commanding man look almost shaken. Like he's barely holding himself back, barely restraining a compulsion and desire that's virtually overtaking him.

"Who are you?" I ask. "I mean, really? Tell me your full name."

"What, and break the rules?" A small smile breaks across his face, and he shakes his head. "It's impossible to keep the secret much longer, Rory. One way or another, you'll find out soon. And when you do..." He rubs the back of his neck, and his warm eyes finally lock with mine. "When you find out who I am, you won't want anything to do with me."

I laugh. "Why, are you a Vaer?"

"No, no," he chuckles and waves the thought away.

"Then what could be worse than what *I* am?"

His smile fades abruptly, and that familiar stoic frown

settles into his face. He doesn't answer, and that concerns me most of all.

I knew there were secrets about Drew that I would never unravel, that this powerful and influential man knows far more than he lets on. But it seems I will get at least one answer about his mysterious past—and when I figure it out, it's pretty clear I won't like what I discover.

CHAPTER FIVE

I walk through the halls of the embassy, lost in my thoughts. With my hands in my pockets, I let my eyes slip out of focus as I weave through the passageways with practiced ease.

This place already feels familiar. A little safe, even, but not enough to let my guard down. I don't know if I would go so far as to call this home, but it's close.

The list of things going wrong is miles long. Irena is still gone. Sick. Maybe dead. I grimace at the thought and shove it from my mind, but what comes next isn't much better—because Zurie is still after me. The Knights are after me. The Vaer are killing dragons to get to me.

Oh, the joys of being popular.

But worst of all, Drew's secret past is truly starting to concern me. It's pretty clear that, when I discover the truth, my world's going to shift.

I'm not too thrilled about the idea.

Before long, I find myself overlooking the courtyard Levi has been using as his home base since we arrived. I lean on the balcony railing to find the blue dragon curled on the ground, his wings tucked in, sleeping as Tucker sharpens a sword at his side.

For a brief moment, cold adrenaline shoots through me. That sword is alarmingly close to Levi's face. I don't believe for a moment that Levi's really sleeping, but to be so near, and with such a deadly weapon—

I tense.

Tucker's mumbling under his breath and, to my surprise, they both chuckle at the same time.

My shoulders relax slightly, and it takes me a moment to process what I'm seeing.

They're... *bonding.*

I frown. That's just weird.

Tucker hasn't seen me yet, lost as he is in his story and the weapons he's cleaning. Careful to stay low and out of sight, I dart down the stairs to get closer, trying to hear what he's saying before he realizes I'm here.

"…and then Dad told me I needed to shape up or ship out," Tucker says with a shrug. "Guess he didn't like the stunt I pulled in Serbia."

Levi chuckles again, thin spirals of icy mist shooting from his nose as he laughs. Eyes still closed, he looks relaxed and at ease despite the weapons master sharpening a sword beside him.

Tucker grins and lifts the blade. It glints in the setting sun as he examines his handiwork. "But he's an ass. We both know that."

Levi nods, eyes still closed.

I'm so thrown off by this whole exchange that it takes a minute longer to realize the worst part of this interaction—Levi knows who Tucker's father is.

William Chase.

General of the Knights. Commander of the strongest anti-dragon terrorist organization in the world.

And they're talking about it in a freaking *dragon embassy.*

"What are you *doing?*" I practically hiss at Tucker, furious, astonished that he would be so careless about possibly blowing his own cover.

Tucker flinches. In seconds, he's on his feet, gun drawn from the hidden holster at his side, the sword perfectly balanced in his left hand as he reactively prepares for a fight.

Levi, however, is calm as always. He opens his eyes and lifts his head, watching me with the relaxed expression of someone who heard me coming a mile away.

It's not *him* I'm mad at, though.

When Tucker's gaze meets mine, he relaxes and holsters the gun. "Rory, you shouldn't sneak up on people like that."

"I could have been one of Jace's guys." I gesture to the castle, huffing in frustration. "I mean, I overheard you. Why wouldn't they? What were you *thinking,* talking about that here?"

He shrugs. "Levi asked about home."

For a moment, I simply gape at the two of them. "You told… about the…" I relax a little, genuinely impressed at the way he placed his trust in a dragon, of all creatures. "Wow, really?"

"Yeah." Tucker shoots me one of his dazzling, disarming

smiles, but I'm determined not to let him off the hook for this just yet. He sets his hands on his waist and nods to the great blue dragon next to us. "He's pretty cool, once you get over the god-awful dragon breath."

Levi snorts in annoyance and flicks his tail, hitting Tucker square between the shoulder blades. The weapons master falls off balance but laughs as he recovers.

"We've got a code and everything," Tucker says so quietly I can barely hear him. "And he has a freaky ability to hear people coming, so he always stops me long before someone gets within earshot." Tucker pauses and shoots Levi a little glare. "Usually by hitting me, come to think of it."

I cross my arms. "You know you can just *think* things to him, right? Might be safer."

Levi chuckles and shakes his head, like this is a familiar conversation, one he's sick of having.

"Yeah, but I can't keep it going for long." Tucker shrugs and sheaths the sword he was sharpening earlier. "Besides, he's a good listener."

"Well yeah, he can't technically talk."

Tucker laughs. "Details."

With my momentary surge of anger now fading, I'm

still kind of blindsided that Tucker told Levi his greatest secret—one he didn't even tell *me* at first. I had to stalk him to figure it out.

I smirk and gesture between them. "So, are you guys dating now, or…?"

Levi bats *me* with his tail this time, but I just take the hit and laugh as Tucker playfully shrugs. Levi's blow is a love tap, if anything.

Briefly, the gorgeous blue dragon brushes his nose against my cheek, and the mental connection between us opens. A surge of affection flows from him into me.

I pat his jaw. "Good to see you too, buddy."

I expect a conversation. Thoughts. Something, *anything* else but silence. Instead, he abruptly breaks the connection and trots off a short distance before soaring into the air without another word.

As the gusts from his wings rustle my hair, my smile falters. I watch as he disappears into the sky without so much as a word.

Just feelings. Just emotions.

Only the dragon side of him spoke to me, just now. And even though he's still my Levi, the implications are terrifying.

With each passing day, he's beginning to seem more dragon than human. I see the feral connection taking over, and it concerns me. If the dragon consumes him, Levi will be gone forever, trapped in his own body and unable to regain control.

No one has ever come back from going feral, but I don't want to lose him.

Tucker sidles up to me, apparently oblivious to the danger Levi's facing, and sets his hands on my hips. With a powerful, fluid movement, he burrows his face in my hair, trailing kisses along my neck. Each brush of his lips on my skin sparks a flurry of gleeful desire, reminding me of all the hours I've spent between his bed sheets.

But we can't do this *here.*

"Someone could be watching," I say, scanning the sky and windows around us as I try to ignore the way his touch burns through my core. "I don't do PDA, babe."

Part of me hates that I care at all. In the Spectres, you screwed who you wanted—as long as it didn't interfere with a mission or a direct order from Zurie.

But here… there are eyes everywhere.

Sure, it's not Jace's business who I spend time with, but it's not like I'm trying to undermine him in his own embassy, either. Everyone thinks of me as his mate—even if I had no say in that matter. Seeing me with another man will just make Jace jealous and undermine his authority. Besides, I have enough to deal with right now as it is.

"Well, *is* anyone watching?" he asks without stopping.

"No," I admit after finishing my scan.

"See? We're fine. I've got you on lookout." He runs his strong palm along my stomach, teasing me as he dips his fingers past my belt, his hot skin igniting sparks along mine as he slowly explores my body.

"Tucker, keep it in your pants," I say with a laugh.

He laughs, the sound dark and deep, his mouth pressed against my ear. "But I want to be in yours."

God, he turns me on.

As much as I want to jump his bones, I'm even more curious to know what's going on with him and Levi. "When did you tell—"

"After the raid on Mason's place." Tucker's hand slips up my shirt, still teasing, still exploring, still pushing my buttons in all the best ways. "Almost dying has a funny way of bringing people together."

"You should tell the others, too." I scan the sky to ensure we're still alone.

I'm always alert. Always in control. I just don't know any other way to be.

"Jace? Drew?" Tucker snorts. "No chance. I like living."

"This isn't the kind of thing you should leave to be discovered." I frown. "They're good at figuring out what they shouldn't know anything about."

"Did you forget the part where this entire building is *full* of dragon shifters? I don't think I would get a warm welcome."

"They accepted me."

He laughs. "Well, yeah, they're madly in love with you."

I playfully smack his shoulder and pull away from him, my skin instantly cold now that he's no longer holding me. But I need to drive this point home, even as those brilliant green eyes of his snare me, trap me, dare me to come closer once more.

"Tucker," I say quietly.

Seriously.

"They need to know," I insist. "Now."

"Are you going to tell them?" His smile falters slightly,

but he lifts his eyebrow in genuine curiosity. It's as though he's testing me, as if he's trying to see the lengths to which I'll go for him.

By now, after everything he's done for me, I would go just about anywhere and kill just about anyone for Tucker Chase.

And he damn well knows it.

"No," I say softly. "But you should. Before it's too late."

"I'll think about it," he says with a small sigh. He looks off, eyes on the ground, clearly fighting this decision. He's going to put it off, but at this point there's nothing else to be done.

I can't force him to tell Jace and Drew the truth. Well—scratch that, I *could*, but I don't *want* to. He'll do it when he's ready, but he had damn well better hurry.

"Are you sure about your sister?" he asks quietly, in a painfully obvious attempt to change the subject. "I mean, after Mason's place—"

"I'm sure," I say with a resolute nod.

How frustrating. I wonder if they're all going to bring this up, but I'll give the same answer every time.

"Okay." He nods, and I'm a little caught off guard by how easy that was.

He wraps one arm around my shoulder and pulls me close, holding me as dusk settles on the mountainside. The last rays of sun are burning the mountaintops, and he simply watches the show in silence.

Tucker gets me. He truly does. My confidence in Irena is enough for him, and he doesn't feel the need to press for information or be convinced.

He trusts me, pure and simple.

I smile, grateful for this ridiculous and wonderful man, and wrap my arm around his waist. We stand there, peacefully watching the beautiful world around us, simply enjoying each other's company.

Tucker trusts me with his life, and I will guard him with all my power. As much as I love riding into battle with him at my side, however, I never want to test the limits of that faith.

If anyone ever hurt this man—well, no one would find their remains.

CHAPTER SIX

I feel him before I hear him.

Jace.

After he snuck up on us in the forest, I've been careful to tune in and pay attention to the sensation—even if it is still murky.

As I stand in the courtyard with Tucker, just enjoying myself for once, I can feel the flurry of longing that bleeds through our surreal connection. I feel him getting closer, and I wonder if this magical mate-link-thing is ever going to make sense.

Knowing where Jace is at all times would be about the greatest superpower ever, if only because it would help me avoid him when he's being an ass.

Seconds later, I hear his footsteps on the balcony above us. Soft, almost imperceptible, but they're unmistakably his.

"Hi, Jace," I say without looking back.

Tucker flinches and looks around, confused. It's a moment or two before he looks behind me, toward the balcony. "How the hell do you do that, woman?"

I chuckle. "I'm magic, remember?"

"Yeah, but not like that."

"Rory," Jace interrupts, his footsteps trailing down the stairs. I still haven't looked back, and now I'm grateful —from his tone, he's clearly pissed about something, but that's not exactly news.

He's always mad about *something.*

Tucker's grip on my shoulder tightens, and I imagine they're glaring daggers at each other. I continue to watch the horizon, ignoring their little spat. The stunning mountains begin to dissolve in the coming night. Above, clouds swirl through the sky as dragons dip and dive, honing their flying skills.

"Take your arm off of my *mate,*" Jace says bitterly. "Or I'll break it off."

"Oh look, it's Captain Buzzkill," Tucker says, and I can

almost hear the frown in his voice. "Welcome to the party."

"Relax, ladies," I snap, the last shred of peace from the beautiful sunset utterly shattered, thanks to their bickering.

I glance between them—Tucker's lean and muscled body, the way Jace's strong jaw tenses as he glares daggers at the weapons expert beside me.

"Jace, what's wrong?" I glance him over, wondering if he just came for a dick measuring contest, or if he has a purpose.

Jace opens his mouth, his brow furrowed in anger, and I know he's about to start something. He glances at Tucker, shoulders squared, looking for all the world like he wants to punch him in the face.

"Please, don't." I simply shake my head, warning him to be smart about this.

For whatever reason, he shuts his mouth again and sighs. Maybe it's the *please* that got him, or maybe he just has other things on his mind.

"Fine." He rubs his neck and gestures toward the embassy. "Look, I need you to come with me. Not because of this." He gestures dismissively to Tucker, as if he's nothing more than a rodent. "Something arrived from our… *friends.*"

I frown. Jace doesn't have friends.

This must be from the mysterious assholes behind the dragon head this morning. They sent us another present, and judging by Jace's expression, I'm not going to like what's inside.

"Go for it, babe." Tucker plasters a huge kiss on my cheek. "I'll see you tonight. My room, or yours?"

Oh, fabulous. I sigh in frustration.

He did that on purpose. It's like Tucker *wants* to get me in trouble with the dragon shifter who thinks he can rule my life.

Jace squeezes his hands into fists, scowling at the weapons expert with barely restrained rage. I wonder if, had I not been here, Tucker would've wound up with a black eye.

With a laugh, Tucker slaps my ass and jogs up the stairs into the embassy.

The dojo master shifts his attention, the full force of his glare now focused on me, and I set my hands on my hips defiantly. "Yes?"

Tucker started this, but I can't back down now.

"I don't understand you," he says softly, the anger dissolving with a hint of hurt.

Before I can see any more of his expression, though, he turns his back to me and heads toward the embassy.

I follow without a word. No, I guess he truly doesn't understand me—and I wonder if he ever will.

We walk through the dojo in silence, Jace a few steps ahead of me and walking at a brisk pace. Though it's effortless to keep up, I wonder if he's somehow trying to test me, to see if I'll grovel or seek his forgiveness.

I won't.

Heck, maybe he's just trying to ignore me. With Jace, it's hard to tell.

Eventually, he comes to a set of double doors I've never seen before. Two guards in the dojo's yellow and black uniforms are posted outside, and they salute with perfect form as he nears.

Ah, these must be his elite soldiers—which means I'm going to see something new.

One of the guards opens the door for us, revealing a large meeting room. Sconces on the walls cast flickering lights over the round wooden table in the center of the room, and one of the twenty ornate chairs has been pulled several feet from the table. Windows line the walls on either side of me, and I imagine we would have a stunning view of the ravine and main courtyard if it were light out.

But that's not why Jace brought me here.

Another pine box sits on the polished surface of the table, and my blood runs cold at the sight.

"Open it," he says with a nod to the box. "And tell me what the hell that is."

I frown at the controlling thunderbird shifter, but my curiosity pushes me forward despite my annoyance.

My fingers brush the rough pine boards, and I effortlessly lift the lid—which means he's already broken the seal and looked inside.

A neatly folded set of black clothes lay on a bed of straw in the box, and my heart nearly stops when I recognize it.

Irena's Spectre uniform.

For a moment, I can't breathe. My heart stutters in my chest. Furious, jaw tense, I slam the lid shut.

"What is it?" Jace asks, the harsh edge slowly fading from his voice. Maybe he sees how upset I am, or maybe he's relaxing now because it's just the two of us in here.

Whatever the reason, he seems to have forgotten his anger—for the moment. It'll come back.

"Irena's outfit," I say quietly, not looking at him. "The last thing I saw her wearing."

Jace curses under his breath, and out of the corner of my eye, I see him rub his temple. "That explains the note."

"Note?" I ask, my voice a bit tense.

Why the hell doesn't he *tell* me these things?

"We found this with the crate." He pulls a folded piece of white paper from his pocket and hands it to me.

I snatch it from his hand to find a few words scribbled on it, the writing tight and elegant.

She doesn't have long.

My blood boils. The fury is so powerful, so over-whelming, that I feel a surge of nausea in my cheeks. Heat burns along my hands, my magic threatening to break free, so I close my eyes to shove the emotions deep down—I can't deal with them right now.

I need to focus.

Carefully, I study the note for clues. The blue ink is flawless. Precise. The script is distinctly masculine, with harsh lines and the occasional blotch in the ink.

Whoever wrote this doesn't waste time, but still cared enough to ensure the note was perfectly legible.

This person wanted to make sure I got his message, and damn it all, I did.

"I can't believe they took off her *clothes*." I'm seething. I pocket the note and toss the lid aside, rifling through the layers of fabric, looking for anything useful.

The good news is her underthings aren't here. They at least gave her *that* privacy, however minimal that might be.

Jace walks up behind me and, in a fluid motion, lifts the note from my pocket. I pivot and reach for it, trying to snatch it back, but he gently grabs my wrist before I can.

His grip is strong. Tight. Immobilizing. I briefly fight to break free, but my heart isn't in it. Not really. We lock eyes as he stashes the paper in his back pocket, his expression softening slightly as I glower at him.

"Give that back," I demand.

"*Now* who's pushy and controlling?" He quirks one eyebrow playfully. "No, Rory. This is clearly upsetting you. Last time you were this upset, you blew a hole in a mountain."

"I'm fine," I lie, turning my back to him.

I'll just steal the damn note back later—if it's even worth my time.

"You were right," he says, changing the subject. "If our mystery friend sent us Irena's clothes, it appears the Vaer are behind this after all. Obviously, whoever sent us this also sent us our little—" He clears his throat uncomfortably. "—*present* earlier."

I pause, leaning on the table, pressing my eyes shut at the reminder that someone died simply because she was loosely connected to me.

It's almost more than I can handle right now.

And I hate how much I *care*.

"Rory," Jace says softly. Tenderly. He holds my shoulders, his strong grip surprisingly comforting. "We'll fix this."

"Damn right we will," I say, my voice dark.

Deadly.

Murderous.

I lift Irena's coat and examine it, looking for more information—anything at all that could help me—but I'm blindsided as the scent of her perfume rolls over me.

We were never supposed to wear scents on missions,

but we could at home. Off duty, when we got the luxury of a few hours' rest.

I put this coat on her to keep her warm through the coma—this wasn't something she was allowed to wear on a mission. Her perfume is light and fresh with a hint of floral notes, maybe rose or lavender, and it always struck me how feminine her choice of perfumes was. She likes the gentle ones, the soft ones, the ones with beautiful bottles and gorgeous celebrity endorsements.

Sometimes, it made me wonder if that was the life she wanted—something soft, something gentle. If she fought with what she was as much as I did.

My anger momentarily dissolves, and I hug the jacket to my chest.

I'm going to fix this, Irena. I squeeze my eyes shut. *Promise.*

Something within the coat crinkles and slides out of the sleeve, falling to the floor. I open my eyes to find another piece of white paper covered in blue ink, identical to the first.

Jace and I both dart for it, but I grab it before he can. I shoot him a triumphant smile as he groans in protest. "Rory, you can't—"

"Just did."

I scan through the note, but this one doesn't have any warnings. No words.

Just coordinates.

Behind me, Jace's footsteps across the wooden floor captures my attention. As I memorize the coordinates —in case he snatches this, too—I feel him come closer, feel the way the air shifts and buzzes with energy as he nears, and I try to ignore the way my body aches to lean into him.

"A trap," Jace says.

Obviously.

I nearly roll my eyes. It's as if he only remembers I'm a hardened assassin when he wants a reason to be mad at me.

I peer over my shoulder to find him inches away. His stormy gray eyes shift from the note to me, and briefly to my lips. His strong jaw clenches slightly, the muscles pinching as he bites back whatever he was about to say.

"Yeah, it's a trap." I swallow my original sarcastic retort as I briefly lose myself in his handsome face.

It's insane how much these men affect me. I hate not having control over my body, hate that I can't suppress the way they ignite a fire within me.

Jace, Drew, Tucker, Levi—I *crave* them, and no one else.

"Obviously, they wanted you to find this and meet them solo." Jace says.

"I wonder what they want to say?" I tilt my head, curiosity getting the better of me. "To set up a meeting—"

"Absolutely not," Jace snaps.

"I'm not an idiot," I snap back. "We wouldn't go in blind. They've killed one of your soldiers, Jace. I think it's time we have a little *chat* with whoever is behind this to let them know just who they're messing with."

I hold the dojo master's eye, daring him to disagree, but he eventually nods. "I suppose you're right."

I *am* right, but I decide not to press the issue.

"I'll have a drone fly by and scan the area," Jace says, lost in thought. "And in the meantime…" Quick as a whip, he tries to grab the note from my hand, but I react just fast enough to keep it out of his reach.

"Rory—" He sighs, hands on his hips, and shakes his head. "Please. I know you've already memorized it."

I briefly grin, wondering if he'll come around after all, and set the paper in his hand. "Fine."

His palm is warm, his skin hot and inviting, and

sparks of need burn through me as my fingertip accidentally brushes his hand. He stiffens, his eyes drifting to mine, evidently just as affected by my touch as I am by his.

In the silence, we simply wait for the other to speak, for one of us to extend the olive branch first.

We don't get the chance.

Outside in the hallway, several men start yelling, their tense voices muffled by the closed door.

The moment shatters, and both of us look away.

Jace, to his credit, simply stares at the door and sighs with frustration. After a moment, it clicks for me.

"You brought me here to keep Drew from finding out about the second box, didn't you?" Despite the gravity of discovering the second box, I can't help but grin at their feud.

"Yeah." Jace crosses his arms and watches the door, clearly expecting it to burst open at any second.

"How's that working out for you?" I chuckle.

"Splendid, if it means he assaults me or a guard, and I can throw him in a cell." Jace grins, eyes glossing over for a moment as he daydreams. "Or, even better, throw him out altogether."

"Play nice." I roll my eyes and walk toward the door. "You might as well let him in."

"Let him *in*?" Jace groans. "You don't know who he is, Rory. Not really. The man you've seen here—the things he's done for you—it's not real. You can't trust this guy."

I pause briefly and look over my shoulder. "Wait, you fought at his side and still hate him?"

"Absolutely." Jace frowns.

I tilt my head in confusion, wondering when the two of them will sort out their issues like healthy, adult men—instead of just yelling insults at each other all the time. "Well, I *don't* hate him, and I'm letting him in."

"Honestly," Jace mutters, rubbing his eyes. "What did I do to deserve a mate who manages to find *every* button I have and smack it with a hammer?"

"It's called karma," I say as I reach the door, chuckling a little under my breath. "And something tells me yours is long overdue."

CHAPTER SEVEN

The coordinates on the second note take us to a forest in the middle of Montana. As my boots pass silently over the forest floor, I scan for signs of life. For the enemy.

There's nothing.

Just wildlife. No cameras. No heat signatures. No indication that anyone has ever set foot in these woods at all.

While others would be relieved to be in the clear, it only puts me on edge. I'm used to the battle. To the hunt. I thrive in a fight. Besides, these are killers we're dealing with. Master manipulators.

They're not going to just forget to show up to their own ambush.

Something dangerous is in the works, and I refuse to walk into someone's trap.

"Clear on the North side," Jace says through the small com in my ear. With my hair down, no one can even see it, and I like it that way. If I am somehow being monitored, our new *friends* need to think I came here alone.

"East side, clear," Tucker says through the shared link. "Guess they saw me flexing these guns and ran off."

I hear a small kissing noise through the link, and I figure my ridiculous weapons expert just planted a big one on his bicep. I pause, wondering if he realized he made a pun, or if that was accidental.

"Shut up, Tucker," Jace says, sounding a little weary.

"No need to be rude," I mutter, grinning a little because I know full well I'm just stoking the fire.

Jace can be a jerk, but that just means he's fun to mess with.

"South side is clear," Drew chimes in, interrupting the dojo master before he can make a retort. "Waiting on the signal from Levi for the West."

I scan the forest again, but I'm alone. Except for the five of us, there isn't a soul out here. The birds sing, and I've spotted a few rabbits along the path so far, so the wildlife isn't afraid of anything in the woods.

And yet, this is clearly where I was supposed to rendezvous with the asshat who's been sending me presents.

It doesn't make any damn sense.

As I slip through the woods, silent as ever, my mind wanders. Why would they give me coordinates to an empty patch of grass in the middle of nowhere? Why lead me from the dojo? Is it because they know Jace will follow, and they want to attack it while he's gone?

Doubtful. As far as I've managed to glean from Drew and Jace, my sudden presence in the dragon world has temporarily suspended the other mini-wars the dragon families have with each other on a regular basis.

No, everyone's pretty much focused on apprehending me, and besides—I pity the moron who starts a war with the Fairfax dragons.

Talk about a painful death.

No, something about this trap strikes me as intricate, and that means it will spring any moment. It was carefully planned and meticulously executed by someone who's used to staying one step ahead, and those are my least favorite enemies.

They're so damn *patient.*

My goal is a field up ahead, and as far as our scans can tell, the meadow itself is also clear—no life, no heat signatures, no submerged weapons, no mines.

There was an odd reading on one of Jace's scans—a large, rectangular mass in the middle of the meadow—but no one is clear yet what it is. It glitches and fades, showing sometimes and disappearing the next.

It could just be an error, but I know better.

There's something waiting for me in that field, even if it doesn't have a heat signature. And I'm chomping at the bit to figure out what it is.

I sidestep a dry twig, careful to remain quiet. With a pause, I glance down at the stick, debating whether or not I should switch things up a bit.

After all, they *expect* me to be silent. Impossibly fast.

Deadly.

With a little smirk, I step on the twig. As the crack shatters the silent forest, I wait, gun drawn, for my prey to come to me.

A bird chirps in the tree overhead. The wind rustles the trees, kicking up a few leaves along the forest floor but, otherwise, nothing happens.

Disappointed, I frown. I was kind of hoping that would work.

As I continue through the forest, my shoulders ache more and more with every step. At least I'm not totally alone—thanks to the four men surrounding this forest, I know I'll make it out of here alive today. Even with their help, though, I can't relax.

The plan is simple. I walk in and draw the enemy's attention while Jace and the others swoop in from behind. Easy. In and out, and once we have our subjects in custody, we'll finally get some answers.

I almost can't believe Jace agreed to this plan. He fought it hard, but in the end, we made it clear we would do it without him if he didn't play along.

It would've been easier if we could have brought the dojo's army, but all of this is technically illegal. Only a few loyal shifters in the dojo's command center even know what Jace is up to, and even they don't have the whole story.

We don't agree on much, but Jace and I both figure it's better this way.

Gun raised, eyes peeled for any movement at all, the hair on my neck stands on end as I stalk through the silent forest.

After all, I'm used to setting the trap, not being the bait.

"Clear in the West," Drew says through the com. "Levi gave the signal."

"Good," I say quietly, trying not to move my lips too much in case someone's watching.

"Just got word from the command center," Jace says. "A heat signature is being picked up at the coordinates, and that rectangular mass is back on the screen. I think it was cloaked before, but they're not bothering with that anymore."

I pick up the pace, trying to close the distance between me and whatever fool is trying to trap me. "The heat signature—is it a shifter?"

"No, something small and mechanical by the looks of it."

"A weapon?"

"No. Hard to tell on the infrared, but it might be a laptop or something similar."

Damn it.

I'm so done with the games.

I bolt through the forest, careful to remain silent and unseen. I want this to end, already.

I just want some freaking answers.

As I near the edge of a small clearing, I pause behind a tree trunk to survey the field. It's still as a summer's day, with the warm sun shining down on the soft meadow grasses as they shiver in the soft breeze.

There, in the middle of the field, is a plain brown table. It looks for all the world like it belongs in someone's dining room, and to have it out in the open like this is surreal.

Unnerving.

But I guess that's the point—to throw me off guard.

The polished gloss on the wood is like warm honey in the sunlight. Two items sit on the table—a cell phone, and an open laptop.

My finger hovers over the trigger, just waiting to see someone I can shoot. As I scan the trees, however, I'm left sorely disappointed.

I'm alone. It doesn't even look like my men have reached the field yet, but they're not far behind.

With a frown, I slip farther back into the shadows of the forest. "So, what's their plan? Shoot me when I walk out there?"

"Not possible," Jace says through the com link in my

ear. "We've surveyed every vantage point and have scanners running the surrounding area. No one's here."

"Just double checked on any possible explosives below us," Drew adds. "My tech is giving the all-clear. What do you see, Rory?"

"A laptop," I say dryly, entirely unimpressed. "And a phone."

"Mind games," Jace chimes in. "They want to throw you off and trip you up."

"Thanks, Captain Obvious," Tucker interjects.

Drew and I chuckle.

The moment of levity is brief, though, and before I know it, I'm frowning again as I survey the meadow.

With a deep and frustrated sigh, I step into the clearing. Gun trained on the laptop, I slowly walk toward the out-of-place table, my eyes constantly scanning my surroundings as I look for any reason to fire off a few rounds.

As I near, the laptop screen turns on automatically. I lift my gun, itching to shoot off a round, but I wait.

There's a few moments of static that gives way to what looks like a live feed of someone lying in a hospital bed.

Irena.

I gasp. Eyes wide, I watch as a strange woman in white scrubs bends over my sister's body, fiddling with the IV. They're in some kind of industrial facility, and the bed Irena lays on reminds me of the one I found Zurie strapped to back in Mason's stronghold. Metal shackles lock her wrists and ankles to the bed, and she's wearing a simple white medical gown.

I grit my teeth, disgusted yet again that they would change her. That these assholes have the nerve to touch her at all.

My eyes flit over the screen, memorizing every detail in case the laptop shuts off on me. I look for anything useful, anything at all I could use to save her.

She's pale, far more so than I've ever seen her. She looks like she's fading, and fast. Her skin is white as a sheet, and her veins almost glow blue in comparison. Her chest rises and falls, but only barely. She stutters now and then, as though every breath causes pain.

The phone rings, shattering my focus, and I nearly blow the thing to hell in my surprise. I manage to restrain my trigger finger barely a second before I shoot the stupid phone into oblivion.

I check the screen. Unlisted number.

It continues to ring, and I shake my head in frustration. These assholes sure love their theatrics.

I grab it with my left hand, answering the call as I train my gun on the laptop out of instinct. "What the hell did you do to her?"

"Well, at least you don't waste words," a man says on the other end of the phone. "I rather like that."

It's hard to tell by just a voice, but I imagine he's maybe a decade older than me at most. His tone is a bit lighter than I expected, nothing at all like the dark growl Mason's voice had. He sounds like an aristocrat, someone used to being obeyed. There's a bit of cockiness to his tone, almost like he's smirking while he speaks, and I wish he were here so I could snap his stupid neck.

"Answer me," I demand.

He doesn't.

Because *of course* he freaking doesn't.

"I enjoyed the little stunt you pulled on Mason," the stranger says. "With the walkie talkies? Clever. I like clever opponents. You're so much more fun than the stupid ones."

I'm tempted to tear him a new asshole for changing the subject, but something he says makes me snap my mouth shut.

Opponents.

To him, this is just a game.

He doesn't care about Irena. About my men. About me.

From his perspective, all he's done is make the first move. I'm merely an adversary. Someone against whom he can play. A trophy to be won or lost, a way to measure his own skill against the rest of the world.

And the way he talks—this is clearly someone used to running missions safely from behind closed doors, where the lives of the men in the field are nothing more than pieces on a board, to be sacrificed at will.

This man is cold. Heartless. Ruthless.

Smart.

He's not going to let arrogance get in his way or cloud his judgment like Mason did. This guy is too good for that.

I have to change my strategy if I want to play against *him.*

As I continue to scan the forest, always alert for possible threats, I take a moment to come up with a new approach.

Careful to swallow as much of my rage as I can, I try to even out my tone. To calm down. "I assume you went through all of this trouble so we could make a deal. So? What's your offer?"

"Ah, so you've already caught on," he says, chuckling. "I knew you were a smart one. A fun one. I'm going to enjoy this."

I grimace to suppress a deep groan of frustration. This guy might not be in any rush, but I sure as hell am.

"Do you know who I am?" he asks.

I rub my eyes, trying to swallow my impatience. "Can't say that I do. Want to share with the class?"

"Maybe later." He sighs happily, and I hear the groan of leather, as if he's reclining in a large and very expensive chair. "For now, let's talk about Irena. Let's talk about our deal."

Finally.

"Fine," I say, trying to sound bored. "What's your offer?"

"Irena's doing poorly, as you can tell from the live feed."

I glance toward the laptop, debating whether or not he's telling me the truth. I want to believe he is, because that would mean I'm watching in real time as her heart rate monitor beeps, proving to me that she really is alive.

But he could easily be lying.

"The illness is rapidly taking over," the stranger continues. "She won't last much longer, and thus, our little game needs to have a swift ending to it. I'm afraid we won't get to play for very long."

"Oh, what a pity," I say wryly, not bothering to mask my sarcasm.

Freaking psycho.

"I'm going to be *very* generous," he says calmly. "Most people would give you twenty-four hours to save your sister. I, however, want to enjoy our game a bit longer than that."

I don't say anything. I'll take all the time I'm given, no matter how the crazy man phrases it.

"In seven days, I will give her an injection," he continues. "Whether it's the antidote or a highly concentrated poison depends entirely on your next move, Rory dear."

I grit my teeth at the pet name, but for now, I choose to ignore it. "Let me guess. You want me to turn myself in."

"Such a boring option, I know." He sighs. "But that's the way it has to be. Even I have superiors, and that's what they want."

"And what do *you* want?" I ask, adding a bit of a sultry tease into my voice. Seeing how I can tempt him, in what ways I can shatter his loyalty.

I would never sleep with this psycho—but a man like this has other desires, and maybe we can make a *real* bargain.

He clearly wants something different than his Boss. Maybe he wants a good fight, or an object I can fetch for him—something that will get me my sister sooner, in some other way than to turn myself in to the dragons I hate most.

"Oh, aren't you fun?" His voice changes, and I can virtually hear the wide grin on his face. "Look at you, already trying to break the rules."

"Bend them, really." I shrug, trying to sound nonchalant even though I want to gut him from ass to ear. "After all, it's more exciting that way."

"True, true," he says, as if we're old friends. "However, I'm afraid dear old Kinsley wants you, and nothing else will suffice."

He doesn't realize it, but he just gave me a clue.

This man called the Vaer Boss by her first name, and with no reference to her title—which means he ranks even higher than I imagined. If he's comfortable talking about one of the cruelest dragons to ever live in such a relaxed manner, I can only imagine what horrifying things he finds completely mundane.

I smirk in victory, but as I do another quick scan of the empty forest, my smile falters. I truly had expected a battalion to descend, for fighters to come at me from all sides, but so far, the silence is eerie.

"So, no." he drones on. "I need you to come to me, and if you do, I will set Irena free."

"We both know you won't do that."

Irena is a Spectre and Zurie's second in command. There's no way they would ever let her go—and that's why she very well might already be dead.

I squeeze my eyes shut, refusing to even consider the thought.

The stranger laughs. "I like you."

"Wish I could say the feeling was mutual."

"So, what will it be, Rory dear? Shall I ask the cooks to make you something special for dinner tonight?"

"You still haven't answered me," I snap, allowing some of my impatience to filter through. "How do I even know if she's still alive? You could be showing me a recording."

"True," he admits. "I guess you can't be sure. You'll have to come see for yourself."

"Look, there are other—"

"See you soon, Rory," he interrupts. "And if you bring your men, I will kill them. There will not be mercy. There will not be hesitation. I only have need for you."

With that, the line goes dead. I look down at it in disgust, only to see a text flash across the screen with the coordinates for where he wants me to go. I memorize it out of habit, even as my mind wanders.

Abruptly, the laptop shuts off. Sparks dance over the surface, frying it. Smoke spirals from the keyboard, and I cuss under my breath, trying to figure out how to stop this.

"No, no, no, *no*," I mutter, trying to pry open the back panel, doing anything I can to save the computer that may have valuable intel on it.

When the laptop starts to beep like I bomb, I realize I can't.

I bolt, barely clearing the field before the tiny explosive embedded deep within the laptop goes off. A blast of heat rolls over my back, knocking me off balance. I roll through the field, looking over my shoulder as what was once the screen soars through the air and into the forest.

"Damn it!" I shout, balling my hand into a fist.

It's not until I hear the crunch of the phone in my palm that I realize I just smashed that, too. I open my hand to reveal a thin piece of metal that was once the phone, the shattered glass of the screen falling to the ground like raindrops.

The sheer destruction I just caused throws me off, and for a moment, I can only stare.

I'm strong, but I'm not supposed to be *that* strong.

...am I?

My magic is building. Fusing with me. Raising the limit of what I can do—and with it, what's at stake.

The Vaer want me for reasons no one seems to fully understand, and that means they know something about me that I don't.

The thought is unsettling, to say the least.

Jace, Drew, and Tucker dart out from separate sections of the forest, converging on the laptop with their guns drawn.

A moment later, each man bolts toward me, but I wave them away as I stand. "I'm fine, guys. Really."

Levi lands in the field a second later, roaring, his wings spread as he prepares for battle.

"It's fine, Levi," I say, trying to soothe him. "It was just a self-destruct on the laptop." I sigh. "Probably so that I couldn't hack it."

"What happened to the phone?" Tucker asks, pointing to the device in my hand.

"I, uh, got a little angry," I admit. I sigh and lift my palm, studying the debris that was once a working phone and my last connection to the man who has my sister.

But if I'm being realistic, it wouldn't have done me any good anyway. With a man this smart, I probably wouldn't have even been able to trace this back to him. He probably covered his tracks remarkably well, and that was likely the only reason he didn't blow up the phone, too.

Tucker and Drew watch me with concern, but Jace looks at me with surprise. His eyes go wide, and even though it's brief, his expression is one of utter shock.

Oh, great. Whatever I just did—whatever is happening with my magic—even put Jace on edge.

Because there's not enough going on right now already.

"We need to get out of here," Jace says, looking around. "It's not safe."

On that, at least we can agree.

Levi takes to the sky while the four of us jog through the woods, back to the waiting chopper that brought us here. Jace takes up the lead, while Drew monitors behind us to ensure no one follows. Tucker and I run in the middle, focused and alert.

They're all mercifully silent as we run, everyone eager to just get the hell out of Dodge, but Tucker begins to gravitate a bit closer once we've put a fair amount of distance between us and the rogue dining table in the meadow.

He keeps looking at me like he wants to talk about what happened, and I carefully monitor the area around us for cameras or other possible equipment.

It's clear.

I hop over a fallen tree, briefly glancing at him as we run. "What's on your mind, Tucker?"

"What happened back there, boss?" Tucker easily scales a tree trunk, his boots kicking up a few dead leaves as he lands.

I frown. "I spoke with a Vaer. He didn't give me his

name, but he *did* give me seven days to turn myself in. If I don't give him what he wants, he'll kill Irena."

"Absolutely not," Jace snaps, looking back at us. "You're not going to—"

"Of course not." I roll my eyes. "It wouldn't do any good, anyway. He would never let Irena free, but he is right about one thing. I don't have any bartering chips in this situation. I do, however, have his location."

"I see where this is going," Drew says, shaking his head. He grins, a wicked little smile crossing his face as he watches me. "You want to go on another daring rescue attempt."

"Look," I say quietly. "I understand if you three want to stay behind."

"Like hell," Jace says, slowing until he's matching my pace. "You're not going into the enemy's—"

"Captain Buzzkill, reporting for duty," Tucker says from the other side of me, giving the dojo master a mock-salute.

Jace frowns, glaring daggers at the weapons expert. "Tucker, I swear to the gods that I will—"

"Guys, stop, seriously." I shake my head in annoyance. "Jace, we need a place to keep Irena safe while we figure out what they injected her with. What this crazy bio-weapon is." My heart skips a beat as I remember the scariest part of what he said. "She apparently doesn't have much time left."

"That could be a lie," Drew points out. "Something to make you rush."

"Or it could be the truth." I shrug. "The point is we have no idea, and I won't gamble with Irena's life."

"Fair enough," the fire dragon admits.

Jace sighs. "You want me to find a dragon facility willing to treat and heal a human Spectre?"

"I could ask Drew if you would prefer not to," I say, a devilish little smirk on my face, knowing full well how many buttons of his I'm pushing with *that* little statement.

Jace gives me an expression that can only translate into *are you freaking serious right now, woman?*

I chuckle. Checkmate.

"I'll see what I can do," Jace finally admits with a begrudging shrug.

Well, at least it's something.

Jace is going to try to stop me from leaving. He'll likely dangle this as an excuse to delay the mission, but it's not as though we have a ton of time. I glance back at

Drew, who subtly nods, as if he and I are thinking the same thoughts.

Hell, maybe we are.

I'm up against someone dangerous, wickedly smart, and fond of theatrics. With enough time to think of a plan, I can use all of this to my advantage—somehow.

I'm good at this. It's what I do. And once I save Irena, I am going to boil the Vaer alive for taking her. They started this—they made this personal—and I'm going to finish it.

Even if I have to face off with Boss Kinsley *herself*.

CHAPTER EIGHT

B ack at the dojo, in the dead of night, I recline in one of the command center's chairs and sigh.

I'm not here because I have anything to steal. I just needed to think, and sneaking around—being places where I shouldn't be—has a funny way of clearing my head.

I scan the dark room, my eyes hesitating over the three monitors that were left on for some reason. Usually Jace turns them all off, but these three display their login screens.

It might be indicative of some kind of trap or monitoring device, but I'm not sure how he would rig something like that. Someone probably just had to rush out and forgot to turn it off. No big deal.

Coming here was risky—I used two of my precious few remaining voids to do it—but I don't really care. I'll be out of them soon, anyway, and since only the Spectres know how to manufacture them, I will probably never be able to restock.

Even though it *sucks* to admit it, I probably need to learn how to live without my Spectre tech.

Bummer.

The manila folder with my name on it—Jace's file on me—sits open on the desk, completely empty, nothing but a taunting reminder of how much Jace keeps secret from me.

He knows more about my power than he wants me to realize, and he seems to have the perfect way of dangling it in front of me while simultaneously not giving me anything to go on.

It's frustrating, to say the least.

"Enjoying your brooding?" a familiar voice asks from the shadows.

Drew.

In seconds, I'm on my feet with my gun in my hand, scanning the empty room, flabbergasted that anyone could get past me.

But the room is still empty.

There's no one here. No silhouettes. No shadows.

Nothing.

Strange. The voice didn't sound like it came through a speaker. It sounded like he was right here, standing out in the open. But he's clearly not.

Quiet as a breath, I steal down the few steps separating the higher platform from the rest of the computers and desks, scanning every aisle for something—or someone—I might have missed before.

It's clear.

I finally walk down the last aisle, gun raised as I survey the empty stretch of chairs and monitors.

Baffled, I look back at the room, trying to figure out what the hell I missed.

Behind me, the wall shifts, and the grating noise of stone rumbling catches my attention.

In the heat of the moment, my body reacts before I fully process what's happening. Before the wall even opens completely, I spin around, my gun raised to where I suspect Drew's forehead will be.

My aim is perfect.

He leans against the doorframe of a secret panel in the wall, arms crossed, one leg propped on the heel of his boot as he watches me with a sexy little smirk.

The mechanical sliding door finally opens all the way, revealing a dark corridor beyond the command center.

For a moment, we just stand there in silence, watching each other as I train my gun on his forehead.

"You're cute when you're on the hunt," he says with a dark chuckle. "I like the way your brows furrow."

With a short sigh, I lower my gun. He knows I won't use it on him, so there's just no fun in pretending. "You shouldn't sneak up on people."

He lifts one eyebrow incredulously. "Says the girl who broke into a top-secret command center."

I shrug.

"Come with me," he says nodding into the dark hallway beyond the secret door. "I want to show you something interesting."

For a moment, I set one hand on my hip, examining the secret door. "Do you know how handy this would have been? I had to come in through the window."

"The window?" He laughs. "You're nimble enough to scale the castle walls?"

I smile, not bothering to mask my triumph. "What, that's not how you spend your Saturdays?"

He chuckles.

I nod to the secret door. "Why didn't you tell me about this?"

"Why didn't you tell me about your late-night break-ins?" He tilts his head slightly, studying my face. "It goes both ways, Rory. I'm sure there's some fun intel in here I'd like to have."

"You're trying to make *me* like *you*, remember?" I chuckle. "You're supposed to do me favors, not the other way around."

"Nah. You already like me." He grins, that wicked smile snaring me, and closes the gap between us. The moment he nears, my treasonous body burns for him, aching as my eyes dart across the thick biceps straining against his sleeves.

I force myself to drag my gaze away from his hard body, rolling my eyes teasingly as I try to mask the fact that he is absolutely right.

"So, are you coming?" Drew's eyes slowly wander my body, not bothering to hide his playful hunger anymore. "Or do you prefer to be carried off caveman-style?"

I laugh and walk into the secret hallway. "Idiot."

"I would hate to take that title from Tucker." Drew grins and follows me, quickly tapping a few keys on a pad shrouded in the darkness.

He doesn't notice, but I watch him like a hawk and note the code he just typed. That might come in handy later—especially if it means I don't have to climb through the damn window any more.

"Don't tell Jace about this," Drew says. "He doesn't realize I know about these passages, and I would like to keep it that way for as long as possible."

I smirk. "No promises."

He chuckles. Moments later, the door begins to slide shut, and I wonder if there's some kind of sensor, some kind of alert that would notify Jace that someone was using the secret door to the command center.

If there is, I figure Drew also knows how to disable it.

And just like that, I'm left wondering about their feud. Why they hate each other. Why they each seem to possess more knowledge, power, and skill than they let on—and why they won't divulge anything to me about each other.

Sure, it's the law of the dojo—but it's pretty obvious Drew doesn't care about the rules.

With a soft click, a flashlight beam cuts through the shadowy corridor. I can see Drew's vague silhouette as he looks back at me, nodding to the left. "Let's go."

For roughly ten minutes, we dart through the dark tunnels and stairwells that connect the various rooms in Jace's dojo.

It concerns me that both Tucker and Drew were able to gain access to the secret passages—Jace's security apparently needs some upgrades.

Even though Tucker and Drew are the best of the best, capable of being where they shouldn't be and doing what they shouldn't do, the dojo is too important. It can't have any weaknesses.

Before long, Drew pauses at a small alcove and clicks off his flashlight. The grunts and moans of people fighting filters in from somewhere nearby, muffled and a bit distant. Thin beams of light cut through the pitch-black tunnel from small slits in the wall, and Drew gestures for me to join him.

Cautiously, I peek through one of the slits to find a massive training floor filled with Fairfax soldiers. Their black and yellow uniforms give the scene an almost chaotic feel as they duel each other, two on two, across the massive floor. Now and then, soldiers will grab weapons from a massive floor-to-ceiling armory on the right side of the room, opposite the tall double doors that no doubt lead to the room's one exit.

Bodies soar through the air as the fighters throw each other, propelled by their enhanced shifter strength. Men and women alike grunt with effort and pain as they take hits or fall to the hard tile that covers the entirety of the massive room.

And there, observing it all, is Jace.

He stands on a circular platform in the middle of the arena, hands behind his back as he slowly paces, surveying the various matches around him.

"O'Brien, watch those elbows," he snaps.

"Sir!" a soldier answers, affirming he heard.

"Ellis, stop holding back!" Jace says, shifting his gaze to a woman in the crowd.

"Sir!" she responds. With just that little encouragement, she tackles her opponent to the ground, instantly pinning him in an arm bar.

"What is this?" I softly ask Drew. "Why are they down here instead of in the courtyard?"

I assumed that's where they practiced, and I never cared enough to follow up on that assumption.

Until now.

Because this... this is something else entirely.

I'm a little jealous. This would be a great place to train.

And, yet again, Jace told me nothing about it.

Drew walks up behind me, pressing his chest against my back as he leans his palms against the wall on either side of me. He leans forward, his mouth almost by my ear, and I try to ignore the heat that burns through me at his touch. At how close he is. At how he teases me, as if he knows full well what his body does to mine.

"Jace is the Grand Master of this dojo," Drew says quietly, his breath tickling my neck and shooting tendrils of hot desire through me. "He's not just some diplomatic figurehead, though I suspect you figured that out already."

I nod.

"What you may not realize is that he's a deadly master of martial arts and dragon fighting. Flight. Stealth. Murder. He's a highly respected killer, one of the best in the world, and any of those soldiers on the mat would gladly die without a second thought if he gave the command. They would do it for honor. For justice. For *him*."

Jace's eyes dart toward our hiding place, and for a moment, I think we've been caught. However, he begins to scan the wall, as if he knows we're here but not where we're hiding.

"And there it is. The mate-bond." Drew sighs. "Don't worry. He can't see us. From what I've read of this connection you guys share, he just feels you. If you sleep with him, though, the mate-bond is finalized. It'll only get stronger."

"That's just freaky," I admit.

"Can't argue there," Drew mutters. "I never would have sent you here if I had known his dragon claimed you."

"Why?" I look over my shoulder, snaring him with my gaze, daring him to tell me the truth.

This is about the most information I've ever gotten out of Drew at one time, and I'm going to milk it for all it's worth.

For a moment, Drew doesn't answer, and I wonder if he's done talking. He simply watches me, his eyes darting across my face. I wait, giving him the time he needs, letting him think it over as he debates what to tell me.

With a deep and weary sigh, he leans his forehead against mine. I turn instinctively, facing him, and his hard body presses against my chest as he holds me close. His skin is hot and smooth, igniting a blast of longing within me, and it takes every last ounce of my willpower not to weave my fingers through his sexy hair. I want to press myself against him, feel him, explore him.

But I refrain.

He sets one hand on the back of my neck, his strong fingers holding the base of my head as his nose brushes tenderly against mine. It ignites more desire, more embers of passion, and I'm painfully close to giving in to him.

"Originally," he says, his voice strained, "I sent you here to train. Jace is an ass, but he does what's right. He would have protected you even if you two didn't share the mate-bond. He honors the law, but he's been known to bend the rules—and he would have, for you, given what you are. No one rivals the sheer skill and numbers of this dojo, though they try to keep their full might a secret. Everyone knows they're a force to be reckoned with, and it was the safest place for you to be while the world hunted you. So, I sent you here to master your magic. To hone your skill so that I could use it for my own means."

His shoulders droop slightly in shame, and I resist the impulse to comfort him. It's important that he tell me everything, and I can't interrupt him—not even with a simple touch.

"I figured that, with time, you would come to trust me," he admits. "That you would leave on your own accord and come to me. But once—" he sighs, trying to push through, clearly not used to sharing his thoughts or vulnerabilities. "Once I grew fond of you, things changed. I came here so I could be near you. I couldn't stay away any longer. That was never once part of the plan."

With that, he pulls just far enough away to look at me. As his dark eyes snare me, our noses almost touching, our lips painfully close, I find myself at a loss for words.

"You would be safe here, probably forever," Drew admits. "If that's what you want."

I don't answer. I don't need to.

He knows me better than that.

"But you're not some damsel." Gently, he presses me against the wall, his solid body too strong to fight even if I wanted to. He's nothing but muscle on a six-foot-four frame, and his dark eyes watch me hungrily.

As my back presses against the cold stone wall, I try to ignore the heat that pools between my thighs. I try to ignore the way I want him to lift me up by the waist so I can wrap my legs around him. I try to ignore the almost uncontrollable urge to kiss him deeply, to give in to the desire I feel for him on such a carnal level.

I ignore it all because, with Drew, I would never be in control. If I indulged him, if I let him in like I have Tucker, I would never control what he does. Says. Knows. Not ever.

Giving in to Drew would mean utter surrender—not just once or twice in bed, but every day. He trusts me more than Jace does, but he's still a possessive dragon.

The thought alone sends chills through me, but not enough to completely quell the fire I feel for him.

"You're not some trophy," he says, his voice dark and deep as he leans over me, pressing his hard pecs against my chest. "You're not something to win and conquer."

With that, something stirs within me—something distinctly *other*.

The magic.

It flutters to life beneath his touch, burning for him as much as I do.

It wants him with a feral hunger that's hard for me to control.

It wants what you want, and vice versa, Jace told me. *You fuel each other.*

Drew presses his lips against my neck, his warm touch sparking a flurry of need that shoots through me with each kiss along my skin.

Out of instinct, I almost tell him to stop. It's too much. Too hot. Too heavy. Too fast.

But I want it. I want it *all*.

He hesitates, and a hot breath rolls over my neck. "Per dragon law, I'm not supposed to touch another dragon's mate. Even if you're not fully bonded yet."

Drew runs his nose over my jaw, and I can't help it—my eyes flutter closed at the sheer ecstasy of his touch. His lips press against my cheek once before he pauses yet again, teasing me so masterfully that I feel delightfully pinned.

"Personally, I don't care much for dragon law," he admits with a dark chuckle. "I care about you. What you want. The way I see it, there are no laws with the dragon vessel—you can make your own way in this world. And whatever path you choose, I'm prepared."

That cuts through my lusty fog, and I open my eyes. We watch each other for a tense moment, his hands in my thick hair as he presses me against the wall.

"Prepared for what?" I finally ask, my voice a bit softer than I would like.

In true Drew fashion, he doesn't answer. Instead, he runs a hand over my cheek and tenderly tucks a lock of hair behind my ear. His thick fingers hold my chin, and without so much as a breath of warning, he kisses me fiercely.

His lips taste *amazing.*

A piercing alarm from the dojo floor interrupts us. I flinch, my hand flying for my gun on instinct, ready to defend myself should the need arise.

Breathless, his eyes a bit glossed over from our, uh, *conversation*, Drew draws a dagger from a hidden sheath around his waist and peeks through the slits in the wall.

I do the same, only to find Jace staring at our hiding place. Arms crossed, his eyes dart over the wall, still searching for whomever he thinks is hiding here. His expression is stoic. Certain.

Angry.

Around him, his soldiers begin to file out of the arena, some of them looking back warily as they follow Jace's gaze.

He knows that someone's here—and I would rather he didn't find out it's me. Not because of Drew, but more so because I'm really not supposed to be here.

"Captain Buzzkill indeed," Drew says, sheathing the dagger. "Let's get going."

He sighs and nods toward the dark hallway, our moment shattered, and part of me feels a bit grateful for the interruption.

Drew has a way of snaring me and drawing me in—so much so that I always seem to forget how little I know about him.

Jace's comment from earlier today rings in my ear.

You don't know who he is, Rory. Not really. The man you've seen here—the things he's done for you—it's not real. You can't trust this guy.

It's hard to tell which of them has more to lose—and which one I can trust. They're both growing on me, but I haven't let my guard down with either. Not really.

My magic craves Drew just as much as it craves Jace. There's no question there. But until I know for sure what Drew wants with me, I have to be careful—and stay the hell away from that intoxicating mouth of his.

CHAPTER NINE

At noon the next day, I sit in Jace's private war room with my heels propped on the table. The last time I was in here, he finally told me the truth about the mate-bond.

Maybe today, I'll get even *more* information out of him.

There's six days left to save Irena, and we still don't have a plan. I need something to go on.

Tucker sits next to me, while Jace and Drew lean against the wall on opposite sides of the room. Both men have their arms crossed as they glare daggers at each other.

I wish Levi could join us, but until he can shift back into his human form, I'm afraid he can't. It's not safe to discuss these sensitive topics outside, so I'll have to update him later.

He'll forgive me for excluding him from this discussion.

Probably.

"I'm rescuing my sister," I announce to the quiet room.

All three men turn their attention toward me, watching me with varying degrees of concern.

"What—like, right now?" Tucker lifts his eyebrow in surprise. "Should I go get my guns, or—"

"*My* guns," Jace corrects with a quick glower at Tucker.

"Well you *stole* mine, so—"

"Confiscated," Jace interjects, frowning.

"We leave in a few days." I shake my head, interrupting their little spat before they can get too deep into it. "Whoever this guy is, he's smart and he knows enough about me to guess what I'll do. He expects me to come to him as soon as possible so that I still have time to find her an antidote. He's trying to make me rush so that I make a mistake."

"Let's recap what we know," Drew says, taking control of the conversation.

I tilt my head toward him in mild frustration, not altogether appreciating the interruption.

This isn't *his* mission. I'm just letting him come.

"This guy's a psychopath," Tucker says with a shrug. "He likes blowing up laptops."

"And he likes theatrical gestures," I add, my mind wandering back over the dining table in the meadow.

"He has Irena and the antidote," Jace says, staring out the window briefly. "But he won't tell you what they injected her with or if the antidote is even real."

I pinch the brim of my nose, reluctant to add the next tidbit. "And, because she's fading, they can't dangle her as bait for much longer. Once they have me, they'll either kill her or give her the antidote to use her as leverage against me." I sigh. "To make sure I behave."

"That won't happen," Jace says quietly. Calmly. Firmly.

I look up to find him watching me, those intense gray eyes unwavering as they drive the point home.

"Thank you," I say softly.

Given everything I have to deal with right now, his vote of confidence is surprisingly comforting.

"I believe I've found a room for her," he continues,

putting his hands in his pockets as he stands and begins to absently pace his side of the room. "I've called in quite a few favors, and I found someone who will keep quiet."

"You're sure?" Drew asks doubtfully.

Jace shoots him a brief and deeply annoyed look, but eventually just nods. "I saved his daughter's life on a mission four years ago. I told him it was my job, but he refused to take that as an answer. By his own admission, he has owed me a life debt for a long time, and he's ready to pay his dues."

"Who is he?" I ask, wary.

"A doctor." Jace lifts his chin, radiating confidence and authority. "An old soldier from my military days. I've fought beside him. He's a good man, and I've made it clear he won't get to know the details of his patient's life. He won't know her name or her connection to you. You can trust him, Rory," Jace adds softly, catching my eye.

I frown, reluctant to trust a stranger, but I have very few options at the moment. At a minimum, Jace's confidence in this guy at least makes me feel better about it.

Kinda.

"I've looked into the coordinates the man on the phone gave you," Drew interjects. "It's an old armed forces base built into a mountain, one the Vaer commandeered a while back. It has very few entry points and some of the fiercest security I've ever seen." He groans and rubs his eyes. "It's going to be a beast to break into this place, much less get out with an unconscious woman in tow."

"Sounds like a fun challenge," I say absently, my mind already racing with ideas. "Can you get me floor plans?"

"Some," Drew says with a shrug. "I have a lead who might be able to do that, but it's risky. There's a lot at stake if he fails."

I catch the fire dragon's eye. "Take the risk."

"So domineering," he says, quirking one eyebrow. The corner of his mouth curves slightly, almost imperceptibly, at my audacity to order him around.

It's a give and take. Neither of us is fully in control around the other.

"So, we have no plan," Jace says, frowning. "And we need to gather more information before we can even begin to build one."

"Well it sounds kind of depressing when you put it *that* way," Tucker says with a slight pout.

Jace ignores the weapons expert sitting next to me and pauses, rubbing his jaw as he turns his attention to me. It seems like he's wrestling with something he wants to say, and he isn't sure if it will start another fight.

It probably will.

He really shouldn't say it.

"Rory," he says, squaring his shoulders. "I will help you and your sister—on one condition."

I groan. This is going to piss me off. I can already tell.

"How about you do it because you want to do something nice for me?" I lean back in my chair, eyes narrowed as I try to point out the thin ice he's walking on right now.

I don't expect him to do things for me. If he doesn't want to help, I'll figure it out on my own—but everything he's said in this room so far suddenly feels very deliberate. Orchestrated.

The promises to help.

The assurance that we can save Irena—together.

He's trying to make me feel dependent on him for this mission to succeed, and that is a mistake.

For him.

He might be the Grand Master of the Fairfax family, and he might command one of the greatest armies on the planet, but that does *not* mean he owns me in any sense of the word.

"Of course I want to take care of you," he says softly. Almost tenderly. "That's what makes this hard to say."

Beside me, Tucker shifts uncomfortably in his seat, and I notice as he leans possessively closer to me.

Jace, however, does not notice.

The master of this embassy is focused on me, his intense expression almost tortured. "If you want my help, you are forbidden to leave the dojo."

His gaze shifts subtly, the lines of his face hardening, the taunt line of his mouth tilting slightly downward as he gives me an ultimatum.

"What?" I ask, almost breathless with shock.

The *nerve.*

"You cannot leave this dojo," he repeats, crossing his arms defiantly. "Not until we have a plan—and not until you've progressed at least a *little* with your magic. I alone will decide when you've reached that level."

Oh, *hell* no.

"Excuse me?" I raise an eyebrow in disbelief at his audacity. "Look, I appreciate what you've done, Jace. The roof over my head, the food, the protection, but don't you think for one *second* that you control me."

"You came here to train," he points out. "That makes me your mentor. And if you want to train with me, you need to do what I say."

The word *mentor* triggers deep rage.

It reminds me of Zurie. Of the Spectres. Of a life in the shadows. Of the chains of obedience.

But most of all, it sparks a deep concern that I might just fall into serving another mentor and lose the freedom I clawed out of a literal hole to claim.

The thought is like cold water, and I get tunnel vision as I glare at the man before me, at the thunderbird who has repeatedly implied he wants to lock me away, to keep me *safe*, to hoard me like a treasure.

For once, I can override the way my body craves him. Right now, it doesn't matter that I feel a deep-set and almost overwhelming need any time he's near.

He has officially gone too far.

"It's clear you don't want to help me," I say coldly. Dispassionately.

That, of all things—the icy cold tone—shakes his resilience.

"I *do*," he says, a whisper of worry starting to show on his face.

If I weren't so livid, I might be astonished that I could crack his stubborn mask with nothing more than a glare, but he's out of line.

"Doesn't seem like it." My voice is cold, and it eerily reminds me of the tone Zurie uses when she's angry.

I shove the thought aside. My problem right now is standing right in front of me, and I need to nip this in the bud.

He sets his hands on his hips and watches me, his eyes narrowed slightly. "Rory, listen. Today, you crushed a phone with your bare hands."

"Hand," Tucker interjects. "Singular."

Briefly, Jace squeezes his eyes shut, as if he's trying to tune out an annoying sound. He continues without addressing Tucker. "The metal and glass didn't cut you. From the looks of it, the movement was instinctive and effortless." He crosses his arms defiantly. "Am I wrong?"

"Get to the point," I say, my voice dark and dangerous.

But this is Jace. He's not going to back down—not from me, not from anyone or anything.

Ever.

"My *point*," he says with an aggravated tone, "is that your magic is growing stronger. Your abilities are increasing. Your magic is testing the limits of what it can do, and that can be catastrophic if not properly controlled. This is what we see with thunderbirds as they come into their magic and as their dragon begins to grow and develop with them—but never to this level."

That disarms me a bit—the idea of a dragon growing within a young shifter, and the idea that perhaps there's one growing in me.

That my magic is more than just raw power—it's a majestic creature, one that might even allow me to shift.

To fly.

That eases my rage momentarily. "Could I really shift?"

"Maybe." A short-lived smile breaks through his stoic expression at the subtle excitement in my voice. "But honestly, I have no idea. No one expected the dragon vessel to be human. We have no idea if this will give you a dragon, or if you just possess the magic of one in human form. It takes years for a dragon to grow within a shifter, Rory—if yours comes at all, it may be ages before we see it."

Bummer.

I frown and lean back in my chair, disappointed. Briefly, I close my eyes and reach deep, looking for the light within.

It's there.

Faint. Distant. Soft.

But still, it's there.

Don't make me wait too long, I say to it.

Patience has never really been my thing.

It grows slightly, just a little stronger, just a little brighter, and I feel energy buzz through my fingers.

I smirk. Apparently, it's none too patient, either. But right now, it's growing. It's weak, relatively speaking, and I need to protect it.

"Let me train you—for real," Jace says, his voice shattering my focus.

As I lose the connection with the magic inside me, I

look up to find him studying my face. I scoff. "What have we *been* doing, then?"

"Tests." He shrugs. "Check-ins, if you will, to see what you can do. It's time for the real training, the lessons I put my elite soldiers through." He looks me over briefly. "It's brutal. It will take all of your focus and energy."

I narrow my eyes in suspicion. "It will distract me, you mean."

He leans against the wall and refuses to answer. Instead, he just looks me over with that stony and unreadable expression of his.

"Fine. *After* we get Irena." I stand, the legs of my chair grating along the floor as it's nearly knocked over. "I have to find her, and I'm not going to let her die just so I can go to magic school."

"She won't die," Jace says with utter confidence. "I'll handle the preparations. This will be an official embassy mission, funded and run by my best team. You won't have to worry about a thing, and you will be *allowed* to join us—provided you can control your magic well enough. Which, again, will be at my discretion." He arches his back, tall and imposing. "Those are my terms—take them or leave them."

The ultimatum is delivered in such an offhand way, so

flippantly and careless, but the rest of us know what he's really trying to do. The manipulation, the tyrannical oversight of a mission that's not even his to run—it sets us all off, igniting a bubbling crock pot of fury.

Tucker, Drew, and I end up talking over each other in our mutual disgust.

"Whoa!" Tucker shouts. "Who the hell are you to—"

"—utterly unreasonable *ass*—" I hear Drew say.

I, however, am seething, and the cold fury is back with a vengeance. "Don't you *dare*—"

"Look," Jace interjects, completely unapologetic. "Thunderbird magic is raw and unmanageable at this stage. Young thunderbirds have killed their parents, burned down their houses, destroyed entire buildings, even towns—*on accident.* If you reach your sister and have an episode, could you live with yourself for killing her?"

"That's *low*," Drew practically growls. "She has demonstrated *far* more control than you're giving her credit for, and I see right through you."

"Shut it," Jace commands, scowling at the fire dragon.

But Drew won't be silenced.

He slams his fist on the table, shaking it. "You're fearmongering so you can lock her away and keep her under observation, like all you mated pairs do." He wrinkles his nose in disgust, and I sit a little straighter at the little tidbit of information he just unwittingly shared.

This—the way Jace treats me—is normal for mated thunderbirds.

Locking away the mate. Keeping her safe. Hiding her from the world.

My nails dig into the wood table as I catch Jace's attention, and he clears his throat. It's a quiet sound, an uncomfortable one, but it's the admission of guilt I need.

He will probably never clear me to join them.

Jace would insist I stay behind while they rescued my sister. He would insist I live my life behind closed doors, never going out, never living a full life for fear I might die.

Deep within me, my magic crackles in the surging heat of my wrath.

"Treat her with the goddamn respect she deserves!" Drew gestures to me, furious and fuming as he yells at Jace. "She's a powerful woman, not some seven-year-old shifter who hasn't grown her wings yet!"

"Her *magic* might as well be." The dojo master glares daggers at Drew. "Her magic is deadly. It tore a hole in the mountain. It ripped open a roof with virtually no effort at all. It's killed people."

I scoff. "How would *you* know—"

The dojo master shifts his attention toward me briefly. "Everyone knows about the incident at that human school, Rory."

I snap my mouth shut and look away, not proud of losing control like I did then.

But this is different.

I'm different. More powerful. More in control. Not perfect, no, but far better than I was back then.

And it's as if he doesn't even *see* that.

Jace glares at Drew once more. "The answer is *no*. She can barely control it, and often it controls her."

"We're done." I make my way toward the door. "I never should have asked for your help. I won't make that mistake again."

As I pass him, Jace grabs my wrist. It's a sudden motion, lightning fast, and it pisses off the fighter in me. I twist my arm and slip out of his grip, but he counters instantly, grabbing my other hand. In one, fluid motion, he pins me to the wall.

His grip is strong, but not painful—firm and controlling, but it's clear he doesn't want to hurt me.

Too bad, because I kind of want to hurt *him.*

"Get your hands *off* of her," Drew demands, his boots thundering over the hardwood floor as he nears.

Jace shoots him one glare over his shoulder. "If you so much as touch either of us, I will consider it an attack on the master of the dojo and finally be able to throw your ass out."

Drew stops midstride, jaw clenched, hands balled into fists. He's practically bubbling with anger, and the only thing holding him at bay is the fact that Jace is the Grand Master. The army of warriors here would die for him in a heartbeat, and I don't want to test their loyalty.

Tucker, Drew, and I—right now, none of us has a say in what happens next.

Jace leans over me, and though I expect anger on his face, all I see is calm concern. As he nears, my treasonous body aches for him, leaning in to him, urging me to give him what he wants.

Like *hell.*

Stupid mate-bond.

He's sexy and overbearing and controlling and protective, and I fiercely want to both screw his brains out and break his nose, all at once.

It's *maddening*.

"Do you agree to my terms?" he asks quietly. Tenderly. "Will you stop fighting me for once and just listen? You came here to train—and now it's time to begin." He pauses, his hard eyes softening a little. "Let me help you."

"If you just wanted to help me, you wouldn't dangle my sister's life in front of my face." I lean in to him, ignoring the urge to glance down at his tantalizing lips, ignoring the way his strong grip smolders against the skin of my arms. "If you just wanted to help me, you wouldn't make ultimatums. You would listen. You would trust me and my training. You would give me some damn *credit*."

In one fluid motion, I swipe out his legs and knock the Fairfax Grand Master to the floor.

He groans in surprise, leaning up on his elbows, looking for all the world like he's going to jump up and tackle me to the ground.

"That's for pinning me," I snap. "And as for your offer,

I'll think about it—and get back to you when I don't want to punch you in the face anymore."

With that, I charge through the doors and slam them shut behind me. The walls shake, but I don't care. Right now, I'm so furious that my veins practically smolder. I want to erupt in fire and singe the world around me, tear it to the ground, let the flames burn through my fury until I can think clearly again.

I walk absently through the hallways, wondering what on Earth I'm going to do.

For all his overbearing and controlling tendencies, Jace is right about one thing—my magic is becoming infinitely more powerful, and I'm only beginning to learn how to rein it in.

But I'm *not* some helpless child. I fought Mason and won, all without an episode. I saved them from Zurie. It's not as though I'm some ticking time bomb, and he freaking *knows* that.

To give into his ultimatum—to hand over control to him—I just refuse to do it. My power is too strong, too limitless, too incredible to allow someone to hold me back like that.

Even if that someone is one of the most powerful thunderbirds alive.

Zurie made me write a blank check—anything she ever asked of me, I had to comply.

Now that I've tasted freedom, I will never allow anyone to chain me again.

Not even Jace.

CHAPTER TEN

I sit alone on the roof of my spire, staring out into the beautiful forest around me. Deep down, I want to appreciate the vibrant greenery, the way the wind ripples through the canopy like waves, but I can't.

I'm still too damn angry.

I came here to cool off and calm down, but so far nothing has helped. My skin buzzes with energy as I press my fingers against the roof, the magic churning within me, but my anger overrides even that.

As I stew in my anger, a shadow bolts into the sky from the courtyard below, nothing but a dark blur through the air.

A dragon.

Whoever this is, he moves dazzlingly fast, so fast that I don't recognize him yet.

I squint after him, a little grateful for the distraction, and I stand as I watch him soar above me. He banks to the left, circling back toward the castle—and, more specifically, toward my spire.

Seconds later, he dives.

It's like watching a bullet race toward me, and I wonder if I should wait for him to land or duck through the window and into the embassy before he has the chance to reach me.

Ultimately, I decide to wait, wondering if whoever this is will attack. Considering how angry I am, it would be kind of nice to have an excuse to blow someone's head off and burn some energy.

You know, in self-defense.

He swoops low, and as he nears, stretches his wings to slow down. Instantly, I recognize the threads of glowing blue light that contrasts with his otherwise pitch-black wings. The radiant blue veins climb up his spine and along his neck.

Jace.

The stunningly beautiful black dragon lands on a

nearby spire, giving me space. I square my shoulders as I prepare for a face-off.

He hesitates, about fifty feet from me, his massive body tense and stiff as we study each other, waiting for the other to move first.

I cross my arms. I can wait all damn *day*.

He sighs and jumps the distance between us effort-lessly. The shingles beneath me tremble as he lands, but I maintain my balance.

Jace takes a few slow steps closer, giving me the first real view I've had of his dragon's face. His midnight scales are sleek and striking, a sharp contrast to the bright glow of the blue fire burning in his throat. A few thin lines of blue light run along his jaw, and the two horns on his face glint like cold black metal in the sun.

Slowly, cautiously, he walks closer, his glowing blue eyes trained on me as he nears.

I'm not sure what to expect, but I wouldn't be surprised if he grabbed me in his claws and flew off with me.

It seems like the sort of thing he would do, just to piss me off.

To my surprise, he reaches his head toward me, stop-ping just inches away, silently urging me to place my hand on his forehead.

To talk.

I sigh and pinch the bridge of my nose, wondering if I have the patience for him right now.

He gently nudges my elbow, and I look over to find his head a little closer. Those beautiful eyes stare into my soul, intense and focused.

When Drew wants to talk in his dragon form, he just presses himself against me, opening the connection without asking. Honestly, I kind of expected Jace to do the same—but he's being polite.

Well, his version of it.

Reluctantly, I set my hand on his forehead.

As much as I hate to admit it, the sensation is heavenly. Light and airy, it sparks a flurry of joy through me to touch him, to be near him, and something about his dragon form is so different—such an odd combination of raw power and unrestrained devotion that I can barely hold on to the dissolving threads of my anger.

After all, even in his dragon form, Jace is still in control.

Rory, his voice echoes through my mind, and for a moment, I simply lose myself in the beauty of the sound. His thoughts are melodic. Tender. Doting. Raw. A dragon's thoughts don't sound like his human voice, and though I find Jace's voice sexy as hell, the tenor and chime of his thoughts are even more alluring.

He adjusts his body, tucking his tail around himself, his wings stretching as he gets comfortable on the sloping rooftop. I briefly admire the blue veins in the leathery wings, studying the way they splinter through the skin and glow with all the fire of a sun.

You're angry with me, he says through the connection, watching me with those glowing eyes.

"No shit," I mutter.

He snorts impatiently, the quick rush of hot air blowing past me like steam. *You shouldn't be.*

I roll my eyes. "If you came here to make me angrier, it's working."

I—ugh, damn it, Rory. He squeezes his eyes shut and pulls away. The movement breaks the connection, and he shakes his head in irritation.

With him goes the beautiful sensation of his scales against my skin, as well as the enchanting buzz of magic that burns through us both.

It's a reminder, for me, that neither of us chose this odd connection we share. His dragon chose me, and it seems as though the growing magic within me chose him.

Neither of us really has a say in the matter.

He sighs and presses his forehead against my chest, much like Levi does. It reopens the connection, and with that delightful surge of energy, I'm able to forget a bit of my anger once more.

You deserve to know the truth, he says with a hint of disappointment. *All of it, especially after what Drew said about the mate-bond.*

"Yeah, right," I say with a chuckle. "Like you would ever tell me the whole truth about anything."

To his credit, he laughs. A few huffs of air escape him, and he leans a little harder into me, like he just wants to be as close as possible. *That's fair.*

"So?" I ask, curious. "Tell me."

Yes, many mates are—well, let's just say they're fiercely protected. Mated thunderbirds usually end up in the capital with our Boss, protected by the full weight of the Fairfax army.

"So, you really do lock them away," I say with disappointment, staring off at the forest. I can't look at him, not after an admission like that.

Yes and no, he says urgently. *There's more to it than that.*

His wing possessively wraps around me, drawing me

near, pressing me harder against his forehead. Instinctively, I weave my fingers along his jaw, and he growls with pleasure at the sensation. The sound ripples through me, consuming me, igniting a possessive pleasure deep within my core.

Not every thunderbird finds a mate, but those who do are watched by the Boss—not just the women, but the men as well.

I lift a confused eyebrow, but otherwise remain silent. I don't want him to stop, not now that he's finally sharing something with me.

Rory, if a thunderbird dragon loses his mate, he goes feral. Instantly. There's no recovery, no chance for redemption. His mind fractures, and he's gone. Jace adjusts his weight, those glowing blue eyes catching my attention, and the severity of what he's saying slowly begins to dawn on me.

He's not just protecting me—he's protecting himself. If he lost me, if I died, he would literally lose his mind. As one of the most powerful dragons in existence, his feral self could decimate whole cities, kill hundreds of thousands of people, and even start a war with the humans.

Over me.

You understand, he says quietly, studying my face. *The reason they're moved to the Capital is because the Boss needs to ensure no thunderbird goes feral. We can't let a powerful but fractured dragon start a war.*

"Why didn't you just tell me all of this?" I ask, frustrated. "Instead of making demands and ultimatums and all that bullshit?"

Because I don't—ugh. His sharp claws dig into the shingles, cracking several as he uncomfortably shifts through his emotions. *Because I'm not used to feeling, Rory! To—to love, or whatever this is you and I have. War, blood, battle—that's all I know! I'm not used to caring at all except for my soldiers and my dojo. To have a mate—to have someone with that power over me—* He squeezes his eyes shut and groans. *None of this was ever my destiny. None of this was ever supposed to happen to me.* He pauses, shifting his attention to me, glancing me up and down before continuing. *But then you came along, and everything changed. I've never had...*

"Never had what?" I scan his face, but he shakes his head and looks away.

He won't finish the sentence, but it's not hard for me to imagine what he was about to say.

Jace Goodwin has never had a weakness. A chink in his armor. It doesn't matter how great a fighter he is —if anyone ever killed me, they would destroy him, too.

My heart pangs at the realization, and it's as devastating as a betrayal.

Just like that, he proves what I've suspected thus far—he doesn't see me as capable. As an equal fighter. As someone who can take care of herself.

After everything I've endured, his lack of confidence in me is utterly baffling.

"What do I have to do to prove to you that I'm not some damsel to trap in a tower?"

He scoffs. *Can you take on twenty shifted dragons at once?*

I roll my eyes. "Can you?"

Yes. He narrows his eyes, and I frown at the unspoken implication he just made.

"So that's what it'll take? Me fighting twenty—"

Gods, woman, no. He sighs, and as frustrated as we both are, I'm surprised when he only holds me tighter. Like he's afraid to let go.

"You and me—" I gesture between us. "—this isn't going to happen unless we get on the same page. You don't get to lock me away. You don't get to make demands of me. I'm not one of your soldiers."

I know, he says with a weary sigh. *We don't understand each other, can't even go a day without arguing about something. Sometimes I don't know why my dragon picked you.*

"Thanks," I mutter dryly.

You feel the same way, he says with a knowing and rather impatient snort.

Yeah. I have to give him that much.

"You see the danger here, right?" I ask softly. "For Irena? How little time she has left?"

I do, he admits.

"You know what she means to me?" My throat tightens. "The lengths that I would go for her? The things I would *do* for her?"

Yes, he says simply.

"And you realize I'm not going to let her die?"

A deeply frustrated sigh escapes him. *I do, yes.*

"So, help me find her." I lean in to underscore my counteroffer to his earlier ultimatum. "Help me heal her, and you and I can train all day long. I'll master my magic. I'll give our training everything I have. But I won't go to the Capital. I won't stay in a tower. If anything happens between us, you'll have to accept that I will never, *ever* let you stow me away. And you will never, *ever* command me."

He watches me for a tense moment, not speaking, not wavering, that steely gaze studying me as though he can see clear through to my soul.

We shall see, he finally says. *But for now, as far as the training and Irena, I can agree.*

"And Irena? When can we—"

Very soon, he promises. *We are at such a disadvantage, Rory. We have almost nothing to go on. I will see what I can do.*

I frown, not satisfied with the answer.

Three days, he says with a little growl. *Give me three days, and then we will discuss everything I've found. Together. And,* he adds with a bit of an eye roll, *I will not make you remain behind. Not with something as important as your sister.*

"Thank you," I say softly, admittedly impressed. "Three days it is, then."

I watch him warily, not entirely sure if this was a victory. But for the moment, Jace and I have made a very tense, very fragile peace.

Hopefully neither of us pisses off the other enough to destroy it.

As the sun sets through my bedroom curtains, I step into the elaborate space and shut the door behind me, only to find a small pine box on my bed.

I stiffen.

It's roughly the size of my hand, and a note lies on top. I snatch the paper, scanning the black ink. This handwriting is different than the other notes, clearly added after the fact.

> *Rory—*
>
> *Jace wanted to hide this from you. I know you can handle it. I'm still trying to trace its origin and get some useful data, but there's no sense in me holding onto it.*
>
> *—Drew*

My gaze flits to the small pine box, my curiosity piqued.

Lifting the lid, I find a small flip phone laying on a bed of straw. A charger sits next to it, wrapped neatly with a little plastic tie.

Cautiously, I flip open the phone and scroll through it. There's only one contact—a Seattle number, by the looks of it, but I highly suspect this is a burner number I won't be able to trace.

To my utter surprise, he actually named the contact.

Ian.

It could be a fake name, but it'll do for now.

Beneath the phone is another note—this one in the familiar blue writing of our sadistic new friend.

Try not to break this one, it reads.

I study the phone, half-expecting it to ring at any moment.

No doubt he expects me to call him immediately, desperate and gasping for information on Irena.

I won't.

I'll wait.

Unlike Ian's other *opponents*, I won't play into his hands.

It seems my rival just upped the ante—he wants a way to contact me, but he has *no* idea who he's messing with.

Or, apparently, the advantage he just gave me.

CHAPTER ELEVEN

As the morning sun burns low along the horizon, I sit on a stretch of cliff facing the distant mountains that surround the beautiful embassy and its lands.

There's five days left to save Irena, and we *still* don't have a plan.

Levi's head lays in my lap, the ice dragon slowly growling with pleasure as I run my hand along the space between his eyes. It's a soothing motion for me, and something about the sensation of his scales along my fingertips helps to quell my bubbling emotions.

Unease, since my training starts today.

Frustration, since Jace is a sexy ass that makes me want to both shake and kiss him.

Bone-chilling horror, since my sister could die at any moment.

You worry too much, Levi hums in my mind. *Just be.*

"Easy for you to say," I mutter. "You don't have crazy dragon magic that can blast holes through mountains if you sneeze too hard."

He chuckles.

"Where do you go all day?" I ask, surveying the forest canopy above us.

Hunt. Through our connection, a swirling flurry of emotions bleeds from him into me. Adrenaline. Excitement. Victory. Hunger.

Mercifully, he spares me the visual details—I don't have to watch a memory of him eating a deer, and for that, I'm thankful.

He chuckles again. *Softie.*

I playfully smack his ear, grinning. In retaliation, he smacks me in the back with his tail. Even though the force knocks me momentarily off balance, I laugh. It was a love tap, if anything. Barely enough to sting, much less injure anything.

He coils around me, his body warm and solid, his wing pressing gently into my back as he holds me close to him. I resume running my finger gently over his fore-head, down his skull and along his jawline, reopening the connection between us.

And this time, a surge of possessive affection bleeds through. I feel him tug on my mind, drawing me into his memories, pulling me deeper into the connection.

In the past, I've fought this. When he pulls me into his mind, everything feels too raw. Too uncontrolled. Too intense.

But today, after how little time I've been able to spend with him lately, I allow it.

Truth be told, I miss him.

The world around me fades to black as I give in, and ghostly silhouettes of his memories blur by. It all happens so fast that it's hard to register more than a mountainside here, or a blurry face there.

He pulls me deep into his mind, where he's trapped and barely holding control of his dragon form.

Slowly, white light blisters through the darkness, and before long I'm standing inches from a familiar face—one I've seen before in his memories, in the moments like this where he's stolen me away from the world for a while.

His messy dark hair frames those piercing blue eyes of

his, and the stubble along his jaw is delightfully tantalizing.

"Hey, Levi," I say with a small smile.

He grins back and wordlessly brushes his knuckle along my cheek. But it's not enough.

Not for him.

His fingers brush along my face. They tease and taunt me, sending delightful chills clear to my core with every touch. Cradling my head in his hands, he pulls me close, brushing his nose against mine.

His touch is soft and sweet, like frost on a petal, and I find myself leaning into him.

My Levi.

"I thought you would fight it," he admits, running his hand possessively through my hair. "Coming in here. You usually hate it."

I grin. "Yeah, well, don't get used to this being so easy."

With a gentle kiss on my nose, he sighs. "So, when are we leaving?"

I tilt my head to the side in confusion. "What do you mean?"

"Tucker told me about Jace's ultimatum. About your

fury." Levi grins mischievously. "I would've liked to see that."

My smile fades at the reminder of how much Levi is trapped in his own body—trapped by the very dragon who's supposed to make him unstoppable.

"Hey," he says softly, gently lifting my chin so that I can't help but look at him. "Don't think that way."

I laugh. I guess there really isn't hiding anything from him while I'm in his head.

"Nope," he says with a chuckle.

I laugh. "Ass."

"So?" he prods, clearly curious.

"We're not leaving," I say with a weary groan. "Not until we have a plan. In the meantime, Jace and I have a truce, of sorts. He'll be training me after all."

Levi frowns. "Rory, he doesn't control you. Even with his impressive knowledge of thunderbird magic—"

"He doesn't," I interject, cutting this off before it can get too far. "We negotiated a tense peace, and that's good enough for right now."

Levi studies me a moment, his eyes shifting between mine as he seems to read deeper, looking further into the statement than I intended for him to see.

"Get out of my head," I chide him, a bit annoyed.

"Sorry," he says sheepishly, grinning. "It's tough to fight. When you look at me, I just want to know every-thing about you."

And just like that, he's charmed me again. Only Levi can get away with saying cheesy stuff like that.

To change the subject, I wrap my arms around his shoulders and grin wickedly. "So, how's your boyfriend?"

Levi laughs, and it's a delight to see the joy on his face. He looks carefree, and I love it. "I assume you mean Tucker."

"Yeah." I playfully roll my eyes. "Duh."

"You know I only want you." Levi brushes his nose against mine, his stubble gently scratching my skin as he drinks me in, tempting me with his lips. I smile, loving the tease, adoring the way his eyelashes brush against my face.

It's insane how he breaks through my barriers. Levi makes me feel, makes me drop my guard, makes me happy and calm when everything else is falling apart.

I should really come in here more often.

His hand drops to my waist, and though he lowers his

mouth to mine, he pauses, tempting me with a kiss he won't give me.

I laugh. "Tease."

In the recesses of his mind, I feel a shift. The air around us becomes heavier. Sadder. Almost mournful.

I lean back just enough to catch his gaze, and his smile is gone. He watches me with sad eyes, his brows twisted upward, like he has news he doesn't want to share.

"What?" I ask, concerned with the sudden change in his energy.

"I haven't known how to tell you this," he says softly. "Especially given the countdown on Irena's life."

"Say it," I demand, my tone as gentle as I can manage.

"It's my dragon." Levi's jaw tenses momentarily as he searches for the words. "He's taking over more and more each day. I lose track of time a lot. I find myself suddenly in a forest I don't remember flying to. Sometimes when a scout flies overhead at the dojo, I feel a surging need to sink my teeth into his neck, to fight, to —" His voice breaks, and he sighs deeply. "Rory, I've held on to my sanity for three years. I don't think I have much longer before it's gone completely."

"Levi, I…"

I'm at an utter loss for words.

In the silence, he sets his forehead against mine and holds me tightly, pressing me against his muscled body, and the surging emotions blur around us like a fog.

Sadness.

Loss.

Grief.

And most heartbreaking of all, intense devotion.

I grip his shirt collar, pulling him close to me, a little afraid he'll dissolve into dust at any moment. "How do I fix this?"

"You can't," he says quietly.

"Like hell," I mutter, louder and more severely than I intended.

He chuckles weakly, but there's no real humor in the sound. "I love your fire, Rory. I have from the minute I saw you."

"Don't you dare give up." I frown, gripping his shirt tighter, trying to make him understand.

"That's not how it works." He looks away. "I don't want you to see this. I should just leave the dojo. I don't want you to watch me lose the last shreds of my sanity, to—"

"Don't you fucking *dare*."

His head snaps toward me in surprise, and I glare with the full force of my rage. My grip on his shirt is as tight as it can be, and I pull him close.

And I kiss him. *Fiercely*.

For a moment, it seems like he forgets everything but me—my body, my mouth, the way sparks dance along our skin as we lose ourselves in each other. He cradles my head with his hands, tender and loving.

"I refuse to let you disappear on me," I say in between kisses. "If you even *try*, I will hunt you down."

He laughs. "You're goddamn terrifying, you know that?"

"Thank you." I grin, pausing only a moment before I press my lips hard against his once more.

I lose myself—in the kiss, in him, in how deeply I feel for this shifter who's trapped inside himself. I lose track of time, of how long he's held me.

Eventually, he sighs and leans away, looking off at something I can't see. "It's almost sunrise. I suspect you have an early training?"

"Yeah," I say, steeling myself, forcing myself to shift

into the right mindset for the brutal training Jace promised. "But I won't go until you promise me."

With that, he smiles affectionately and once more brushes his knuckle along my cheek. "I swear to you, Rory Quinn, that I will remain by you until there is nothing left of me."

Before I can reply, I feel a tug at my navel. I'm pulled backward, through the darkness, past the whispers of memory that are slowly dissolving to nothing in his mind.

Levi is convinced he doesn't have much time left—and after the interactions I've had with him lately, I'm concerned he might be right.

But I refuse to lose my Levi, and I will fight tooth and nail to bring him back. No matter what it takes, he will be human again.

I'm too damn stubborn to give up on him. I just hope *he* doesn't give up on *me*.

CHAPTER TWELVE

As much as I hate to admit it, Jace was right.

His training is brutal.

I fall to the ground yet again, my body covered in bruises and blood as the sun begins to set. Even my lungs hurt from the fall.

I gasp, briefly curling around myself, biting back the pained groan that's trying to claw its way out of me.

But Zurie's training was worse, and this is nothing I can't handle.

I stand, teetering a bit as my world temporarily tilts. The forest around me shifts and slides, and for a moment, I can't tell what's up and what's down.

I'm still dizzy after that last blow, but I'm not going to tell *him* that.

Leaves crunch beneath my boots as I regain my balance. Jace stands roughly ten feet away, fists raised, ready to land another blow. We circle each other in the little clearing he found for me, where I can make mistakes with my magic without killing anyone.

Well, except maybe him.

White light curls around me, darting over my arms and legs like ribbons, and I take a moment to check in with the magic in my core. It pulses, erratic and wild. Violent.

But as I pause to touch it, to soothe it, it calms ever so slightly.

So far, this is the only thing that works—the only way to quell the rising tide of aggressive fury this magic can unleash on the world.

And doing this—reaching inward to touch it—has an annoying way of distracting me.

I notice a fist coming for my face, and I barely have time to roll out of the way. I slide across the dirt, kicking up dust as I train my focus once more on the thunderbird who has burrowed his way into my life.

"You just tap out when you're done, now, Rory," he says, heaving and just as out of breath as me.

He's shirtless, and his hard abdomen is incredibly distracting.

Worst of all, he *knows* it, and I'm pretty sure he took off his shirt on purpose, just to mess with me.

He grins—cocky, infuriating, and hot as hell. With a subtle twist of his hand, he wipes a thin trail of blood from the corner of his mouth.

At least I'm giving him a run for his money.

"Oh, I'm just getting started," I say, feigning strength in my voice that I don't have.

We've been doing this since dawn, and we have yet to take more than a five-minute break here and there.

Nonstop.

No food.

No interruptions.

No rest.

Just brutal, intense sparring. My only task is to not have an episode—and, of course, to stay conscious.

As Jace's magic fizzles beneath his skin, dazzling sparks shoot across his body, arcing over his hard biceps like lightning across his muscles. Every spark is a reminder of the raw power burning within him—the magic that makes him so like me.

He's mastered his power. Hopefully, he can actually help me master mine.

If he can stop turning me on long enough to actually do it, of course.

I dart toward him, as fast as I can, with the intent of tackling him to the ground.

It doesn't work.

At the last second, he wraps an arm around my shoulders. I feel the motion, knowing full well he intends to take me to the ground and probably pin me in an arm bar. To avoid the blow, I twist in his grip before he can lock my arm in his.

With a strained groan, I toss him over my shoulder and take him to the dirt first, pinning him to the soil and grass with my knee as I lift my hand to strike a blow to that gorgeous jaw.

After all, *he* wanted to train *me*. No sense holding back.

Fast as lightning, he pivots and tilts his hips, throwing me off balance. My fist hits the dirt instead of his face.

It only takes a moment, but in that brief gap of time, he

throws me on my back. I gasp as the wind is kicked out of me yet again, and before I know it, he's on top of me.

His eyes are wild with the thrill of battle. He grins, full of fire and mischief, entirely focused on the match.

He roughly grabs my wrists, pinning me to the leaves on the forest floor, and his touch is electric.

Energy and a carnal yearning buzz through me as my treacherous body angles toward him, my hips unconsciously lifting to press against his thighs.

"Seduction, huh?" He grins, and his gaze briefly drifts toward my waist. "I thought you would be above tricks like that." He leans over me, his solid abs pressing against my navel, giving me a taste of my own medicine.

For all his talk, though, he still lets his guard down. The sultry twist of my hips against his thighs distracted him, and his expression is a little foggy, now. Distracted by every shift of my legs beneath him, by my every breath as he pins me to the ground.

He knows full well I have no control over my body, not when it comes to him, but I find myself grinning anyway. "It worked, didn't it?"

With that, I hook my leg around his and throw him onto his side. He rolls, but he's not fast enough. As tired as we are, we're both moving slower than we would like, but I have the slight advantage.

I'm just naturally a hair faster than he is.

Just enough to get the job done.

I curl my leg around his and dig my knees into the dirt, pulling on every ounce of my enhanced strength to keep his wrists above his head. He laughs, and I can't help but admire his smile.

For a man who frowns as much as he does, he has such a dazzling smile.

"Is this how you feel every time you lose a match to me?" He laughs, narrowing his eyes playfully, taunting me in the one way he knows for sure will get under my skin.

I roll my eyes. "Ass."

"Check on your magic." He knocks aside my hands and tries to flip me again, but I roll out of his reach before he's able to.

He begins to circle me as I indulge his order and check once more on the bubbling magic in my body. With every step, he's looking for an opening, another chance to attack.

All he really has to do is wait—because as soon as I

touch the magic within me, I lose touch with the world around me.

It's infuriating.

We're trying to make these check-ins with my power unconscious, something I can do even while utterly exhausted and distracted.

Still, he has an uncanny way of knowing *exactly* when to strike.

But I'm a fast learner.

He darts toward me, and I duck out of the way just in time. I quickly check with the magic in my core, and it's burning bright as ever despite my exhaustion.

"Do you really think I have a dragon?" I ask, wondering if this magic will ever be more than a pulsing light within me.

"Possibly." He shrugs and throws a punch at my temple, but I easily duck out of the way.

"How would I know?" I lift my hands, palms out, ready to parry his next blow. "I mean, if a dragon starts growing?"

"Look for a second pulse." He shrugs, his eyes on my shoulders as he no doubt tries to anticipate my next move. "Energy and emotions that aren't wholly yours."

"Am I a thunderbird?" I dart toward him again, but this time I feign to the left at the last minute and land a blow hard on his spine.

He grimaces from the blow, rolling out his shoulder as he tries to shake the pain. "Damn, Rory. Good hit."

I wink at him. "Want another?"

He chuckles and resumes his fighter's position. "We have no idea what you are, Rory. I've never seen a thunderbird with your level of potential. That's what makes this training so crucial."

With that, he takes my arm and flips me. I land hard on my stomach and gasp in pain. My vision briefly spots, the white and black dots dancing across the forest.

"Yikes." He leans over me with a concerned expression on his handsome face. "I think that's enough for today," he says, offering me a hand.

It takes a moment for my vision to clear completely, but even a girl as stubborn as I am knows when to call it quits.

I nod and take his hand, letting him help me to my feet. He drapes my arm over his shoulder and begins to lead me back to the dojo.

"You, uh," he clears his throat. "You did good today. Better than I expected."

Through the bruises and jolts of pain, I chuckle. "God, does it really hurt you that much to give a compliment?"

He laughs. "Just say thank you. Jesus."

Covered in bruises and blood, the two of us limp our way to the back stairwell, near Levi's courtyard. I pause at the base of the stairs to look around for my ice dragon, but all I see is Tucker sitting alone amidst a pile of semiautomatic rifles.

"Hey, guys," Tucker says, glancing us over. "Did the wood-chipper survive your encounter, too? Or did it get destroyed trying to eat the two of you?"

"Har freaking *har*." It's a dumb joke, but I still can't suppress the grin that tugs at the corners of my mouth.

"And where did you get *those*?" Jace asks, voice suddenly tense as he glares at the weapons expert.

Just like that, Jace is back to normal—a little soft toward me, and pretty much just angry at everyone else.

Tucker, to his credit, just blows Jace a sarcastic kiss.

"Where's Levi?" I ask, scanning the courtyard once again. I'm tired, sure, but I'm positive I didn't overlook a massive blue dragon.

"He's gone most evenings, lately," Tucker says, his smile faltering. "A lot, actually."

Beside me, Jace tenses. I glance him over, and he's doing an awful job of trying to hide his concern. He scans the horizon, frowning deeply.

Briefly, our eyes meet, and I already know what he's thinking. He knows this is a bad sign, and he's afraid Levi's going fully feral.

And if Jace is thinking it, that's a *massive* concern.

When we first came here, the other dragons wanted to kill Levi the moment they realized he couldn't shift into his human form. They were ready to rip out his throat, and they wouldn't have felt the slightest remorse.

Not for a feral dragon.

Only Jace's order to stand down kept them at bay. And if Levi snaps for even a moment—if he lets on at all that the last threads of his control are slipping—well, I'm beginning to suspect not even a command from the Grand Master would protect my ice dragon from *that.*

CHAPTER THIRTEEN

That night, I lay in Tucker's bed, with nothing between our naked bodies but the sheets. His head rests on my shoulder, and I gently weave my fingers through his hair as we lay in the silence.

It's nice to have a moment of peace.

A nagging thought burrows into my mind, and I tilt my head toward the flip phone sitting on the end table beside me.

No messages. No calls. Not even a text.

Nothing.

With a sigh, I close my eyes, trying not to dwell on the phone or my new opponent's theatrics.

Tucker's warm body presses against me, hard and

covered in muscle, and I debate waking him up for round two. After all, we might as well take full advantage of my birth control.

His hand weaves around my waist, and though I love his touch, I wince as his fingers pass over one of the many bruises I got from my day of training.

"Sorry, babe," he says groggily. Still half-asleep, he kisses my neck apologetically, making comically exaggerated smooching noises.

I chuckle. "Didn't mean to wake you up."

"Nah, it's fine." He rolls over onto his back and sighs. "Sleep is for the weak, anyway."

"I dunno." I shrug. "Sleep sounds pretty great right about now."

"Yeah, especially after your run-in with the woodchipper."

I laugh. "You're so ridiculous."

"You love it." He peppers more kisses along my shoulder, igniting my skin with longing and desire.

"Yeah," I admit. "I do."

"So, how is Jace as a teacher?" Tucker leans on one elbow, looking me over with unabashed curiosity.

"Merciless." I rub my eyes. "Efficient. Effective. It's funny, but the only time we're not arguing about something is when we're literally in a fistfight." I chuckle. "Even if it is just a sparring match."

Tucker laughs. "Do you figure the mate-bond thing is just... I don't know, wrong? How could two people so wildly different—"

"I know." I groan, my voice fading a little in my frustration. "I know."

"You clearly need another orgasm to sleep." He gives an exaggerated sigh, like he has to make some great sacrifice. "All right, then. Let me do my civic duty."

With a swift motion, he kicks off the sheet covering me. As it flies off the bed, he grabs my knees and pulls them apart, settling between my legs, his rock-hard cock already teasing my entrance.

I laugh. God, how I love this adorable idiot.

The chime of his phone interrupts us, and he groans for real this time. He reaches across me, his cock still tantalizing close to my sensitive folds, and checks the screen.

"Shit," he mutters. He hunches over the phone, scowling, all his adorable charm gone in an instant.

Whatever just popped up on his screen killed the mood entirely.

I sit up, leaning against the headboard as I study his face. "What is it?"

Briefly, Tucker scans the room around us. "You're sure there's no recording devices in here? Nothing at all?"

"Nothing," I confirm. "I check every time I come in."

"Good." His shoulders relax somewhat, and he rubs the back of his neck. "The Knights are getting impatient. Dad has been texting me—that's when you know it's bad. He usually doesn't bother with me except to tell me when I screw up." Tucker looks down at the phone. "They want news and updates. I don't know how much longer I can keep this ruse of ours going, babe."

"Then don't." I lock eyes with him, intent on making him see reason. "This is dangerous, Tucker. Don't push your luck."

"I can't," he says stoically. "I know it seems like they're not a real threat right now, but they haven't given you much trouble because I've kept them at bay." He watches me warily and gently shakes his head in frustration. "They've only stayed quiet this long because I've dangled you in front of them without giving them anything useful. It's worth it to keep this going as long as possible. It buys you—and Irena—time."

I sigh. Fine. I have to give him a point there. "When do you have to meet with them?"

"Tonight." Tucker runs a hand through his hair. "That's what the text was about. They're getting irritated."

"I'm coming."

"Like hell—"

"Tucker, I can come with you or follow you," I interrupt, glaring at him. "What will it be?"

He clicks his tongue in mock disappointment. "You're so damn *bossy*."

"You love it." I smirk. "Let's get going, shall we?"

He raises one eyebrow in confusion as I hop out of bed and begin to dress. "Well, someone's certainly eager."

"Jace probably has extra sentries posted to keep an eye on me," I say as I tug on my pants. "We're going to need extra time to avoid them."

Tucker leans an elbow on the headboard, a bemused expression on his face. "So, when you swore to remain on the dojo lands in exchange for his help and training..."

"I mean, it's *close*." I shrug. "We won't go *that* far off-property."

Tucker laughs and grabs his shirt off the floor. "One of these days, he'll learn he can't really control you."

"Yeah, right." I scoff. "Either that, or he'll give up and just zip-tie me to a bed."

"Oh, good idea." Tucker grins. "Want to grab some zip-ties on the way back?"

I laugh and shake my head.

Oh, Tucker.

Never change.

CHAPTER FOURTEEN

O ut in the dark forest that surround the dojo, I press my back against a thick tree trunk as yet another dragon flies overhead, scanning the exposed path I was just on, no doubt vaguely able to sense where I am.

Briefly, Tucker and I share a deeply frustrated look. The security here is tighter than it has ever been, and we both know why.

Jace.

Sexy. Domineering.

Control freak.

He knows I'm going to defy his orders to stay in the embassy, and he wants to catch me in the act. I'm not entirely sure *why* he wants that so badly, but that's not at the top of my list of problems right now.

"Your boyfriend's kind of an asshole," Tucker mutters to me.

I scoff and gesture toward the path, urging him forward so we can get the hell out of here.

Tucker obliges me and jogs through the forest, a pistol strapped to his waist. Odd, since he usually hides his weapons, but I figure it's part of the show. To remind the Knights we're meeting who's boss.

There's no telling what they might try, especially if they're getting impatient with him.

As we hop over a log, he turns to me, his voice low. "Have you told Jace about our exit?"

"Hell no," I say with a humorless laugh. "I want to know I have a way out of this place whenever I need it. When he's not being such an idiot anymore, maybe I'll tell him."

Tucker chuckles and sidesteps a twig, running silently through the forest beside me. I smirk, impressed with how quickly he learns.

Hell, with a few more lessons, he could even pass for a Spectre.

Our trip through the forest is quick and quiet. The occasional rush of air overhead is the only warning that dragons circle the skies, looking for me. Several of them intently scan the forest nearby, no doubt sensing my presence even though they can't pinpoint exactly where I am. Jace probably already knows I'm gone—but I don't really care.

Tucker's safety is more important than facing Jace's anger.

At around two in the morning, we arrive at the dark clearing just outside the embassy lands. The moon is almost full, and it casts a silvery glow across the flattened meadow grass in the once-lush field.

The voices of two men filter over the forest floor, their muffled tones unclear but unmistakably out of place.

They're here. The Knights.

Wordlessly, I tap Tucker's shoulder and point to the tree I'll be in, should he need backup.

He nods, his expression hard, his shoulders tense. Carefully, he scans the trees around us, no doubt looking for possible hidden Knights, but I already checked. We're clear.

I'm no good with feelings, but I brush my finger over the back of his hand, gently reminding him that he's not alone. I'm here, and I won't let anything happen to him.

Not that he really *needs* the protection. For all his dumb jokes, he's still a hardened warrior who grew up surrounded by rifles and blood.

But still.

His eyes flit down to my hand and, a moment later, the corners of his mouth gently tilt upward. His shoulders relax ever so slightly, and he plants a rough kiss on my cheek. I grin and climb the tree without a sound, as eager as he is to get this over with.

Time to check in with the organization that even Zurie despises.

Two grown men sit in a modified military field vehicle, a massive anti-dragon rifle mounted on a circular platform in the back. With no roof, that leaves them exposed to a dragon dive—but it also allows them free range of movement for the gun to fire on its rotating platform.

I don't recognize either of these men. One bald, one redhead. I frown, scanning their faces, wondering why the organization would send new faces on a familiar mission. Dressed in all black, the men sit with their rifles on their laps, nervously watching the skies.

"Hey, ladies," Tucker says as he enters the field.

The two men nearly jump out of their skin, and the bald one instinctively aims his rifle at Tucker. A moment later, they both sigh in exasperation.

"You scared the shit out of us," the bald one mutters.

"You, maybe," the redhead snaps impatiently. "Status report, Captain. I want to get the hell out of here."

"Why are they so pissed?" the bald man interrupts, pointing to the skies. "They're circling the forest like they're hunting for someone. You get found out?"

"You give me too little credit, Hitchens," Tucker says, clicking his tongue in disappointment. "No, there are reports that a Vaer got onto the property. They're hunting it down."

"You find anything useful, yet?" the redhead sneers. "You've been here, how long, exactly? And we have nothing to go on. The General is getting impatient."

"That's his default state." Tucker laughs and crosses his arms. "And you'd best watch your tone with me, Reynolds."

The redhead snorts. "I don't give a shit if you're the big guy's son. You're failing, and I finally want my chance to prove I'm better."

"But you're not," Tucker says with a smirk. "Why waste everyone's time?"

The redhead scowls at Tucker, mouth open, ready to chew him out and start something petty, but the bald man interjects. "Captain, you need to give us something useful. The General, well—" He scratches the back of his head. "He's making threats."

Reynolds hits the bald man hard in the arm, like he said something he wasn't supposed to divulge.

"I'm close," Tucker says, his voice dropping all pretense of humor. "This girl has some strange ability, something they're keeping quiet but carefully honing." He looks around, as though afraid someone might overhear, really selling this new lie he's probably formulating on the spot. "It's big. War-crime-big. They want to harness it, but I think we can beat them to it. Once I have more details, we can act."

"How about we just come back with you now?" Reynolds offers, his nose wrinkled in disdain. "You bring us in, show us around a bit? Why won't you tell anyone else about this secret entrance you found? Seems suspicious to me."

"Suspicious?" Tucker barks out a laugh, like that's the stupidest thing he's ever heard. "Are you serious? You have the stealth of a Clydesdale, Reynolds. You'd get us all caught and kill any chance of this mission's success. Get the hell out of here and report back to my *father*," he adds, emphasizing his connection to the General. "And he can smell your bullshit from a mile away, Reynolds, so try to keep it to a minimum." Tucker glares at the redhead.

"Yeah, sure," Reynolds mutters. He taps the side of the car, and without another word, the two drive off, kicking up dust as they hightail it out of dragon country.

Tucker holds his ground, arms crossed, glaring at the car until it's out of view. When they're gone, his shoulders finally relax, and he runs a hand through his hair.

His expression shifts from stoic disgust to deep concern, and he looks up at my tree.

I jump to the ground, keeping to the shadows just in case, and gesture for him to join me. He slips into the forest, scanning the trees around us nervously, and rubs my shoulders, pulling me close. His warm touch sends off a flurry of joy through me—the need to be close to him, to hold him, the delight of having him there.

But I suppress it so that I can remain focused.

"They're not going to give me much longer," he mutters.

I frown. "That didn't seem any different—"

"Reynolds has it out for me." Tucker shakes his head. "That asshole wants my job, and he would love nothing more than to put a bullet in my head. Any excuse, any opportunity, he'll take it. If Dad sent him with only one witness to keep Reynolds in line, they're trying to send me a message."

I raise one curious eyebrow. "And that is?"

"Deliver," Tucker says, staring intently into my eyes. "He's done playing, and he's done being patient. Very soon, he's going to give up on me."

I hold his arms, trying to comfort him. "And what exactly does that mean?"

"That depends on how much they figure out," Tucker admits with a deep frown. "Knights aren't a forgiving bunch. They'll probably kill me, but they might try to drag me home first. For *debriefing*." He sighs and watches me. With a gentle smile, he runs his fingers through my hair. "But you know I won't let them hurt you, right?"

I want to laugh and remind him who he's talking to— the Spectres aren't afraid of Knights.

But I refrain. He meant well.

"I know." I rub my thumb along the stubble on his jaw,

allowing a bit of my fondness to bleed through. "Thank you."

He nods, shooting another uneasy glare over his shoulder at the open field. "Let's get the hell out of here."

We jog through the forest in silence, pausing to hide any time we hear a dragon whoosh overhead, and that makes for slow going. When we're finally in the embassy once more, we glide through the shadows of the secret hallway.

It strikes me, then—I'm fairly certain Tucker's hallway isn't connected to the ones Drew took me through. They have different walls, different floors and ceiling heights. It's clear they were built at different times.

Interesting.

Eager to get back to the room and get some sleep, I push onward. Of course, if Tucker gets his way, we probably won't sleep for another hour or so. I grin, already anticipating the sexy mischief he probably has planned for me.

I, however, want to simmer on this new development. There's a chance the General might enlist Zurie's help in this matter—and if he does, I'm not sure what that would mean for me *or* Tucker.

We might both be in deep trouble.

Together, we slip out of the secret tunnel. Wordlessly, we weave through the halls toward our rooms, avoiding the cameras as much as possible.

But as we round a corner, I spot a familiar silhouette leaning against the far wall. The muscled shifter has his arms crossed, propped against the wall as if he has nowhere to be and nothing to do.

Drew tilts his head toward me, smirking. "Have a nice trip?"

I stiffen. He had been absolutely still, barely breathing, intentionally lying in wait. I didn't even hear him until it was too late.

There's no telling how long he's been here, but one thing is abundantly clear—he knew exactly where I would be.

The question is *how*?

Even though my chest tightens, wondering what he's doing here, I force a cocky smile. "We took a little walk."

"A *romantic* walk," Tucker corrects with a goofy grin.

Drew's gaze flits briefly toward Tucker, but it's clear he can't be bothered with the weapons expert next to me.

The dragon shifter stands, making a grand show of slowly sauntering toward us. Toward *me*. "How is it that you keep managing to shake me?"

Interesting.

Drew was tailing me, trying to see where we went, and it seems we lost him. That's why my every movement is made with intention, precision, and caution. I never know who's following.

Thank goodness, too—I can't let anyone discover Tucker's connection to the Knights.

They would kill him.

Casually, I set my hand on my hips. "I don't know what you're talking about."

"Sure." He grins and rubs the back of his neck. "Sure, Rory. You continue to surprise me, so I've got to hand it to you." He grins, passing me, and doesn't bother looking back. "I admire that."

As Drew disappears around the corner, Tucker's cocky smile disappears. He looks at me, deeply concerned, but I shake my head.

We can talk about this later.

A little more eager to get back to the room, we steal silently through the castle's corridors. As we scale the circular stairwell to our suites, I hear the shuffle of boots on tile.

I hold up my hand, gesturing for Tucker to stop, and he watches me with a concerned expression.

I guess he didn't hear it. Huh. We'll need to work on his senses next, then.

Our eyes meet briefly, and I strain to hear anything else from the landing at the top of the stairs. If we have company, that probably means trouble.

Yep—another shuffle. Another step. Multiple pairs of boots, by the sound of it. But no chatter, no rustle of clothes, nothing else.

Several people are lying in wait for us to return.

It must be Jace.

Damn it.

Deep in my core, I feel the familiar pull toward the thunderbird who runs this dojo. The feeling is fuzzy and vague, like looking through a dirty window to see someone's silhouette instead of their face—but the sensation is there, all the same.

Silently, I run my hand through my hair, deeply frustrated—Jace noticed I left after all.

The only way back to our rooms is through those

doors. I checked. The wall outside the rooms doesn't have enough handholds to scale and climb through a window.

I bite my lip, debating my options, and I get a wickedly mischievous little idea.

I grin.

Tucker raises one very confused eyebrow, and I imagine he has absolutely no idea what's happening right now. I chuckle quietly and gesture for him to come with me—only this time, I take the stairs more slowly, like I have nowhere to be and nothing to do.

Tucker follows suit, and I have to say, I'm grateful for the way he just goes with the flow. It makes things so much easier.

"Gorgeous night, though," I say, as if we're in the middle of a conversation.

"Sure, but didn't all those dragons seem like overkill?" Tucker smirks, briefly looking at the top of the stairs, no doubt beginning to catch on to what we're doing. "I wonder if Jace ever lets them sleep. What a slave driver."

We round the bend to find Jace facing us, blocking the way to our doors. Arms crossed, he frowns at us, eyes narrowed with knowing and judgment. A dozen of his guards stand at attention behind him, watching us with equally grim expressions.

"Speak of the devil!" Tucker says cheerily. "What's the occasion? If they're making a grocery run, get me some jelly beans."

"Can it, Tucker," Jace snaps, his eyes shifting to me. "You left the facility."

"I went on a walk," I correct him, one hand on my hips. "Through the building."

"Don't lie to me."

"Don't make accusations when you have no proof," I snap back.

Behind him, one of his guards turns away, trying and failing to hide a knowing smile.

Good. That's all the proof I need—Jace is trying to get me to confess. He has nothing.

Jace rubs his neck and lets out a frustrated sigh. "Rory, I'm trying to keep you safe, but you keep resisting me. It's just making this harder."

"I don't know what you're talking about," I lie. "After all, who would dare disobey the great Jace Goodwin?"

With a mischievous smirk, I pat his arm, ignoring the tendril of desire I get from touching him. Totally at ease, I walk around him and head toward my door. The guards step aside for me as Tucker follows, and before long, we're at the doors to our individual rooms.

"Night, Tucker!" I shout obnoxiously from my door as he walks into his room.

"Night, babe!" he shouts back, emphasizing the pet name just to piss Jace off.

Jace Goodwin can try all he likes to control me. It's just going to make it funnier when he fails.

CHAPTER FIFTEEN

With Jace's hands on my waist, it's so damn hard to concentrate.

And, with only four days left to save Irena, I absolutely *have* to focus.

The day after my romp through the forest with Tucker, I aim into the abyss, into the swirling mist that disguises the seemingly endless fall into the canyon below. With Jace's firm grip on my body, I feel the bond we share kicking up a flurry of lust and longing within me.

Feelings I would very much like to *ignore*.

"Good," he says softly in my ear, his deep voice driving me wild. "Just like that. Focus."

Today's training is designed to strengthen the connection I share with the magic growing within me. We've been at this for over six hours, trying to create a controlled blast. One I command, from start to finish.

Just *one.*

With an uneasy breath, I close my eyes and dip into the burning energy at my core. It sparks and fizzles, frustrated from a day of ups and downs and uncontrolled surges.

But as I touch it, as I feel into it, the frustration ebbs. It calms ever so slightly, and I feel myself naturally relax into it. *Feel* into it.

Just one, I beg of it.

Heat rushes through my arms, clear down to my fingertips. I feel the light surge within me once again, responding to my request. It fills me, sizzling through every muscle, every vein, until my body hums.

With light.

With heat.

With raw *power.*

And there, very faintly in the middle of it all, I hear a pulse. A heartbeat, one that isn't my own.

I smile.

My eyes snap open, the magic aching to be freed, and I aim at a boulder in the void. It's a massive rock, possibly the size of a car, and it juts out from the canyon above the mists.

The tension builds in my arms, my wrists straining from the sheer force of power that I'm barely holding back.

"Release," Jace commands. "Now."

I comply.

A surge of white light bursts from me, cutting through the air. It hits the boulder like a missile, shattering the rock into shards and dust. The ruins crumble into the abyss, falling toward the sea below, leaving small gaps in the fog as it slices through the thick, white clouds.

My power recedes, pulling into my core once again, leaving my muscles weak and weary. I manage to stay on my feet, and though my body screams for rest, I soldier through the fatigue.

After every uncontrolled episode, I find myself a little stronger—but with this being my first truly controlled one, I'm surprised to find that my body is even more resilient than usual. With a short break, I could easily be at this once again.

"Yes!" Jace says excitedly, releasing his grip on my waist

to pump his fist in the air. "Amazing! Holy shit, you did it!"

"You sound surprised," I say with a weak grin, slurring a little from my exhaustion.

He wraps his arms around my shoulders and swings me, celebrating my victory.

I grin, caught off guard by the man's excitement. "Since when do you laugh?"

"Since you achieved in one day a technique that takes years to perfect," he answers. He chuckles and sets me down, grinning at me as his eyes scan my face. "How do you feel?"

"Surprisingly okay," I admit, eyeing the abyss. "That felt almost easy."

He grins and crosses his arms. "Well, don't get cocky. There's a lot of work left for us to do."

"Right, cockiness is your thing." I jokingly set my palm on my forehead. "How could I forget?"

He laughs, shaking his head. "You should be nicer to me, you know."

"Oh?" I playfully lift one eyebrow.

"Definitely." Slowly, he saunters toward me, closing the

gap between us as our mysterious mate-bond connection takes hold of me once more.

My smile falters as my body naturally leans into him, aching for him as it always does, longing for him to hold me close—it takes everything in me to suppress the urges, but they're becoming harder and harder to ignore.

When he's barely an inch away, he leans in, his hungry eyes wandering over my face, my neck, my lips. If he planned on following up on his original comment with more witty banter, he seems to have forgotten what he wanted to say.

Tenderly, he sets his fingertips against my jaw, cradling my face as though he's afraid I'll break. His skin is rough and warm, igniting blips of desire within me. I fight the urge to close my eyes, and I swallow the soft little moan that so desperately wants to escape me at his touch.

"Sorry to interrupt," a woman says from nearby.

I nearly jump out of my skin, disgusted with myself for not hearing her approach. Out of instinct, my hand goes to my waist, toward the dagger that's not there. Since Jace likes to throw me around in our sessions, and I don't want to accidentally stab myself, I left it on a log nearby.

A woman about my age, maybe just a few years old, leans against a nearby tree, dressed in a white shirt and blue jeans. Her soft blonde hair cascades around her face and neck, her skin like porcelain. She watches me with sharp blue eyes—eyes that are focused, clear, and give me the impression she's seen just about everything, and nothing fazes her anymore.

"Boss?" Jace asks breathlessly, either not bothering to or outright unable to mask his surprise. "When did—"

With a charming smile, she shakes her head and clicks her tongue in mock disappointment. "Don't use my title, Jace. Not here."

That snaps the master of the dojo out of his bewilderment, and he abruptly clears his throat. "Right. Rory, this is Harper. Harper, Rory."

"A pleasure," the blonde says with a regal nod.

"Same," I say curtly, not entirely meaning it.

Cautiously, I glance between her and Jace, not entirely sure what the hell just happened.

Jace is a man of authority. Law. The rules of the embassy run his life, and he almost never lets anything shake him. Ever. And yet, he was so caught off guard by this woman showing up that he actually *broke* one.

Jace broke a *rule.*

The thought is baffling.

But more mysterious than that is the fact that I'm currently in the presence of the Fairfax Boss—and I can kind of understand why he was so thrown off-guard.

Someone new—and very, *very* important—arrived in his dojo without him knowing.

Jace sets a protective arm over my shoulder, though he looks at the Boss. "When did you get here?"

"Just now." Harper nods back toward the dojo. "They told me to wait in the dojo, but you know how fidgety I get."

He chuckles, relaxing a little. "I think there are drug addicts who can sit still longer than you."

She laughs, her face lighting up at the jibe.

I squeeze my hand into a fist, not altogether comfortable with the sudden appearance of a dragon Boss. She seems harmless enough, relaxed and at ease.

But those eyes—I know a warrior when I see one.

This Harper woman may look calm and approachable, may laugh and joke and play, but my intuition tells me this is a commander who knows her way around a gun and a battleground.

And I'm not taking any chances.

"Rory, it really is a delight." Harper shifts her gaze to me, that charmingly warm smile still on her face. She reaches out and shakes my hand, setting her other palm on the top of our joined hands as if to drive home the sincerity of her words.

I nod, not really one for formalities.

In my peripheral vision, I notice the barest hint of movement. The gentle shuffle of a boot over the dirt. A rustle of fabric. I briefly shift my gaze, hunting for the source of the sound, but neither Jace nor Harper seem to notice.

There, in the depths of the woods, is Drew. Yet again, he's watching—and I suddenly wonder how often he's slipped my notice.

Hmm.

He leans against a tree, arms crossed, eyes narrowed in suspicion as he stares at Harper. Shoulders tense, jaw clenched, it's clear he recognizes her and isn't too fond of the fact that she's here.

Interesting.

"Would you like to go for a short walk?" Harper asks me. "I would love to pick your brain."

"About what?" I raise one eyebrow in curiosity, a tad surprised at her honesty. Most others would ask to take a walk under the guise of "getting to know each other" or "just enjoying the day."

Points for Harper, then. I admire someone who doesn't try to lie to me.

Jace lets out an annoyed little groan and crosses his arms. "Harper, you're really breaking protocol here."

"Oh, hush." She playfully waves away the thought. "Let me have a little fun, just this once." She shifts those big blue eyes at him. "Pretty please?"

Now, this is just weird.

I know Jace is in charge of the embassy, but I just heard his own *Boss* ask *him* for permission.

No wonder he gets so pissed when I ignore his orders.

He sighs, apparently giving in. I expect him to just give her the go-ahead, but he turns to me. "Are you okay with this?"

I tilt my head in surprise.

Huh.

"Sure." I'm not really worried. This is still embassy ground, and so much of dragon culture depends on the laws of their neutral zones.

Besides, if she gives me any nonsense or threatens me, I'll just hurt her. Maybe throw her into the abyss and see what happens.

I don't care if she's the Boss.

"Fine, then," Jace mutters, grinning. "But Harper, you owe me an extra shipment of that espresso I like. We haven't gotten any in ages."

"A brutal negotiator, this one." Harper nods toward Jace and rolls her eyes.

"I'll be close," Jace says quietly, his hand on my shoulder in reassurance. "If you need anything."

I nod, and that's apparently good enough for him. He quickly grabs my dagger off the log and gives me a knowing look before walking off, back toward the embassy.

Ugh. No weapons around the Boss, I guess.

Bummer.

Harper weaves her arm around mine, like we're old friends going for a walk through the woods. She begins to lead me on the same path Jace just took, walking at a slower pace as she takes in the sunlight glittering through gaps in the canopy above.

Ahead of us, Jace walks at a brisk pace. As he rounds a

bend in the path, he briefly looks back at me with a reassuring nod before disappearing into the trees.

In the heavy silence that follows, I wait. I'm not afraid of the quiet.

"Hope I didn't scare you," Harper says with a smile. "Nobody likes to be snuck up on, especially when they're training. Sorry about that."

"I'm surprised you were able to," I admit.

She shrugs. "You were distracted by the mate-bond, I'm guessing. It does weird things to us. Based on the way you move, though, I figure I wouldn't be able to in most situations."

I smirk. No, probably not. But my mistake is still unforgivable, and I won't make it again.

"He's such a hardass," Harper says with a nod down the path after Jace. "Always has been."

"How long have you known him?"

"Forever, feels like." Harper shrugs. "We grew up together in the Capital. He always swore he would never find a mate, didn't care for it, what have you." She looks me briefly up and down. "In some ways, I feel bad for you—he can be such a pain in the ass."

I laugh. I can't help it. If anyone can understand, it's

Harper. The way he relaxed when he saw her, the way he teased her—it would make sense that they grew up together.

"He's your brother, then?" I ask.

"Cousin, but might as well be a brother." She grins. "An annoying, overbearing, overprotective little brother."

My smile falters.

"He means well," Harper adds softly, watching my face. "He really does. It's just—he's been here so long that he doesn't really know how to be anything but the master of the dojo."

I give her a playful smirk. "Did he bring you here to put in a good word for him?"

She laughs. "Nah. I've wanted to meet you since I first heard about you, Rory, but he made me wait. And wait. And *waaaaaait.*" She grins. "To think, the dragon vessel taking refuge in my own embassy? And I couldn't even go *meet her*? It was agonizing, but I get it. He wanted you to feel comfortable first. For him to keep me away is really saying something—he loves that he can boss me around here, making up for all the shit I give him back home in the Capital."

I chuckle. These two remind me of my lifetime with Irena—the banter, the teasing, the unspoken affection.

Harper leans in. "Between you and me, whenever we're not here, I make him call me Boss instead of my name. Just to screw with him. That's why he slipped up—old habits."

I smile, admittedly charmed by her, but I'm left wondering what she really wants. Why she's really here. She said herself that she wanted to pick my brain, but it sounds like she knows everything already.

My name. Who I am. What I am. Why I'm here.

And she probably knows because Jace told her.

The thought alone wipes the lingering smile from my face, and I'm left with a sickening sensation in my chest. This all feels a little like treason, for a man who says he wants to protect me to give all this sensitive data to one of the most powerful dragons in the world.

Because at the end of the day, she's still the Fairfax Boss. She's still a leader, and she rules one of the dragon families who stand to gain quite a lot if I ally with them.

Briefly, I wonder if he's told her about my previous life as a Spectre—because if he has, that would be the ultimate betrayal.

I would never, *ever* forgive him.

"What is it you want to know?" I ask, not bothering to

mask the chilly tone in my voice. "It seems like you already know everything about me."

Her smile briefly falters, but to my surprise, she looks more apologetic than offended. "Rory, this must all be overwhelming."

I shrug. "I can handle it."

"Clearly," she says, her grip tightening ever so slightly around my arm. "I'm surprised. Most women would shatter if they were in your shoes. They would be in their rooms, sobbing."

"I'm not most women," I admit.

She grins. "Neither am I."

"I figured."

"How about this?" She resumes her cheery demeanor. "I won't ask you anything for now. We can deal with that later, if you still want to. For now, you ask me questions. What can I tell *you*?"

I frown, wondering if this is a game. After all, the Palarne Boss offered me a similar deal—*come with me, and I'll tell you everything.*

Still, if she truly has information, it would be foolish for me to pass up an opportunity to learn more about what I am.

And since no promises have been made... why the hell not?

"What is the dragon vessel?" I ask. "I mean, really?"

"Well, the short answer is it's *you*," she says with an elegant shrug. "But the deeper answer that you probably want is this—the vessel is the person who possesses the magic of the dragon gods. According to lore, they were stripped of their power centuries ago. No one remembers how or why, if it was taken or willingly given, but the story goes that whoever is worthy will wield their power as a living god."

"Jesus," I mutter, a little blindsided. "No pressure."

"Right?" She shudders. "If that's true, I don't even know how your body can handle all that energy. It would dissolve most people into dust."

I wrinkle my nose at the image. "Thanks for that little visual."

"Sorry, I'm morbid." She grins cheerily once more. "Anyway, that's just the story. Truthfully? No one knows what the vessel really is, or what it means for you to even exist. None of us were expecting an old legend to ever come true."

"Is there anything else to the story?" I ask, trying to sound disinterested, like I'm not desperate to get any clue possible to better understand my strange new abilities.

"Officially, no." Harper briefly cranes her neck to look around us, as if she wants to share something that no one else should hear.

I follow suit, only to find Drew hidden deep in the forest. He hides behind a tree, only part of his head visible. Still intently watching, he gives me a knowing nod as our eyes meet.

Harper doesn't seem to notice him and leans in to me. "Unofficially, there have been rumors that you're currently in what's called the *fusion state.* It means the power hasn't formally fused with your body, and once it does, there will be no way to remove it."

"You mean, someone could remove it now?"

The thought sends cold dread clear to my toes, and I can't help the way my body tenses with concern at the thought of someone ripping this magic from me.

I'll gut the poor fool who tries.

"Again, I'm not really sure," Harper admits.

Cautiously, I examine her face, looking for the tells of a lie. But she's entirely relaxed, entirely at ease, her eyes slightly out of focus as she loses herself in thought.

She told me the truth.

I relax ever so slightly, grateful she's not trying to swindle me with this. I already have so many enemies —I really didn't want another.

I don't trust her, of course, but I also find it hard to hate her.

She's—well, kind of adorable.

"I will say this," Harper adds softly. "There are rumors that a few of the families have access to something that might be able to steal your magic." She looks at me with deep concern in her eyes, the smile gone, replaced by a deadly serious expression. "The Andusk and Bane are after you for that sole purpose, guaranteed, and I believe the Darringtons might be as well. The Vaer hate you, too, but I think you already know that."

I frown, already somewhat familiar with each of those dragon families. The Andusk tried to attack me already, and I figure those vain and materialistic dragons want me for the fame and notoriety I would bring them. They would parade me around like a jewel.

I've run into the Bane dragons before, and I despise them. They're petty crooks who view laws as guide-lines that hold other people back. For them, it's all about seeing what they can get away with, what they can steal, and who they can swindle.

But the Darrington dragons—I suppressed a shudder. They were not to be messed with. As the eldest and most powerful family, angering them is largely considered to be a death wish. Zurie rarely sent us into Darrington territory, and when she did, it was only when she could guarantee one hell of a payout.

"I'm no fool," Harper says, interrupting my thoughts. "And unlike Jace, I won't bother telling you what to do. But for your own safety, try to stay out of trouble, at least until the fusion period ends."

"And that is?"

"The first time you shift." She sighs, her soft blue gaze drifting toward the ground. "*If* you ever do, of course."

I frown, not a fan of all the unknowns in this scenario.

Harper scoffs. "And, of course, there's this meeting the other Bosses all want to have. Like you don't have enough on your plate."

"It seems stupid," I admit.

And, given the danger Irena is in, this little meeting is pretty low on my list of priorities.

"Yes and no." Harper shrugs. "Leaving the embassy puts you in danger, but there's one of you and seven of us. Well, six—the Vaer aren't and never will be invited. They've broken too many peace treaties in the past, and none of us honor their word. They won't be there. But the rest of us, well…" She sighs. "No one will do anything stupid if it means five other dragon Bosses declaring war against them for taking you."

"It will be good to know who I'm up against," I admit.

To meet them. To see how they hold themselves. To see how their soldiers obey them.

It will tell me so very much—and even though part of me is hesitant to go, the adventurous assassin in me wants to know *everything* about the dragons who so desperately want me sequestered away in their Capitals.

Besides, I've been feeling so cooped up here. I want to get out. Stretch my legs.

"Look, we can't make you go," Harper says. "I mean, I'm sure Jace will try, because he's a hardheaded idiot sometimes, but we can't *really* make you. I would suggest you at least consider what he has to say. He's smart, if misguided. When he gets an idea in his head, he can occasionally do the wrong thing for the right reason. And as much as I sometimes want to smack him, he really does have a good heart."

I chuckle. "I guess so."

Deep down, I like this woman. She's smart, capable, and there's more to her than meets the eye.

But I have to remember who she is.

What she is.

Harper Fairfax is one of the most powerful dragons in the world. The Bosses have to be strong, and to keep her title, Harper has most likely defended it with blood and battle, just like Jace did with Guy Durand.

Even though she seems casual and approachable, so much of dragon politics is a lie. A sleight of hand, nothing more than a misdirection meant to disarm and undermine opponents.

No matter how charming Harper is, I intend to keep my guard up. She might be able to get Jace to tell her things, but she won't get *anything* from me.

CHAPTER SIXTEEN

It isn't long before Harper has to leave, and I have to confess I'm kind of grateful. Being around a dragon Boss for hours left my nerves frayed, as I was constantly looking for any indication that she was playing me.

As I briskly walk through the halls of the embassy, headed down a familiar path that ends in the roof of the spire I've grown attached to, I catch glimpses of a black military chopper in the main courtyard far below. A familiar blonde figure pauses at the door, briefly looking back toward the embassy—in the vague direction of my room—before climbing in.

I grit my teeth, feeling like there's more to what Harper knows about me. I don't like it one bit.

Much to my surprise, the flip phone in my pocket vibrates, interrupting my thoughts.

I study the screen, and the antiquated caller ID shows Ian's name.

It looks like our little game of chicken has ended. Time to see what he wants.

Without saying a word, I flip open the phone and set it against my ear.

"I'm disappointed," Ian says with an exaggerated sigh.

For a moment, I hesitate and allow the silence to settle between us. To flush him out.

To test him.

The muffled creak of leather filters through the connection. "Rory, there's a reason I gave you this phone. I know I'm not on speaker. Let's kill the theatrics, shall we?"

"Oh, *I'm* theatrical?" I bark out a harsh laugh.

"Day four, and no sign of you." He adjusts in his seat, and I can practically hear the tension in his voice. "Did you stop playing?"

"No," I admit, my voice light and relaxed. "You should know better than that, Ian."

"Ah, yes," he says, chuckling. "Did you like that? Have you figured out who I am yet?"

"Why? Eager for a bit of brief fame?"

"How delightful," he says, and I can hear the grin in his voice again now that he realizes the game is still afoot. "The claws come out."

I pause, wondering just what I can goad him into admitting.

"Irena's not faring well today," he says before I can say anything. "It would be a shame if we had to cut things short simply because I have no more bait."

"How lazy," I say, trying not to let my anger filter into my voice. "If she were dead, you wouldn't *tell* me that."

"Wouldn't I?"

Interesting. He's trying to trip me up and make me second-guess myself. He wants to get under my skin and make me doubt the deductions I glean from each of our interactions.

It won't work.

"Tick tock, Rory dear," he says in a chilling tone.

With that, the line goes dead.

I grit my teeth, angry that I barely got a word in—but I

suppose that was the idea. Rile me up. Ruffle my fears. Hurry along the game.

With a deep and frustrated sigh, I close my eyes and wait until I'm centered. Calm.

As much as I hate the idea, I just have to be patient.

This is part of the game. If I call him now, I'll look too eager. Too willing to play. If I call him, it has to be with something significant—something to string *him* along.

Every conversation is another chess piece moved across the board, and it has to be done with strategy.

I glance out the window to find the chopper still there, Harper peeking out an open door as she speaks with one of the embassy guards.

A bit of peace and quiet would be lovely right now, and I've grown rather fond of the roof of the tallest tower.

As I reach the window and climb out onto the shingles, I pause when I notice the man sitting silently on the shingles. He reclines with his back to me, utterly comfortable, his massive and muscular body blocking most of my view of the forest beyond.

"Hey, Rory," Drew calls over his shoulder, not bothering to look back.

I smirk. "Have I become predictable already?"

"A little," he admits, finally tilting his head enough that I can see the playful grin on his face.

"I'm impressed," I admit, sitting next to him. "Neither Jace nor Harper saw you out there."

"I'm quiet when I want to be."

"Not enough to hide from me," I point out.

"Maybe I wanted you to see me."

I tilt my head, not bothering to hide the annoyed expression on my face. "That's cute."

He chuckles.

"Thanks for the phone," I say, scanning the horizon out of habit.

"Did the guy call?"

I nod. "You know any Vaer named Ian?"

"About twelve of them." Drew snorts sarcastically. "It's not exactly a unique name."

"Yeah, well this guy certainly acts like he's important." I pause, absently biting my lip as I think it over. "He has power. Money. Influence. How many shifters named Ian are high up in the ranks?"

Drew hesitates. "Are we sure he's even a shifter?"

I pause, debating inwardly. "I believe so. The Vaer aren't fond of anyone outside their circles, and they're not always loyal even to each other. Whoever this Ian guy is, I doubt he's human. They wouldn't trust a human with someone as important as Irena."

"Maybe," Drew says ominously.

"You disagree?"

"It's a risk, that's all." He shrugs. "Be careful not to assume."

"Fair." I nod. "Still, if you can find anyone named Ian in the upper echelon of Vaer society, it would be a lead."

I tense, aching for something to go on already.

We're running out of time.

For a moment, we sit in silence, watching the sun set on the horizon. The wind kicks up, rustling the trees, reminding us that up here in the sky, we can have a moment of chilly silence. Below us, the helicopter blades spin faster, the chopper finally lifting into the sky.

"I see why you like it up here," he says.

"Helps me think," I confess. "But since you're here, I guess we can talk."

He shrugs. "I like the quiet."

"Maybe, but there are some things you need to tell me."

"Oh?" He laughs, giving me a brief once-over, charmingly astonished as always that I would dare demand something of him.

"You know her," I say with a nod toward the helicopter as it finally takes off.

The chopper's tinted windows are too far away for me to make out expressions or detail, but the vague outline of a face watches us as it flies off in the opposite direction.

"I know *of* her," Drew corrects.

I shake my head, not satisfied. "When she joined us in the forest, I saw that look of recognition on your face." I stare him down, daring him to lie to me. "You *know* her."

He holds my gaze, never one to back down, and for a moment it looks like he's not going to answer me.

I frown, not bothering to mask the deep aggravation I feel with this man.

"Fine," he mutters, looking off. "Yes, we've met. Briefly."

"And?"

"And nothing. I don't trust her. I don't trust any of them." He gestures toward the embassy, seemingly referring to everyone in the dojo with one sweeping brush of his arm.

"How have you had the opportunity to even meet her?" I watch his face, studying every line, looking for any indication of a lie. "When did it happen?"

"Why are you so interested?" he asks, clearly irritated.

"Call it a hunch," I say dryly.

Something in my tone seems to catch his attention, and he tilts his head toward me, watching me just as intently as I watch him. "What do you think I am, exactly?"

"Annoying," I admit. "Frustrating."

Drew laughs and looks off into the distance, going silent once more. Just like that, he thinks he's diffused the tension and gotten off the hook.

He hasn't, but I wonder if there's any point in pursuing the topic. The more he avoids the truth, the less I trust him.

My heart twists at the thought, and I look away.

"What's so awful that you don't want me to know, Drew?" I ask quietly, a bit of my wounded heart seeping through into the question. My voice is softer than I intended, a little more sincere and curious than I wanted it to be.

He opens his mouth to answer but pauses as his gaze lands on me. His jaw clamps shut, and he sighs, rubbing his eyes as he no doubt tries to find the words.

"The world outside of the embassy is not the one you see in here," he says. "Titles matter. Hierarchy matters. Class matters. Money matters."

"So?"

"So, I've done terrible things," he admits, looking at his hands. "Out of obligation. Out of loyalty to the family that raised me. To keep my title."

"Hmm. So, you *do* have a title."

"Don't play dumb," he says with a wry grin. "You know I have authority out there. You already pieced together the clues I gave you, and you probably picked up on some I didn't mean to give."

Yep.

But I'm not going to tell him that.

"Look," I say, absently picking at a loose thread on my pants to distract myself. "It sounds like we've both been in terrible positions where we had no choice but to act against our moral fiber. If anyone understands, it's me. What I don't understand is why you think hiding so much from me will make me trust you." I catch his eye, trying to drive home my point. "Drew, the more you hide from me, the less likely I am to listen to you."

"I know," he admits softly. Stoically.

With those two little words, he betrays so much.

The tortured way his jaw tenses, like he wants to say more but physically can't. The way he leans in, like he wants to pull me close. The way his eyes drift to my lips, to my neck, to my chest.

He abruptly clears his throat and reaches into his pocket, pulling out a folded piece of paper. "This came for you. Jace was going to hide it from you, too, so I stole it."

I pluck the note from Drew's hands, only to find familiar writing on the page—with a picture of my ghostly pale sister shoved between the folds.

Tick, tock.

"I'll kill this asshole," I mutter, crumpling the paper in my hands.

"I'll help." Drew sets a hand on my thigh, and a soothing warmth seeps from him into me. My heart stutters at his touch, and as much as I hate to admit it, his comforting presence makes me feel a little bit better.

As dusk rolls over the dojo, a foreboding sense of finality settles into my shoulders. Soon, I'm going to learn the truth about Drew—and when I expose the skeletons in his closet, I wonder if I'll still feel this way.

CHAPTER SEVENTEEN

As the night ticks on, I'm getting more and more concerned.

Levi isn't back yet.

I pace the courtyard where he usually sleeps as the stars glitter in the night sky above. It's close to midnight, and I haven't seen him all day.

That's unusual, even for him.

I'm getting antsy. Truth be told, these past few days have been almost too much for me—too much of the politics, too much of the law, too much of a reminder of the world out there that's salivating for a chance to hunt me down.

To pin me.

To trap me.

To drain away the magic that's *mine.*

Part of me wonders if this intuitive concern is just me aching for an adventure, for some adrenaline, for a trip beyond the walls. The confines of Jace's dojo have begun to feel a little like a prison, and though I can technically leave, I wonder how long that will be the case.

After all, Harper said it herself—Jace might have good intentions, but he often makes misguided decisions.

The patter of boots on stone catches my attention, and I pause. Ear straining, I listen as the muffled steps race toward me from somewhere behind the courtyard's walls.

The silhouetted of a man pops into view, leaning against the wall as he pauses for breath. He's draped in shadow, but as his head turns toward me, I recognize the outline.

Tucker.

"What is it?" I ask, my voice tense.

He's nearly vibrating with anxiety. Something happened, and whatever it was, it isn't good.

"We have to go." Tucker points back toward the forest. "Now. Levi's in trouble."

I stiffen. "What?"

"He was headed back toward the dojo," Tucker says, still gasping for breath. "I waved him down, wanted to say hi, because I'm a charming and amazing friend," he adds casually, running a hand through his hair. "But as he angled toward me, a net shot through the air and snared him. He went down *hard*. I ran toward him, but all I found was a crater where he landed. He's gone, and Rory, someone *took* him. There's a trail—tire imprints, boot prints, the works. I can track them, but it looks like we're facing at least forty men. We have to go. Now."

"Damn it." I rub my neck, my mind racing.

This could be a hit designed to lure me out of the dojo, but I doubt it. Not many people know about my connection to Levi—and of those who do, I'm not sure who would have the resources to snare him in particular, and with so many soldiers at their disposal.

Zurie likes to handle things on her own. Solo, with maybe one or two other Spectres at most. She keeps to herself and cleans up her own messes.

And that's all I am to her—a bit of chaos she has to tame.

I look at Tucker, completely focused. "How far onto the embassy grounds were you?"

"Along the edge, on the north side."

Overhead, three familiar dragons soar in tight formation toward the embassy. I've seen these three before—they're some of the most active scouts around the dojo, and usually the ones I have to avoid any time I sneak into the command center.

"Something tells me Jace knows about this," I mutter, racing up the steps toward the building.

Before I can reach the door, however, it flies open—and Jace stands in my path.

"*There* you are," he says sternly, as if he's been on the hunt for a while.

"Levi—"

"I know," he interjects. "We're on it, Rory."

"Good. Then let's go."

"*My* team is on it," Jace says sternly. "I'll handle this."

"And you expect me to do what, exactly?" I gesture up to the castle. "Wait in my room like a good girl?"

"I don't care where you are," he says flippantly. "As long

as it's within the embassy. My team is capable, Rory, more than—"

"Your *team* wanted to rip his throat out when they met him," I remind the Grand Master. "Your *team* wanted to kill him for being feral without bothering to realize he's still alert. Sentient. Aware." I step in, closing the gap between us, my cold fury seeping through my veins. "And don't think for one *moment* that I didn't notice the expression on your face the other day. I'm not letting him die, Jace—but *you* might."

In my periphery, Tucker watches our exchange with his arms crossed and a stern expression on his face. Like me, he won't let anything happen to Levi.

"That's entirely unfair," Jace says, his voice deep and dark. "I have been nothing but accommodating to you *and* him from the start."

I scoff. "That's a generous way to put it."

"You're staying," he barks.

"I'm going!" I snap back, the depths of my fury finally digging deep into my core. A burst of white light arcs across my body, and I feel it expand within every vein.

For a moment, I glow with my rage—and even the Grand Master takes a step back.

In the silence, the crackle of magic across my skin spikes through the air.

"What do I have to *do* with you, woman?" Jace asks quietly, his brows knit together with anger. "Chain you to the *bed*?"

"Try zip ties, first," Tucker says with a chuckle.

I glare at the weapons expert, but he just smirks and shrugs.

Without another word, I stalk off toward the dojo's armory. Tucker has some dangerous toys, sure, but I need the big guns. I plan to load myself down with everything I can carry—and given my newly enhanced strength, that's a considerable amount of firepower.

As I thunder through the dojo, my hands balled into fists, Drew steps out of a side hallway and joins me without a word. He never looks at me, never says a thing, but I already know what he wants.

For whatever reason—be it for Levi or for me—he's coming, too.

Good. The more soldiers I have on my side, the better. Especially if we're facing a small army.

Levi's in trouble, and the brutes who took him won't play by the rules—not if they're stealing dragons from within an embassy's territory.

This is war, and it's going to be bloody.

Nothing will stop me. I'm going to save Levi, and if Jace can get his head out of his ass long enough to grab a gun, he can come, too.

CHAPTER EIGHTEEN

Through the scope of a Fairfax-issued rifle, I survey a meadow.

It's deadly quiet. In the chilly night, nothing chirps. Nothing rustles. The only sound is the agonizing wheeze of an injured dragon, lying wounded and bleeding in the middle of the field.

My every impulse is to run to him—in the silvery moonlight, it's easy to recognize Levi. His beautiful scales. The majestic curve of his neck. The massive wings.

But this is clearly a trap.

Chains cover his body, brutal barbs that slice through his stunning blue skin. I grit my teeth in anger, and it's abundantly clear there will be no mercy tonight.

These people came onto embassy land, kidnapped a dragon I adore, tore his body nearly to shreds, and are now lying in wait with their trap set.

Tonight, they're going to *die.*

I scan the edge of the forest, only to find forty-three of them sloppily hidden among the trees. There's probably another dozen or so hidden among the canopy, simply invisible due to my vantage point. Those I can see shift their weight and adjust in their seats, some of them in the branches with their scopes trained on the meadow as well.

Though this would be a fairly simple victory for me, I hesitate.

Based on their lackluster stealth and cloaking ability, it's easy to assume these are nothing more than well-equipped amateurs.

And yet, somehow, these bumbling idiots were smart enough to not only capture a dragon as swift as Levi, but also knew to take him off of embassy land. This strip of the forest is owned by humans—which means Jace and his dragons can't technically shift.

They're not supposed to *shoot* anyone, either, so we're still breaking laws by being here. But it's a lot easier to go unnoticed in their human forms, sneaking under the canopy, than it would be if they shifted.

This puts the dragons at a disadvantage, but these fools don't seem to realize they're dealing with an army as brilliantly trained in hand-to-hand combat as they are in dragon fighting.

Either they're stupid, or I'm missing something. Both options make me a little nervous.

Jace kneels beside me, his rifle aimed toward the forest floor as he glares into the field. We briefly exchange a tense look, but this isn't the time or place to argue.

He doesn't want me to be here, but he knows I would show up anyway, regardless. Short of locking me in a cell—and probably not even then—there's nothing he can do to force me to obey.

And, if we're being honest, he absolutely *could* lock me in a cell. He's probably tempted to do it, in fact, and he very well might follow through one day.

But right now, Levi's life is at stake, and Jace seems to be agreeing to yet another tense peace with me in an effort to save him.

"Negative," Jace whispers into the earpiece he's wearing. "No need for backup. Secure the embassy."

He pauses, no doubt listening to someone on the other end of the line.

Apparently satisfied, Jace leans toward me, his voice low. "Stay here."

I suppress the urge to roll my eyes.

Right. Sure. Whatever you say, Chief.

Without waiting for me to agree, he gestures to the twenty-five soldiers behind him, ordering them to fan out. We left most of the military back at the dojo, just in case this was merely a diversion, but twenty-five expert soldiers are more than enough to handle this.

Quietly, they tear through the shadows, converging on the soldiers from both directions.

Without a sound, Tucker slips up next to me from the pitch-black forest, the butt of his military-issued rifle pressed hard against his shoulder. He nudges my arm with his elbow and signals toward the nearest group of enemy soldiers.

Let's join the party, the gesture says.

I nod. *With pleasure.*

Drew slips out of the shadows as we stand, taking the lead and silently stalking through the woods ahead of us. I frown in slight annoyance, but it doesn't matter. Even if he's in front of me, it won't stop me or slow me down.

Before we can reach the soldiers, bullets rip through the night on the far end of the meadow. Men shout. The orange flash of guns going off rips through the darkness, and bodies thud to the dirt.

Drew, Tucker, and I all run a little faster to join the chaos.

Movement overhead catches my eye, and I tilt my gun upward as a barrel aims down at me. Drew follows suit, and in unison, we each fire off two rounds.

A man grunts. The branch creaks, and Drew takes a step back, nearly pressing himself against me as the dead soldier falls to the ground, right where he would have been.

Drew briefly tilts his head, checking on me, and I nod for him to continue. The shifter carries on, a little more careful to watch the treetops this time.

I pause briefly by the man's body, scanning his face and uniform, but there's no logo. Nothing about him looks familiar.

Tucker does the same, but his eyes widen with recognition.

"Shit," he hisses.

I glance at him, but he's already scanning the branches above us, shoulders tense.

"What?" Drew demands quietly.

Tucker shakes his head. When Drew returns his attention to the forest, Tucker looks at me, a concerned expression on his face.

Something is definitely wrong. He just doesn't want Drew to know, and he can't tell me until we're alone.

I let Drew continue ahead of us, slowing my pace and leaning toward Tucker in the hopes he can lower his voice enough that the dragon shifter ahead of us won't hear.

He takes the hint.

Leaning into me, he sets his mouth close to my ear, the rough stubble along his jaw brushing against my hair. "They're Knight rebels," he whispers to me. "They know who I am, and they hate the General."

"Damn it," I mutter.

Tucker nods, lifting his gun, scanning the forest for more of the soldiers. I can't let any of these guys see him—or it might be game over for his secret.

A short distance from us, the chaos spills out into the field as Jace's well-trained fighters make quick work of the sloppy amateurs who captured Levi. One by one, the nameless soldiers begin to fall as the master fighters quickly clear them out.

But something isn't right.

These men are unfamiliar with stealth and barely capable of hand to hand combat, and yet they somehow captured and restrained a dragon as powerful as Levi?

It doesn't add up.

This—the trap—I get the feeling it hasn't even sprung yet.

I pause. "Guys, don't—"

I hear the gun go off before I see where it came from, and purely on instinct, I grab Tucker's shirt. Yanking him toward me, I use every ounce of strength I possess to throw him off balance.

And I'm lucky.

I'm lucky he didn't fight it. I'm lucky I caught him off guard because the bullet sails through the air, right where his head was a moment before.

The three of us duck for cover, each taking refuge behind a tree.

"I am going to give you *so many orgasms*," Tucker says breathlessly from the tree next to mine. "You are the fucking *best*."

As much as I enjoy that delightful little promise of his, I

tap my finger to my lips, telling him in the politest way to shut the hell up.

We're not out of trouble yet.

"Oh, Rory," a familiar man's voice growls. "Have an entourage now, do you?"

I grit my teeth, nose wrinkling in disgust.

Diesel.

That *ass.*

I peek around the corner of the tree, eyes straining against the shadows of the forest. And there, deep in the woods, is a familiar silhouette. He lifts a gun, aiming it toward my tree, and fires.

Quickly, I duck behind the trunk as the bullet shatters the bark next to my face. My grip tightening on my rifle, I tense, preparing to take out one of the greatest Spectres alive.

This ought to be fun.

"I thought we were friends, Diesel!" I shout, forcing a hint of mock wounding into my voice. "What's with the gun?"

"There's a big bounty on you now, kid. Dead or alive." He chuckles. "Dead is easier. Nothing personal."

Fast as lightning, I kneel and twist, pressing the barrel of the rifle against the trunk for balance. I lift my gun, scope trained on the outline's chest as he aims at me again.

Perfect. One shot, and I can end him once and for all.

The hair on my neck stands on end, however. A chill creeps down my spine, and I lift my scope in time to see a boot sailing toward my face from the branches above.

It's too fast. All I can do is register that it's there. Even though I try to duck the blow, I can't possibly get out of the way in time.

The shoe hits me in the face.

Hard.

I tumble backward, sliding across the dirt, my gun clattering against a tree from the force of the blow. My world spins, but I've been hit harder.

As spots dance along my vision, I force myself to stand and draw a pistol from the holster at my waist.

Whoever attacked me lands on the dirt and lifts a gun. The silhouette is feminine, with curves and a thin waist, but her face is shrouded in shadow.

"You're so predictable," Zurie says, her frosty voice biting through the night.

My blood runs cold, but I hold my ground. "So that was your plan, huh? Use some amateurs as a diversion?"

"Pretty much," she says. "It worked, didn't it?"

I can't see much of the forest behind her, shrouded as it is in shadow, but I do hear the grunt of Tucker taking a blow. Drew groans with effort, and it seems like Diesel has the two of them cornered. No gunfire, thankfully, but that could change at any moment.

Looks like I'm on my own.

Zurie and I circle each other, slowly creeping toward the moonlit meadow. The light will give me the upper hand—she excels in the dark, as if she's able to see even when there's no light at all.

She passes into a silvery beam of moonlight, and I catch the familiar sight of her grim, determined face.

"And Diesel?" I nod. "How did you rope him into this?"

She shrugs. "He doesn't like you. I didn't even have to cash in a favor."

Wow.

Diesel must *really* hate me, then.

I'm almost to the meadow. Almost to the light. I need to stall her, wait until we can ease toward a better fighting ground, one where I stand a chance.

"Why did you tell me Irena's dead?" I demand, letting a bit of my anger drip through. "Why lie?"

"Because she might as well be." Zurie grits her teeth, her hand tightening around the handle of her gun.

She's—*angry*.

At *Irena.* At the golden child.

I frown, baffled. "Why? What did she do?"

Zurie hesitates, briefly scanning my face as if she can't believe I would ask such a stupid question. It barely lasts a second, though, and it's followed by understanding. She laughs derisively. "You really didn't figure it out?"

"You know how much I hate games," I snap.

Zurie grins, eyes narrowed, sly and judgmental as ever. "She betrayed us, Rory. She turned us in. To Mason. To the Vaer. It was *her.*"

For a moment, I can't breathe.

If Zurie wasn't having so much fun gloating, it would have been the perfect moment for her to attack.

But this—no, it's a lie.

It has to be.

To screw with me.

I scoff, correcting my aim, tilting the barrel of my gun toward her face this time. "Bull—"

"The Vaer aren't known for honoring commitments." Zurie pauses in the woods, no longer letting me slowly guide her toward the field. "She was an idiot to make a deal with them, and it backfired. She turned you in, Rory. She turned us both in."

I search Zurie's eyes for signs of a lie, but in the darkness, I can't be sure. She taught me how to do this, after all. She could be masking her tells, and even though her stern face looks genuine, I don't believe her for a second.

"Irena would never do that," I insist.

Without missing a beat, I lift my gun, aiming for the space between Zurie's eyes.

And I fire.

Zurie rolls out of the way as my bullet shatters the bark on the tree behind her. "I hope you had fun," she chides, recovering. "Because it's time to fix you."

She fires her pistol, and I dive out of the way barely a

moment before a tranquilizer dart digs into the tree behind me.

Unfortunately for *her,* I'm carrying bullets. Not darts.

I aim for her chest and fire again, but I'm operating at a disadvantage here. This is the woman who trained me, who knows my every move, who can tell what I'm about to do as I decide to do it. She can read me, almost effortlessly, and she manages to yet again leap out of the way.

She fires another dart at me, and this time it grazes my shoulder. It scratches through the fabric of my shirt, but the needle breaks off, a bit of it embedded in my skin.

For a moment, a rush of wooziness burns through me. The world briefly spins. I stagger, but I push through the disorienting haze.

She's not going to win that easily.

I rip the half-submerged needle out of my arm as she charges, trying to recover with time enough to fire, but I lift my gun a second too late.

She hits my elbow hard, and I groan in pain as the gun is knocked from my hand. Fist raised, she aims for my temple. I block, spinning, and kick her hard in the gut.

She doubles over, and I take my opening to knee her in the face.

Zurie falls on her back, blood streaming from her nose, but she's only down for a moment. In seconds, she jumps onto her feet, wiping the blood from her mouth in a fluid motion.

"You're faster with that magic," she mutters approvingly. "Impressive. Too bad you can't keep it."

She raises her gun again and fires—but I'm through playing games.

Fast as lightning, I reach into the depths of my soul, deep into the core where my magic burns hot, and summon my incredible power.

I lift my hands, my fingers surging with heat, and fire a blast of brilliant white light at the woman who spent half of her life training me.

The magic burns the tranquilizer dart to ash, dissolving it into dust as it tears through the air. The white light sails toward Zurie, and I have to confess, part of me wants it to hit her. Part of me wants my magic to end this, to destroy her, to know once and for all I'm safe.

But I never will be. Even if Zurie dies, Diesel will just take over—and he's worse than Zurie could ever be.

And if Irena really betrayed us, well—

No. I can't think about that now.

Zurie dives out of the way with seconds to spare, hitting the ground hard as the brilliant white light shatters a tree. The massive trunk groans as it topples, splintering, the branches crashing through the canopy as whatever remains of the giant oak falls to the ground beside us.

My former mentor gapes at the tree, but only for a moment. She turns her head toward me, gritting her teeth, practically fuming.

I don't give her the opportunity to speak.

"I'm giving you one chance, Zurie," I say, seething. "Call a truce. Leave me be and call off the others. I will *never* come back to you. I will *never* be your obedient little assassin ever again. If you come for me—if you back me into a corner like this even one more time, you will die. And if you ever *dare* to touch one of my men, I *will* end you. It *will* be war. We will hunt each other until one of us is dead."

Slowly, Zurie stands. She watches me with chilly detachment, the way I've seen her survey warzones before. Studying. Dissecting. Analyzing.

Like I've done so many times before, she's weighing her options.

"You damn *traitor!*" Jace yells, his voice echoing off the forest. "I knew it, Tucker! I'll *kill* you!"

My chest tightens, and I can't help myself. I look over my shoulder, careful to keep my former mentor in my periphery.

In the meadow, Tucker is shoved onto his knees, his arms held behind his back by three of Jace's soldiers. He struggles against them, twisting in their grasp, but he's vastly outnumbered. There's nothing he can do. They glare down at him, one of them pushing his head toward Jace's boots.

And, to my horror, Jace aims a gun at Tucker's head.

"No," I say breathlessly.

I have to stop this.

But if I let Zurie go—

"I'll consider your offer, Rory," Zurie says with a wry grin. She darts off into the forest, not waiting for me to reply.

I've heard *that* before. It's what she tells the difficult Spectres and Knights when they give her a ridiculous offer. It's what she says when she wants to string someone along, dangling a carrot in their face just long enough for them to comply—so that she can shoot them in the back when they're no longer useful.

It's a no.

I swallow hard, torn between saving Tucker and letting my greatest enemy leave.

Jace cocks the gun.

Damn it.

I bolt into the field, letting Zurie slip into the night. Jace might have just cost me *everything.*

"Stop!" I shout, my chest tightening as I race toward him. "Don't you *dare!*"

Jace tilts his body just enough to see me, never lifting his gun, moments from sending a bullet through Tucker's brain.

Tucker manages to peek up from between two locks of his hair, his face twisted in anger and rage.

"He's a Knight, Rory!" Jace shouts. "A *Knight.* I knew there was something wrong with him." The Grand Master sets his finger on the trigger. "And I don't allow traitors to live."

CHAPTER NINETEEN

"I know!" I yell, skidding to a stop between Tucker and Jace. "I know, all right? I've known he's a Knight."

The moment I step between the two men, Jace instinctively turns the gun away from me. It's almost like he doesn't even realize he did it—but it now points to the ground.

I am not, however, in the clear.

Jace watches me with cold fury. He's still as a stone, body rigid and tense, and I wonder what's going through his head right now.

"You *knew?*" he says, his voice dangerous and dark.

The full force of his intense gaze bores into me, as chilling and startling as any warning glare Zurie ever gave me—it's strikingly similar to the expression she would don just before punching me in the gut, breaking a bone, or knocking me down when she felt I had underperformed on a mission.

It makes my blood run cold.

For the first time, I see Jace as the world sees him. Fierce. Ferocious. Imposing. Inches away from murder.

This is what it's like to face the Grand Master's wrath —and I can't say I enjoy it.

Drew darts out of the forest, about fifty feet away. The movement catches my attention, though Jace doesn't so much as flinch. Drew's eyes lock momentarily with mine, and for a second, he seems to pause to take in the scene.

But then his gaze drifts to the gun so close to my leg.

That sets him off.

His brow furrows with anger. With hate. It's like something in him snaps, something fierce and protective. His eyes get sharp and cold. Without so much as a word of warning, he lifts his gun and aims at Jace's chest.

It's not a good move.

Ten of the soldiers around us swarm him, trying desperately to restrain the muscled shifter.

But Drew is a tank. A man of muscle and strength, someone who doesn't go down easy.

He elbows one soldier in the face, and two more replace the one he knocked out. Another knocks the gun from his hand, only to get a fist to the jaw.

Five more soldiers rush to help their comrades.

One by one, blow after blow, they eventually manage to subdue the fire dragon—but at a price. Four of them lay unconscious around him, and it takes eight soldiers with enhanced dragon strength to wrangle him in.

He drops to his knees, four hands pushing his head down even as he manages to glare at Jace with all the hatred and fire of a sun.

I could have used this distraction to take Jace's weapon. I could have taken out the soldiers holding Tucker hostage and run, but it would mean no redemption— for him or for me. It would mean abandoning Levi and Drew.

I won't do it, no matter how soft that makes me.

The dojo master tilts his head only slightly, like a hunter focusing on its prey, and looks at one of the soldiers holding Tucker hostage. "Back up. Out of earshot."

"Yes, sir."

The soldiers nod in unison and drag Tucker backward. The weapons expert tries to stand, but they don't give him the chance. The three soldiers holding him drag him mercilessly across the grass, his heels digging into the dirt as he wrestles in their grip.

"Jace, there's more to this than meets the eye," I say softly.

He takes a step toward me, and the cold clink of the gun in his hand is a sharp reminder of how close Tucker just came to a quick and bloody death. The barrel is still aimed toward the ground as the thunderbird shifter leans toward me. "How long have you known?"

I meet his gaze, unwilling to so much as flinch. I will not show weakness, not with so much at stake.

But the time for guarding Tucker's secret is over, and I have to share at least some of the truth.

"Shortly before the attack on the Vaer," I admit.

"Damn it, Rory." Jace shakes his head, the hard lines of his jaw tensing as he briefly looks off into the forest. I can imagine how many bodies are littered along the floor of the woods, and I suspect he took out most of them.

"I tailed him into the forest and out of your territory," I continue. "I saw him meet with Knights. Saw him give an update."

"On what?" Jace's voice has a menacing growl to it.

"Me."

Jace glares over my shoulder, in Tucker's direction, and I hear the creak of skin over the metal gun in his hand as he tightens his grip.

He could still shoot.

"Out there, in the forest, I was going to kill him," I say simply. "I was about to kill all of them."

That, at least, catches Jace's attention. "And why didn't you?" He gives me a brief once over, a hint of disgust in his voice. "Is he that good in bed?"

I grit my teeth at his tone, resisting the impulse to punch him in the throat. "Shove your jealousy up your ass for two seconds and *listen,* Jace."

"Listening," he snaps, narrowing his eyes.

"He lied to them." I nod toward Tucker. "Even though he didn't know I was there, he gave them a false report. He covered for me and has done so for most of the time I've known him. They have so much false information, they won't ever know what's true and what isn't. All thanks to *him.*"

"I don't believe you."

"Why the *fuck* would I lie?" I resist the impulse to shake him by his collar, but only barely. "I held a knife to his throat, ready to end him if he didn't tell me the truth. I don't suffer traitors either, Jace."

We glare at each other, the minutes creeping by, each daring the other to show weakness. To cave.

Neither of us do.

Jace leans in, our noses almost touching, but there's nothing romantic about this. His warm breath rolls over me, and for a moment, we both seem capable of suppressing the overwhelming mate-bond that clouds our judgment most of the time.

"Rory, you betrayed me." His voice is quiet. Tense. Wounded. "Not only did you bring a feral dragon into my home, but you brought a *Knight*. And, somehow, also thanks to you, I've had to play host to the shifter I hate most in this world."

We both briefly look at Drew, who's massive biceps bulge against his sleeves as he wrestles with the grip of the remaining soldiers barely holding him at bay. Beside him, one of those he knocked unconscious groggily begins to stir.

Jace grabs my chin, and I expect it to be rough—but it's not.

Gently, he tilts my head until I can't help but look at him. "I've never trusted any of the men you brought here," he says quietly. "Least of all Tucker, and I was *right* to think he was up to something. I was *right* to assume he's no good. But the most painful part of all of this? The worst part?" He pauses, jaw tensing as his eyes rove over my face. "The worst part is that now I don't even know if I can trust *you*."

I won't lie. As much as I don't want to care what he says, that stings.

"You know why I lied?" I gesture toward the field, covered as it is with soldiers and hostages. "This. This is why. I *knew* you would act like this." I want to knock some sense through that thick skull of his, but I somehow manage to refrain. "I knew you would try to kill him, no matter what I said."

That's not the whole truth, but it will have to do for the moment so that I can make my point.

"You're overreacting," I add, rather curtly. "Just like I knew you would."

He laughs humorlessly. "*I'm* over—Gods, Rory, you have *got* to be kidding."

"I'm entirely serious." I point at Tucker, keeping my voice low despite the urgency in my tone. "In the Vaer stronghold, he took out dozens of shifters on the catwalks to ensure *you* didn't die." I square my shoulders, ready to knock Jace off his high horse. "He continues to meet with the Knights to lie to them and feed them the sort of misinformation that leaves them scrambling for a new plan each time. He alone is the reason we haven't had a Knights attack on the embassy since I arrived—they're waiting on intel from *him*, and he continues to *lie*. For you. For me. To keep us all *safe*."

"He's one of *them*," Jace says with a sneer. "How can you possibly trust anything he says?"

"I trust him more than I trust you," I admit.

It's the sort of honesty that claws its way out of you when you don't want it to—the truth, yes, but phrased in a hurtful way far harsher than you intended. And, of course, at the absolute *worst* time.

Jace grabs my arm, his tight grip on my bicep almost painful, but I don't flinch. He pulls me close, his hard chest pressing against my body, that disappointed scowl almost burning into my soul as he stares down at me.

I can tell that hurt him. Deeply. It was the kind of comment that leaves a lasting wound, all without blows ever being exchanged.

But it's the truth—and it doesn't have to be.

"He doesn't try to lock me away," I point out. "He doesn't withhold information from me or outright *lie*, all in some misguided attempt to keep me safe." I give Jace the same disgusted once-over he gave me not long ago. "He's a brilliant fighter and a loyal asset to this team, and you would be an absolute fool to kill him after all he's sacrificed to be here."

"No, I would be a fool to let a Knight live," Jace says menacingly. "*Especially* the General's son."

Ah, shit.

He knows.

"That's right." Jace nods, apparently seeing something in my expression I didn't mean to give away. "Yet another secret you've kept from me. You knew that, too."

"Can you blame me?" Though he still has one arm pinned to my side, I gesture toward the field with my free hand. "Look at this. I knew you wouldn't react well. There was no way for me to tell you. Absolutely none at all."

"I'm keeping my people safe," Jace sneers, not really acknowledging my point. "I'm keeping you safe, whether you like it or not. This is what it takes to lead."

"Safe from what?"

"From organizations that are actively trying to kill us!"

"You accepted me," I point out, locking eyes with him. "You know what I am. What I was trained to be. You pretend to forget about it every time you talk about *keeping me safe,* but in the back of your mind, you know exactly what I can do. Who I can break." I take a step toward him, chin lifted in defiance. "Do you know how many dragons I've killed, Jace?"

His mouth settles into a grim line, and it's clear he neither knows nor *wants* to know.

"I'm not proud of any of it, and neither is he." I briefly nod toward Tucker. "He was forced into this life, just like me. Neither of us wanted any part of these organizations. Neither of us wanted to kill. And neither of us had any damn choice in the matter."

Jace's grip tightens on my arm, but he doesn't say anything.

That's a good sign.

It means he's listening. Processing. Considering what I have to say.

It also means I might still be able to salvage this.

"He and I had the same childhood," I add quietly. "We faced the same dilemmas. We had the same terrible, impossible choices to make." I poke Jace roughly to make my point, my fingertip pressing against the hard muscle of his abs. "If you kill Tucker, you might as well kill me."

"Don't say that," Jace says softly, shaking his head. "*Damn* it, don't..."

Begrudgingly, he lets me go. He takes a step backward, never finishing his thought. He runs his hand through his hair, the other still holding the gun, and turns his back on all of us.

As he sets his free hand on his hip, I hear a rough and shaky sigh escape him. He stares up at the moon, seemingly debating his options.

I'm tempted to get on my soapbox and lecture him, but I've said enough. Anything more would be overkill, and probably of the unhelpful variety. I tense my jaw, suppressing the urge to speak, forcing myself to wait.

It's agonizing.

"Let the asshole go," Jace commands, his voice carrying through the field.

Behind me, I hear the grunt of Drew shaking someone off of him. I almost laugh that the soldiers knew exactly who Jace was talking about, but there's still too much at stake to relax.

As I turn my head, Drew runs toward me, his intense glare focused on Jace.

"Are you all right?" the fire dragon asks quietly as he nears, stopping beside me. His voice is dark and low, like he wants nothing more than to tear Jace a new asshole and just wants any excuse to go do it.

"I'm fine," I say curtly, returning my attention to the Grand Master.

We're not out of trouble yet.

Jace pivots on his heel, his gaze skipping over me as he points at a few of the nearest soldiers. "You eight, get Levi to the medic ward. Patch him up but keep him sedated until he heals completely. He might lash out if he wakes up too suddenly."

I frown, not loving that option. "Jace—"

"Don't." He holds a finger toward me, squeezing his eyes shut, like he doesn't want to hear my voice right now.

Since Tucker's life still hangs in the balance, I comply and snap my mouth closed.

It's just a bit of sedation—Levi will be okay.

Jace sighs, rubbing his jaw, and finally shoves his pistol into the holster at his waist. "I will grant a *very* fragile, *very* temporary pardon to the Knight," Jace says through gritted teeth. "Get him on his feet."

With a rush of relief, I look over my shoulder to find the three soldiers who were holding Tucker step backward. He abruptly stands, roughly brushing off his shirt as he glares daggers at them. He no doubt wants to break all their noses, but he is thankfully holding back.

For the moment.

"You," Jace finally says, his voice drenched with anger.

I return my attention to the Grand Master, only to find him pointing at me.

"You and I have a *lot* to discuss," he snaps. He whistles abruptly, the piercing sound splitting through the night, and nods back toward the dark castle in the distance. "Now."

With a steadying breath, I indulge him. He waits until I near, and together, we head back toward the dojo with him slightly in the lead. He has me firmly in his peripheral vision, and I have the eerie feeling he'll be watching a little closer from now on.

That, I have to confess, is *not* good.

CHAPTER TWENTY

As I sit in the war room adjacent to Jace's suite, the sun cracks over the mountains in the distance.

Day five of Irena's countdown.

My chest seizes with anxiety. Nerves. Concern.

Technically, today is the day he promised to go over his intel with me, but so far he hasn't brought her up at all. I *hate* waiting. *Hate* the fact that only Jace and Drew can get me the information I need to formulate a plan.

Unless they get me something concrete—and *soon*—I might have to do this on my own after all.

I rub my eyes to get rid of the sting from my sheer

exhaustion, since the Grand Master hasn't let me out of this room since we got back.

I've decided to give him another title—the Royal Pain in My Ass.

Jace sits beside me, his elbows on the table as he rubs his forehead. Tucker sits on the other end of the long, rectangular table, as far from me as Jace could put him, and Drew leans against the wall behind me.

Any time I look over my shoulder, the fire dragon is glaring daggers at Tucker. He's been doing that pretty much nonstop since he realized what Tucker is.

For a few moments, none of us speak.

We've been in here for hours, giving Jace the info he asks for. I tried to keep our exit a secret, but it just wasn't possible—and, as we speak, crews are down there, patching it up, locking the sconce, destroying the one exit I had out of this place.

Awesome.

"I can't believe you hid a secret exit from me," Jace says quietly. Deeply injured. He won't look at me and hasn't since Tucker told him about the secret wall. "A chink in my armor, something that could compromise my entire building, and you didn't say a word."

I subtly look over my shoulder at Drew—at the shifter who has access to the web of tunnels and secret corridors behind the walls—but he gently shakes his head.

Guess we're keeping that secret, then.

No way *that* could backfire.

Too tired to fight this, I just sigh. "Jace, of course I wanted to tell you. You have weak points of entry in your fortress, and you can't allow that. But Jesus, man, look at us." I gesture between the two of us, even though he won't turn his head my way. "The only time we get along is when we're literally fighting in an arena. You want to hole me away in the Capital, keep me in some tower—"

"I *never* said that," he snaps, finally shifting those stormy gray eyes toward me. "Not *once*. I don't know where this tower nonsense even *comes* from."

"The tower isn't the *point*," I bark back. "It's a fun little metaphor for the life you want me to lead! Good lord, man." I rub my eyes. "I'm talking about the commands, the orders, the militant control you try to keep over my life—for goodness sake, I'm not some porcelain doll."

He glares at me down the bridge of his nose. "You are the key to destroying me. If anyone ever killed you, they could—"

"I'm a goddamn Spectre!" I shout, slamming my fist on the table.

The wood cracks beneath my fist. Though the table doesn't shatter, the crack slices halfway along the surface.

"I'm awake!" Tucker flinches, briefly looking around the room as if he's not entirely sure of where he is. "Who said I was sleeping?" He rubs his eyes. "I agree with her." Eyes still closed, he gestures vaguely in the direction of Drew.

In unison, the rest of us just sigh.

"You shouldn't shout things like that," Jace chides, his heart clearly not in it. He doesn't even seem to care about the table I just ruined. He crosses his arms and leans back in his chair, studying the wood grains in the table's surface. "No one else knows. Just us. I would like to keep it that way."

I shrug. Hopefully, my outburst made a dent in that thick skull of his. But his comment rings a little bell in the back of my mind, and I raise one eyebrow in curiosity. "Not even Harper?"

"Especially not Harper." Jace rolls his eyes. "I protect the secrets worth keeping."

Hmm. I nod in gratitude, fully aware of the trouble he would be in if she ever found out the truth—and the fact that he was hiding it from her.

His hypocrisy is palpable, of course, but I decide not to start a fresh new argument. We won't get anywhere, and I just want this conversation to end.

"How's Levi doing?" I ask to break the silence.

Jace pulls a phone out of his pocket and glances down, tapping the screen with his thumb. His eyes scan something for a moment, probably a report. "Stable."

I let out a sigh of relief.

The four of us are silent, and a large part of me just wants to go to bed. To rest. To let this settle, and to hopefully find Jace more forgiving when I wake.

The other part of me is concerned he'll kill Tucker in his sleep, though, so I'm hesitant to leave until I know everything is safe.

Leaning my elbow on the table, I rest my head on my fist. "Look, Jace—"

"There's nothing else to say." He shakes his head, pinching the bridge of his nose. "Truly, nothing. I see where you're coming from, even if I don't agree with you. And as for him—" Jace nods toward Tucker as the weapons expert tries not to nod off again. "As far as I'm concerned, this isn't over. I don't believe he deserves a pardon, but I won't act until I have proof otherwise. Which I will be looking for," he added with a brief glare toward me.

I'm not happy with that, but it's a truce I can live with for the moment.

"I guess this means you won't be helping me save Irena, then?" I ask, leaning back in my chair so I can study his face.

He leans his tired head on his hand, watching me, so many thoughts buzzing behind those stormy gray eyes of his that I can practically hear the hum of all the things he wants to say.

"I'm tempted to order you to remain here," he admits, tapping his pointer finger on the table. "I'm tempted to lock you in the dungeon if I have to, but you'll still find a way to put yourself in the line of fire." He rolls his eyes. "You always do."

"Thanks," I say dryly.

"So, yes, I'll help," he finishes, a bit begrudgingly. "But we do it my way."

"And that means?"

He gives me a terse look. "We act with strategy. We absolutely will *not* take this mission like you did with Zurie's rescue."

"Hey, I *had* a strategy." I shrug. "You're just mad you weren't part of the original plan."

Jace groans in frustration but doesn't say anything.

I hide a little smirk.

Checkmate.

"Let's look at what information we have, then," Drew says from behind me, dragging out a chair so he can sit down at my side. He leans in toward the two of us, his expression intense and focused.

It's like he doesn't even need sleep. It's baffling—I don't know how he has the energy to discuss any of this.

But I press on. We need to iron out a plan, and we need to do it as soon as freaking possible.

Because Irena—

As I think of my sister, my heart sinks. I can't believe for one moment that Irena would betray us—and certainly not *me*.

It doesn't add up.

"What?" Jace asks, his eyes scanning my face. "What's wrong?"

I shift my gaze toward him, wondering if I should tell them.

Briefly, I look at Tucker as he fights to stay awake at the far end of the table, and this whole nightmare serves as a valuable reminder of what happens if the dark secrets—the big ones—are kept too long.

With a sigh, I tense and prepare myself for the worst.

"Right before he threw me into the pit, Mason said someone betrayed me and the other Spectres to the Vaer," I say softly, looking at the table, refusing to look anyone in the eye as I say the words that feel almost impossible to comprehend. "Someone gave him everything—our names, safehouses, the works. Out there in the forest last night, when I faced off with Zurie, she told me *Irena* was responsible." I rub my eyes in frustration. "With everything that was going on, I couldn't tell if she was lying or not."

Jace shakes his head, furious. "Do you have even *one* normal friend or family member? Just *one* that isn't a direct threat to my dojo and dragon life in general?"

I glare at him, hardly in the mood.

"Do you believe her?" Drew asks simply, showing no emotion.

"No, I don't..." As I trail off, I shake my head on impulse, without thinking it through, but I have to pause and force myself to consider the possibility.

To blindly ignore the idea would be foolish. I have to at least think this through.

After a moment, I tap my finger on the table as I think over the question a little more carefully. "If I'm being honest, I don't know," I confess. "I don't *want* to believe her. Zurie is hardly reliable, and it would make sense if she lied to mess with me." I frown. "To throw me off my game."

And that she did.

"Who do you think the traitor is?" Jace asks, leaning in. "If not Irena?"

"Diesel," I admit.

Everything points to him. Motive. Means. Opportunity. He doesn't have access to all of Zurie's missions, but the two of them grew up together, trained together, and yet she was chosen as the Ghost instead of him.

Though he tried to hide it throughout my life, he has always held a bit of a grudge for that.

"He's a pleasant fellow," Tucker says, yawning as he stretches at the far end of the table. "Jace, can I join the party yet, or—"

"No," the Grand Master snaps, no doubt just to be spiteful.

I roll my eyes.

"That's quite a dilemma," Drew says, ignoring Tucker as he props one foot on the elegant wooden table and leans back in his chair.

Jace shoots him a nasty look, like he can't believe Drew could act so uncivilized. If Drew notices, he doesn't care.

"I'm still going to save her," I say, shaking my head. "I need to ask her myself."

"If she's the traitor, she won't *tell* you," Drew points out with a bemused laugh.

"She will," I say, straightening in my seat. "Zurie's hard to read, but Irena—I'll know in a heartbeat if she's lying."

"And if she's guilty?" Jace raises one eyebrow quizzically. "If she did betray you?"

I sit with the thought, not entirely willing to process it,

but there's only one answer to a question like that. "Then she's dead to me, too."

My heart clenches at the thought, but I'm resolute. Zurie is a terrifying enemy—I don't need another one just like her. After rescuing Zurie, only to have it back-fire, I learned my lesson.

Hardened Spectres like Zurie don't forgive—and they won't ever let me live in peace.

If Irena really was trying to kill me by handing me over to the Vaer, then she's not who I thought she was—and I'll stop her before she has the chance to follow through.

Drew leans forward with a heavy sigh. Beneath the table, his hand slides over my thigh, squeezing lightly in a soothing display of solidarity. I catch his eye and manage a weak smile in gratitude.

"We're doing this, then," Jace says, a hint of disbelief in his voice. "Fine. What information do each of you have thus far?"

"I'm working on getting the blueprints," Drew says carefully. "My contact has to make a few more very risky trips to get all of them, and there's no guarantee he'll succeed. So far, though, he's made good progress. He's been sending me what he has bit by bit."

I tilt my head, annoyed that he hasn't told me this yet.

"What?" Drew asks with an incredulous frown. "I need to make sure they're *real*. Don't give me that look."

"Fine," I mutter, crossing my arms stubbornly.

"Wait," Jace interjects with a suspicious glare at Drew. "After the light drone recon I've done so far, it's clear this place where she's being held is a fortress. It's a military compound far superior to Mason's little smuggling outpost. How the hell are you getting blueprints?"

"I have methods," Drew says dryly.

In unison, Jace and I both frown with annoyance and disbelief.

Deep within me, something shifts—a little flare of doubt, and it's slowly getting stronger.

A while back, I jokingly asked Drew if he was a Vaer—and he very quickly said no. But he seems to have so much access to the very information we need. So much intel. He admitted himself he has authority outside the dojo walls, and Jace said this was the dragon he hated most in the world.

When it comes to dragon-on-dragon violence, who do most shifters hate more than the Vaer?

However, given how tired I am, I just don't want to think about this right now.

I press on, returning to the conversation at hand. "We need to find a way into this fortress of theirs and then, more importantly, find a way back *out* with an unconscious assassin." I lean my head on my hand, weary and aching for sleep. "Not to mention, we need to find the antidote while we're in there. If we don't, she will die. We just don't know how much time is left, and we have to assume she's a breath away from dying."

"And all without official help." Jace adjusts in his seat. "None of this is entirely legal, mind you. Even Harper would question who we're rescuing and why. It would leak your connection to the Spectres, and that's something I can't risk. Any help from the Fairfax family has to come from favors I cash in so that the people involved are willing to do what they're told and not ask questions."

That catches my attention. "You're still willing to cash in favors for me? After—well, after last night?"

"Of course," he says quietly, though he frowns a bit as he says it.

I'm not sure if he's trying to convince me… or *himself*.

"Do we have the guy's name, yet?" Tucker asks. "Anything about him at all besides the fact that he's insane?"

Ah, crap.

Yet another thing I've been hiding from everyone but Drew—the flip phone.

The name.

I clear my throat, wondering if this is just going to start another fight, when Drew interjects. "All we have right now is a first name. Ian."

Drew and I catch each other's gaze, and I nod slightly in gratitude. He winks.

"Keep looking," Jace orders Drew, his eyes glossed over in thought. "We need more than a first name, especially since it could easily be fake."

Drew nods, his eye twitching a little at the order, but he thankfully doesn't press the issue.

"There's a lot missing in this plan." Drew points out. "And we only have, what? A couple days left?"

"A lot missing?" Tucker asks, standing and walking over to us. "What do we even *have*?"

Jace sits upright, scowling. "Hey, don't—"

The scrape of the chair across from me drowns him out as Tucker sits near us, a grin on his face. "Sorry, what was that?"

"Let it go, Jace," I say quietly, just wanting to get on with this. "Please."

The Grand Master frowns and leans back in his seat, but his furious gaze lingers on the Knight sitting barely five feet away.

I tap my finger on the table to get their attention. "We need to find the least guarded entry points into the base, take out the guards, and infiltrate the facility," I say, trying to get us back on track. "And remain unseen through it all."

Drew nods. "Somehow, we have to disable security long enough to avoid being swarmed by guards. Last I heard, there's a battalion there that's two hundred strong, maybe more." His jaw tenses. "All shifters."

"Fabulous," I mutter.

Jace absently scratches his cheek. "Once we're in, we have to find Irena, figure out how to unhook her from their machines, and get her into a transport pod." As the list of things we have to do adds up, he sighs in resigned exhaustion. "We also need to figure out how to transport an unconscious woman out of a military zone, secure a medevac chopper, guard it, and then get the hell out of there."

"Easy," Tucker says with a sarcastic shrug.

"When can your doctor arrive at the dojo to get every-thing ready for her arrival?" I ask, leaning in toward Jace.

He shakes his head. "Irena is *not* coming here."

I nearly flinch in confusion. "But—"

"She's going to a secluded wing of a dragon-only hospital." Jace frowns. "And before you get upset with me, I'm not doing this to punish you."

"You sure about that?" Drew says in a gravely tone.

Jace ignores the fire dragon and intently leans toward me instead. "If we bring her here, she might die. We don't have a hospital here." He gestures vaguely at the room around us. "A medic ward, sure, but that's bare bones. We can't give her the advanced care she needs. We just don't have the facilities."

I sigh.

He has a point.

"But I need to be there," I point out. "When she wakes up, when—"

He nods. "You will. The doctor will keep me informed of her progress, as well as her brain activity. We'll know she's coming-to long before she wakes up."

"But—"

"I promise," he says firmly.

I grit my teeth, hands balling into fists as I force myself to look away from him. She *should* be kept close. She *should* be kept near so that I can talk to her right away.

But, as much as I hate to admit it, he's right. At least I'll have access to her.

"I need sleep," Jace says, standing. "Drew, handle the blueprints, but know I'll be checking them for authenticity before we plan *anything* concrete."

Drew shakes his head in aggravation, clearly wanting to say something, but he manages to bite his tongue.

Thank freaking goodness.

"I'll handle the rest." The Grand Master heads for the door without another word.

"Hello," Tucker says sarcastically, pointing to himself. "Weapons expert over here. I can—"

"You can shut the hell up," Jace snaps. "Rory may trust you, but I don't. You don't get to do *shit.*"

"Jace," I chide, my tone firm and commanding.

"Don't start with me," he says, shaking his head in frustration, refusing to even look my way.

"And I'll, what, sit patiently?" I ask, not bothering to

mask the scathing disdain in my tone. "Wait for the big bad Jace to save the day?"

"You will *train*," he corrects me. "You will master that damn magic until I'm confident it won't obliterate my whole dojo."

Sure.

And until then, he'll use it as an excuse to keep a close eye on me.

To keep me under watch. Under lock and key.

I grit my teeth, biting back the scathing remarks clawing at my throat. It won't do any good, especially not with how exhausted we all are.

"I need to sleep." Jace gestures toward the set of double doors that lead to the hallway, silently ordering us all out of the war room in his suite.

That's all the push I need.

I leave, giving him only the barest glance as I walk into the corridor.

He's willing to help but only if it's done his way. He'll listen but interrupt shortly after asking a question.

God, he's so *infuriating.*

When Drew, Tucker, and I stand in the hall, Jace shuts

the double doors to his suite behind us without another word.

I sigh, hands in my pockets, wondering if I can stop my racing mind long enough to sleep as well, or if I'm going to toss and turn for the rest of the day.

Drew crosses his arms, his imposing broad shoulders blocking out a good chunk of the hallway behind him, and glares at Tucker. "If that had happened in my homelands, you would be dead."

"I know," Tucker says quietly, nodding.

"I would have done it," Drew admits, eyes narrowing. "I wouldn't have paused long enough for her to interfere." He nods toward me.

"Dude, I'm *right* here," I say, spreading my arms wide in case he missed the fact that I'm freaking *listening* to this nonsense.

"The Knights are brutal, Rory," Drew snaps, his gaze shifting to me. "Abuse. Torture. They would do unspeakable things, force themselves on you, or happily break you in half if that's what it took to get what they want out of you." His furious glare returns to Tucker. "And he's—"

"Not with them," Tucker snaps, squaring his shoulders, looking for all the world like he wants to throw down with Drew in the middle of the hallway. "Why do you think I risked it all to lie? You think my Father is going to just *let me go*? Are you an idiot? He'll hunt me down and kill me for treason even though I never, not *once,* wanted this life! I didn't sign up for this, but do you think that matters?" Tucker snorts derisively. "Of course not. He won't care that I'm his son. Why do you think I sacrificed everything to keep her safe?" He gestures toward me.

"Right here," I say again, deeply frustrated with these two.

"I'm lucky to be alive," Tucker continues, ignoring me. "You don't think I realize that? I do. The fact that I'm here leaves me so damn confused—I thought for sure I was a goner." His gaze drifts toward me, and his expression softens.

It's a silent show of gratitude. He's sacrificed his rank, authority, and the life he had before, all to keep me safe. But back there in the field, I repaid him in full. I put my life and my freedom on the line.

For him.

And I would do it again.

"I'll be watching you," Drew says, nearly growling as he glares at Tucker.

Tucker snorts, clearly irritated. "Well, try to at least cover your eyes when I jerk off, then."

With impatient huffs and growls, both men turn on their heels and walk down the hallway in opposite directions. Fuming, they mutter under their breath and leave me in the corridor with my face in my hands.

I groan in frustration.

Men.

CHAPTER TWENTY-ONE

To my surprise, I sleep straight through the day. When I finally sit up, rubbing the sleep from my eyes, it's dark again. I check the clock beside the bed—one in the morning.

Damn. I can't remember *ever* sleeping that long.

My muscles ache as I stand and dress, my body already humming with antsy energy from laying too long in one place.

I need to burn off some energy, and I wonder if I can get down to the secret training hall below the embassy. If I can, maybe I can train a little and use the time to clear my mind.

Namely, to think of a plan to save Irena.

As I dress, I notice a small envelope icon on the flip phone's small screen. Curious, I tap a few of the keys and play the voicemail.

"Bold move, Rory," Ian says on the recording. "Only a couple of days left, and you ignore my call? I'm starting to think you don't want her. And if that's the case, I'll just get rid of her." He pauses, probably for effect. "There's other ways to lure you in."

I squeeze my eyes shut, careful not to take out my anger on the phone this time.

"Make your choice, Rory dear," he says curtly. "And do be quick about it, please."

The recording ends, and I resist the urge to throw the phone across the room.

I'm tempted to call back, to play his game, but I force myself to wait. I can't make a decision like that when I'm angry, and I need to burn off some steam, first.

Briefly, I pick Tucker's lock and check on him. He's sprawled across his bed, snoring lightly, and it's a relief to see him alive after yesterday's close call. Whatever happens over the next few days will determine if he's safe here—or if I need to find him someplace else to lay low for a while.

Unable to stay idle for long, I quickly steal down the

stairs. To my surprise, the halls are mostly empty. A few guards stand outside the command center and a few other secure locations, but that's about it.

With a few glances out the nearest window, I quickly realize why.

The skies teem with dragons, each of them on alert, at least one head turned in any given direction. As I near the panes of glass, a few dragon heads even turn toward me, no doubt sensing my presence.

I shudder. I sure hope that eerie ability of theirs starts to fade as I connect with my magic, since I would hate for dragons to sense me—even vaguely—for the rest of my life.

The fact is, Jace has his people on high alert, and I don't blame him. Not after what he witnessed in the forest.

With the corridors empty, I take my chances and sneak down to the secret rooms below the dojo—primarily, to the vast training hall Drew showed me.

It's slow going, even in the middle of the night, and I have to duck my fair share of cameras or passing soldiers. Eventually, I find myself facing the massive double doors that lead into the cavernous training hall where Jace holds lessons for the elite soldiers in his army.

As I near the towering entrance, I strain to hear any signs of life beyond the doors—the grunts of late-night sparring, the shuffle of clothes, the patter of boots on the tile as someone tidies after a match.

Nothing.

Gently, I push against the large circular emblem of a dragon painted across both of the doors. The entrance swings open, and I peek in to find the massive hall empty.

Good.

The wall of weapons fills the far end of the room, covered in everything from daggers to bows and arrows. Between me and the vast arsenal, however, is Jace's rounded platform. It rises from the floor, easily four feet high, and the whole room practically begs me to walk in.

I step into the space, looking up at the vast ceiling with a smile. Astonishing that it can feel so open despite the fact that we're deep underground, but I figure that's the point. This space is big enough for at least a dozen dragons to shift and fight.

And with more than enough space for me to train.

I grab a six-foot bo staff from the wall of weapons and spin it in my hand, loving the way the balance shifts as it rotates in my palm. I grab it abruptly, slicing to the left, launching into a familiar Spectre form Zurie taught me long ago.

Irena and I would run this sequence of movements every morning, slicing through the air, using the walls to launch into flips, whacking the shit out of imaginary opponents before starting our day.

Typical sister bonding.

As I spin the staff over my head, I step on the edge of the platform in the center of the room and flip effortlessly into the air. The world spins around me, and I land easily on my feet. The far end of the staff hits the ground hard, the snap of wood on tile cracking through the massive space.

I pause, ear twitching as it picks up movement, and I glare at the door just as it opens.

Drew walks through the entry, that trademark smirk on his handsome face. "You learn fast."

"How so?" I stand, setting the butt of the staff against the ground next to me, breathing a little heavier from the routine.

He gestures to the training hall. "I showed you how to get here *once*, and yet you're already down here training in the middle of the night." He chuckles. "And I thought I was the only one with a knack for breaking rules."

"*Bending* the rules, if I recall." I grin and nod to the wall of weapons. "Care to join me?"

"Sure." With a mischievous grin, he grabs a second staff from the row of dozens just like it. "But when I kick your ass, remember you invited me."

"That's mighty big talk." I spin the staff in my palm with practiced ease. "Let's see if you're as good as you think you are, shall we?"

The imposing dragon shifter circles me, holding his staff firmly, eyes scanning my body as he no doubt looks for a weakness to exploit.

He won't find one.

I play it coy and cocky, at ease in the massive space, feeling more in my element than I have in quite a while. This place reminds me of sparring in the caverns beneath Zurie's mountain home, of jiu-jitsu training with Irena, of having perfect precision and flawless control over every motion as I learned new routines, new attacks, new methods of killing my prey.

None of this *the magic controls me* nonsense. Just effortless perfection, every time.

Drew attacks first, and I easily block the blow. The

sharp thud of our staffs hitting snaps through the massive room, and I feel the reverb shoot up my arms.

Without my enhanced dragon strength, I probably would have had to drop the staff—it was a hell of a blow.

But I'm stronger, now. More powerful. More confident in my ability than ever before. Sure, it might take a bit more effort to rein in my magic, but I wouldn't give it up for the world.

I *love* the newfound power I wield.

With a teasing smirk, I look him dead in the eye. "Not bad."

"You're cute when you get cocky." He chuckles. "But what happens when you get knocked on your ass?"

With a quick and sudden thrust, he swings his staff at my legs. Thanks to his accidental warning, I jump in time to avoid a rather painful hit. It's a close call, though, and I clear the staff by mere centimeters, moving *just* fast enough to not fail.

He follows up the blow with another and another, swinging at me with rapid-fire precision as he tries to take me down. I duck and roll, sidestepping each attack, always a hair too fast for him to hit me.

The crack of wood hitting stone thunders through the

space as he misses yet again, his staff coming down hard on the floor.

Drew grins at me, breathing heavily, the thrill of a good fight igniting the fire in his warm brown eyes.

I hesitate just out of reach, chest heaving from the exercise, and effortlessly spin my staff around my head. "Had enough?"

"Hardly."

He launches into another attack, and this time I can't avoid it—I have to parry. Our weapons thud against each other, but he doesn't pause. He pushes forward, launching blow after blow, and it's all I can do to keep up.

He's *good.*

"You find Ian's last name yet?" I ask, trying to distract him.

"There are a few options," Drew admits, swinging his staff at my thigh.

I block the attack and dart out of the way of the next one.

"Ian Rockwood is a Captain in their army," Drew says, squaring me up, looking for the chance to land another blow. "Owns a few gambling dens and runs a small cartel in South America."

I shake my head. "Not our guy. Doesn't have enough imagination."

"Fine," Drew says, twirling the staff in his hands as he circles me. "A guy named Ian Banner brokers arms deals for the Vaer, mainly in the Middle East."

"Does he go on the field?" I ask, swinging the staff at Drew's head.

Drew ducks. "Yeah."

"Not our guy, then."

Drew watches me, skeptical. "How are you so sure?"

"Our Ian is a cocky bastard who doesn't like to get his hands dirty," I say, twirling my staff as I look for an opening in Drew's posture. "Our Ian sits in a chair and coordinates everything from the comfort of his office. From what I can tell, he doesn't like getting dirty."

"Huh," Drew raises his eyebrows, clearly impressed. "You got all that from talking to him?"

I nod. "Is there anyone on your list like that?"

"Eh." Drew shrugs, thinking. "Maybe one."

"And?"

"Ian Rixer." Drew frowns, his eyes taking on a cold glint. "Evil bastard. I can't get much information on him, just that he's a Major who manages the Vaer network across the Eastern Seaboard. His daddy knows the Boss, but I'm not sure how."

I grin, and everything in me screams that this is him.

That's our guy.

Ian Rixer.

I can't believe he gave me his real name.

In my quiet moment of victory, however, Drew decides to go for the kill.

Figuratively speaking, of course.

With a short grunt of effort, he abruptly shifts direction, thrusting the butt of his staff up toward my face. I dodge, thrown off balance, and roll onto the ground—only to watch as he swings the staff toward my face with all his force.

I jump backward, barely dodging the blow. His staff splinters as it hits the ground, fracturing half of the weapon virtually to dust.

Out of breath, I stand, gaping at the shattered weapon in his hand. He lifts it lazily, bored as he examines it, as if this has happened dozens of times before in his practice sessions.

How the hell did he get this good?

"Who *are* you?" I ask again, determined to get an answer this time.

He sighs and rubs his face, tossing the destroyed weapon aside. "I would really rather just have fun, Rory." He grins and nods to the wall of weapons. "What else do you want to play with?"

I chuckle. He certainly knows how the way to my heart, that's for sure.

In almost any other circumstance, I might let him change the subject and go play—there are a set of scimitars on the fourth row that I'm itching to try out, after all.

But the more I think about it, the more concerned I am that he might in fact be a Vaer.

And that—well, it feels unforgiveable.

I have to know. And since we're quickly running out of time to save Irena, I need to know *now*.

With a frown, I set one hand on my hip and tilt my head expectantly, knowing full well that my expression makes clear what I don't want to say—*this is your last chance, Drew.*

To be honest.

To tell me the truth.

"Fine," he mutters, reading my expression. He reaches a hand toward me, palm up, and nods to my weapon. "Give me your staff. I'll put it away so you can't hit me with it if you don't like my answer."

I hesitate, one eyebrow raised skeptically, but I eventually indulge him. Besides, there are loads more weapons to choose from should the need arise.

The trick would just be to get one before he does.

"My family gets away with whatever they desire," he says ominously as he sets my staff back on the wall. "Anything. We are almost never held accountable when we break the law, as long as we're clever about it. It's made us, well—" He sighs and grabs the remnants of the staff he broke. "Overconfident, I guess you can say."

I cross my arms, waiting for him to stop speaking in riddles and answer my question, already.

"Our wealth and power allows us to push boundaries," he admits, surprisingly self-aware. "It's something I've always hated, watching as the people around me constantly strive for more. *More* land. *More* money. *More* politicians in our pockets." He looks at the ground and sneers. "It's never good enough for any of them."

With a few powerful strides, he walks his shattered staff to a nearby trashcan and tosses it in the bin.

So far, the things he's describing could apply to a few of the families I know of.

Andusk, maybe. Or perhaps the Darringtons, or even the Bane.

And the Vaer, sure, but I silently hope I'm wrong about that one.

Nothing he's sharing is all that helpful, and it feels like he's just delaying the inevitable.

I shift my weight, trying not to sound overly eager as I attempt to piece together the few clues he's giving me. "Is that why Jace can't stand you?"

"That—huh." Drew runs his hand through his hair. "That's part of it, yes, but our feud goes deeper. For him, it's personal." Drew sighs, frowning, rubbing the muscles on his wrist and stretching his fingers after our match. "And I'm not proud of the part I played in it."

With a little jump, I hoist myself onto the edge of the empty platform in the center of the room, watching

Drew intently. Careful not to make a sound, I silently wait for him to continue.

Drew sidles up to me and lounges against the tall platform as he stares up at the ceiling. "Jace and I—our families have been at odds many times before. Jace's brother, Garrett, was involved in a clash with my family that should never have happened. We were trying to push the Fairfax family out of a very lucrative business deal so we could take it over. I hardly even remember what it was for."

"I can imagine that would piss Jace off," I admit.

"That's not why Jace hates me," Drew says with a shake of his head. "It's what happened next."

A chill snakes down my spine, and I get the distinct feeling I am *not* going to like what I'm about to hear.

"My family knows full well that people fear us, and those in charge of this little takeover—my brother Milo, primarily—were determined to use that to their advantage."

Drew abandons his place beside me and paces in circles with his hands on the back of his head. "Garrett was sick of us, sure, but he truly hated Milo. None of us ever really knew why, and Milo still won't talk about it. I heard through the grapevine that Jace was trying to get his brother to leave this be, to give us the deal and walk away before people got hurt, but the arguments grew into fist fights. Into brawls. One by one, the meetings and negotiations started getting bloody. Then they started shifting, and before we knew it, we had tense face-offs with forty shifted dragons, circling and drawing blood."

Drew rubs his face in disappointment. "It wasn't even about the stupid deal anymore. It became about pride. Neither side was willing to give an inch, and no one would give up."

I sigh. This is the sort of thing that only ends in bloodshed.

Drew pauses, arms crossed, and looks at me intently. "The last fight had over a hundred dragons between the two sides, and twenty-three died. Fairfax dragons, mostly. And, among them, Garrett."

I grimace and sigh with disappointment.

"Yeah," Drew says with a frown. "He tried to take me and Milo on at the same time. I try not to speak ill of the dead, but that was just stupid." Drew shrugs. "On the field, no one but me and Milo saw who dealt the final blow."

"Who did?" I ask.

Drew holds my gaze for a moment, his face still and

stoic. "Milo," he eventually confesses. "But everyone assumes it was me, and I let them."

"Why?"

"Milo—ugh." Drew frowns. "He can be such an idiot. Prideful. Headstrong. Manipulative. A fine politician, honestly, but he isn't any good as a fighter. If the Fairfax dragons knew it was him, they would come after him. Of us, I think he's the one who could be taken out in an assassination. If they tried to kill me, they know they would fail—and a lot of their men would die. But Milo? They could do it."

Drew's jaw tenses, and he quietly grunts in disappointment as he pauses to imagine what would happen. "But killing Milo would have consequences, even if killing Garrett didn't. It would lead to war, but some Fairfax dragons don't care. Garrett was revered, and many would be willing to die if it meant they would at least have their revenge." Drew shakes his head. "But they know they can't kill me. So, I let them think I did it. I let them hate me, even though I was trying to make him stop."

"Aren't there laws against this kind of thing?" I gesture to the training hall around us. "There seem to be all kinds of treaties, agreements—"

"Since it was me and Milo, well—" Drew sighs.

"Because of what we are, we get preferential treatment."

Oh.

Oh, no.

"You're an heir," I say quietly as the realization hits me. "They're grooming you to be the Boss of your dragon family."

"Milo is the current favorite, but yes." Drew nods. "My Father, well, he keeps hinting that it's not guaranteed."

"Tell me your family," I demand, standing. "Tell me. Now."

I don't know of any Milo or Drew in the Boss families —but we never had to study the heirs. The list of possible heirs for any given family is always a dozen or so long, and the current favorite can change on a whim. Since it was rarely important to the missions Zurie sent me on, we never bothered to learn all the names.

Drew's eyes flit to me, his expression sharp and authoritative at my demand. "It's technically illegal to do that, here. That's why even Jace hasn't told you, though I suspect he desperately wants to." Drew pauses and, after a moment, shrugs. "That, and I threatened to reveal a few secrets of his own if he dared."

I gesture to the room around us. "We both know you're not exactly fond of rules, Drew. Don't let *that* stop you."

His jaw tenses as he watches me silently, no doubt toying with whether or not to follow through.

Oh, he's going to. One way or another.

I'm about to dig into him, to give him a piece of my mind, when the air vents shut off.

The soothing rush of air filling the room becomes a painfully quiet eeriness that settles on the massive space.

I tilt my chin upward, careful to keep Drew in my periphery as I examine the air vents along the ceiling, but there's no indication of anything wrong with them. No smoke. No fire.

They just… stopped.

The hair on my neck stands on end, and my intuition screams that something is very wrong.

"That's not good," he mutters, scanning the ceiling.

With those three words, his entire mood shifts in an instant.

His back straightens, those broad shoulders of his squaring up for trouble. All at once, he's ready for war, and I get the feeling he knows what's happening topside.

"This isn't over," I say sternly before heading to the door.

He ignores the comment and reaches the exit first, peeking his head into the empty hallway, tense and alert.

Instead of scanning the halls, I watch him. His tension. His mood. He's on edge, ready for a battle, a hint of knowing in his eye.

I didn't make it this far in life by letting my guard down. If he tries to lead me in a trap, I don't care how much he claims to care for me—or how much I deeply care for him.

If he tries to trick me—if my growing suspicions are correct, and he's a Vaer—I will have to take him down.

CHAPTER TWENTY-TWO

As we sneak through the dark halls of the dojo, I'm a little surprised at how often I have to correct Drew's stealth.

He's powerful, sure. Strong. Imposing. But he has some *serious* work to do when it comes to patience and controlled, undetectable movement.

With a mischievous little grin, I wonder how much it would piss off Drew if I asked Tucker to train him.

Sometimes, it's just *too* easy to get under a dragon's skin. Prideful creatures.

My first goal is to find Jace, and the route I'm taking will eventually lead to his suite. It's a bit of a gamble, assuming he's still there, but it's all I have at the moment.

We near another hallway, one that runs by his bedroom. I press my back against a wall and strain my ear, listening for who—or what—might be around the corner.

Impatient as ever, Drew shifts his weight anxiously and tries to sidestep me, to just look into the hallway and be done with it. I smack him in the stomach to get him to stop. He grunts lightly and shoots an annoyed look at me, but I press my finger to my lips.

Once more, I listen—*there*. The shuffle of fabric and boots on the tile. Two—no, three men.

I catch Drew's eye and hold up three fingers, nodding at the corner he was trying to go around blindly.

He lifts his eyebrows in surprise, pursing his lips briefly and apparently impressed. With a nod, he gestures for me to continue.

The soldiers' footsteps begin to retreat, and I almost follow. But as I instinctively pause, my senses catching something my brain missed, I listen again for signs of trouble.

There—the hiss of air through a grate.

I frown, scanning the dark hallway, until I see it—a soft yellow haze seeping from the vent on the floor.

Crap.

I elbow Drew in the side to get his attention and point at the golden fog, silently asking him what the *hell* that is.

He grimaces and pulls on his collar, gently lifting his shirt over his mouth, and I follow suit. It won't be a ton of help in filtering out toxins—or whatever the yellow haze is—but it might help us avoid inhaling at least *some* of it.

Carefully, Drew slips a nearby curtain off the rod and balls up the fabric, stuffing it into the grate as tightly as he can to block the yellow smoke. A thin ribbon snakes out of one gap, but he otherwise did a great—and thankfully *silent*—job.

As the strangers' footsteps recede, I peek into the hallway to find three soldiers rounding the next corner at the far end of the hall. Each of them wears a gas mask and a crisp, wine red uniform with a gold stripe on his left leg. What's more, however, is that each soldier also carries an advanced military rifle with what looks suspiciously like a laser scope.

Oh, that's just freaking *super*.

This is a full-on, military-style hit.

The gas, the soldiers—this is a premeditated, calculated mission to infiltrate the dojo, and it's not hard to imagine what—or *who*—they might be looking for.

Can't I catch a damn *break*?

Two soldiers in the dojo's black and yellow uniforms lay sprawled across the floor in the middle of the hallway. With the immediate threat now gone, I tense and run to them, kneeling to check for a pulse, hoping that this gas isn't lethal.

Beneath my finger, I feel the first soldier's steady pulse. I let out a sigh of relief and check the next one. He's alive, too.

Thank goodness.

I may be pissed at Jace, but that doesn't mean I want any harm to come to his dojo or the people who live here.

"Rory, we need to go," Drew says, his hushed tone shattering the silence.

I flinch, a little caught off guard—since this is supposed to be a stealth mission, damn it all—and shake my head. "We need to find out what's going on."

"I *know* what's going on," he snaps back. "I know these people."

"How?"

"I'll explain on the way." He grabs my wrist and tugs, shooting an anxious glare down the hall at the side corridor the guards in the red uniforms had just walked down. "Let's go."

"Drew, I'm not—"

"Fine," he mutters. "This is for your own good, so don't you dare hate me."

With that, he grabs me and flings me over his shoulder in true caveman fashion. His hand firmly on my ass to root me in place, he jogs down the hallway in the opposite direction from the three soldiers.

"Drew!" I hiss quietly, smacking my fist on his muscular back. "What the *hell* do you think you're—"

"Quiet," he chides. "You'll get us caught."

"*I'll* get us—" I groan in frustration. "You're the one who spoke during a silent recon mission!"

It takes everything in me not elbow him in the back of the neck to make him drop me—though, honestly, I'm not entirely sure that would even work on someone as solidly built as Drew.

The man is seriously a *tank*. One made of rippling muscle and brimming with witty comebacks, but still.

He pauses at a random wall. A second later, the soft chirps of buttons on a keypad hit my ears, loud and piercing in the otherwise deathly silent hall.

Determined to get down, I wriggle in his grip, half tempted to just kick him in the face and be done with this.

Not to be outdone, the dragon shifter slides his hand down my legs and pins my thighs to his chest, so that pretty much only my knees and ankles have free motion any more.

I can't move. I can't wriggle. I can't break free.

It's *astonishing* how strong he is. Every time I think I learn Drew's limits, I discover another level to his strength.

And not always in a fun way.

My heart stutters, and I feel the momentary sting of claustrophobia as I'm rendered utterly immobile. After a lifetime of Zurie's brutal training, the idea of being at someone's mercy is making my pulse skyrocket—even if that someone has fought for my best interests up until now.

The lack of control, the lack of free movement—it makes me want to kill something.

"Drew, let me *down*," I demand, barely able to keep my voice quiet anymore.

"I will," he promises as a hidden door in the wall slides

open. He ducks inside, carrying me into the shadowy corridor as the secret door closes behind us.

But he doesn't.

He trots down a flight of steps in the secret hallway, and for the life of me, I have no idea where he's going or what he's doing.

Drew, the mysterious and silent dragon shifter that he is, must think he's doing something noble right now. I get that he doesn't share his feelings, rarely shares his thoughts, and never wants to divulge much of anything, but this is beyond what I'm willing to put up with.

He can carry off someone else macho-caveman style.

I'm *done*.

"Drew," I say, seething. "I swear to all that is freaking holy I will beat you *senseless* with a *fish* unless you tell me what you're doing! Right now!"

"We're leaving," he says simply, pausing at the end of the corridor as it forks into two directions. After a moment of silent debate, he jogs down the path to the left without saying anything else.

"Leaving?" I ask, incredulous. "I'm not leaving, not without Tucker and Levi."

"Those people up there don't care about Tucker *or* Levi," Drew snaps. "They probably don't even know about either of those men. They want you, and they're going to rip this place apart until they find you." He hesitates, looking back over his shoulder, the way we just came. "I know there's another exit to the forest down here, if I can just remember—"

"You had better give me answers, Drew," I say, my voice dark and dangerous. "Real ones. Ones that make *sense*."

I'm about out of patience.

I'm about out of *calm*.

My magic burns within me, sparking as it pushes against my palms, eager to break free.

To defend me at any cost.

With my bubbling fury, I can barely rein it in.

"I'm—" He groans and pauses, sucking in a sharp breath. "Rory, I'll explain everything."

"Then do it," I demand. "Now. Starting with who the hell you really are."

"I'm…" He groans. "I'm a Darrington."

I freeze, squeezing my eyes shut as the reality of what he just said washes over me.

A Darrington.

The most feared dragons in the world. The most powerful family, with the most connections of any dragons alive. The most wealth, the ones who can get away with murder.

Or in this case, abduction.

Suddenly, everything makes sense in the absolute worst way.

"What's the plan here, Drew?" I ask, seething, my heart shattering at the thought of the man I've been growing so fond of betraying me so completely. "Are you going to take me back to Jett Darrington? To the Capital? Hand me over?"

My throat tightens, and as angry as I want to be, all I can feel is hurt.

"Listen, Rory," Drew says softly, jogging down the hall again. "I'm—"

He turns a corner and pauses. Something he sees makes him stiffen, and I wonder what it could be.

Jace, maybe. Or Tucker. Someone to distract him long enough for me to break free, to—

"Father," Drew says tensely, his voice lowering an octave. "What a pleasant surprise."

With those simple words, my last shred of hope burns to ash in my chest.

Drew, to his credit, finally puts me down. He sets me on my feet, never once looking at me, his intense gaze focused on the hallway ahead of us.

But I'm not about to stay and witness their little reunion. I don't care about meeting the Darrington Boss or getting more information about how I fit into his grand scheme—not right now, anyway. A Spectre knows when to retreat, and this is my freaking cue.

Fast as a bullet, I pivot, ready to bolt, but Drew grabs my arm. I grimace, astonished he was faster than me. His grip is impossibly tight, and no matter what I try, I can't move.

He has me pinned to the spot, but I don't go down that easy.

Furious, enraged, and ready to kick ass, I land a perfect blow in the back of his knees.

I give it everything I have, but even a lifetime of training, my flawless precision, and the force of the dragon gods smoldering in my body isn't enough to do more than knock him slightly off balance.

He teeters for a moment and instantly recovers, not even grunting with the effort.

Shit.

Drew tugs on my arm, dragging me closer, angling his body so that he mostly shields me from the other people in the dark hallway.

Finally, I look over my shoulder to find two men standing alone in the corridor, their faces illuminated by one of the bare light bulbs hanging from the ceiling. Both men have a gas mask under their arms and wear the same wine red uniforms as the soldiers above us, though theirs have more golden threads woven into the hems and intricate patterns of gold on their chests.

They look like mirror images of each other, though the elder man must have a good thirty years on the younger one. Strong shoulders. Piercing brown eyes. Jaws lined with rough beards.

The older man I know all too well—Jett Darrington, the merciless dragon Boss. The younger man can only be Drew's brother, Milo.

As I study the uniforms, something clicks in the back of my mind. The soldiers upstairs—

I look at Drew, piecing everything together. The soldiers up there, the ones that knocked out the entire embassy, belong to *him.*

To his family.

My throat stings with betrayal, and the hurt swiftly fizzles into barely contained anger as I fight with Drew's grip on my arm.

His father and brother carry themselves like hardened warriors, and from the stories I've heard, they're not opposed to violence.

But I will *not* let them take me. I don't care what I destroy or who I kill.

"She's feisty," Jett says with a chuckle.

As a last-ditch effort, I dip into the magic burning in my chest. It bleeds into me, filling my veins, ready to appear the moment I give the word. I don't have perfect control over it yet, but I can wield it well enough to help me now.

With a wounded look at Drew's stoic face, I wonder if he'll make me do this—if he will truly make me kill him.

The thought makes my throat burn with grief. Horror. Guilt.

"Good work, son," Jett says with a nod of approval. "If she really is the dragon vessel, a little concussion won't hurt her." He gestures toward the opposite end of the hallway. "Knock her out, since she's being difficult. Let's go."

My magic sparks and sputters within me, ready to attack.

"Do it, and you'll *die*," I snap, glaring at Drew.

Drew, to his credit, chuckles. It's the first time he's broken that stoic glare since we came across his father, and I have no idea what it means.

"You would, too," he says softly. "Kill me, I mean."

I tense, readying for battle, biting back the searing sting in my throat at his betrayal. "Damn right, I would."

It's a lie.

Well, partly.

Bringing myself to kill him would rip me to shreds, but I'm a woman of war. It would be brutal. It might break me, but I've endured shattering grief before. One way or another, I'll find a way to recover.

Eventually.

Hopefully.

"Do it," Drew says, his eyes scanning me. "Show them what you can do."

For a moment, I simply gape at him in confusion. "You *want* me to kill you?"

He smirks. "You can't, but I want to see you try."

"Drew!" his father snaps impatiently. "Stop playing with your new toy. We're leaving."

That breaks me.

It makes me snap.

The idea that I barely exist to this asshole. That I'm just something to claim, nothing but property to keep in line and control.

My magic pushes against my fingertips, begging me to let loose. Ribbons of white light shimmer across my skin like the northern lights, aching to break free.

Though Drew still has a firm grip on my arm, I twist as much as I can, aiming my hands at his muscled torso.

My palms flatten against his shirt, the threat real and very near, but he just watches me.

Waiting.

Daring me to do it.

Bastard.

My throat aches. Tears burn at the corners of my eyes.

I can't believe he's going to make me do this.

"Damn it," his father snaps. "Milo, go grab her."

Absolutely not.

In that moment, as Milo takes his first step toward me, I release the power in my blood. The burst of white light tears through the shadows, blinding me, filling the space with crackling energy.

But never—not once—does Drew's hold on me loosen. He teeters momentarily, thrown off balance, and I hear the feint hiss of breath as he sucks in air through his teeth, trying to mask the pain.

And yet, he doesn't let go.

When the brilliant white light finally fades, he's still standing beside me. Though his shirt has burned away, revealing the hard muscle beneath, he is otherwise unharmed.

No blood. No bruises. And still very much alive.

He watches me, that stoic expression back, like he's just waiting to see how I react.

I gape, unable to process what I'm seeing. My body spent and exhausted from the blast, I teeter in his grip. And, in a blistering instant, my grief and sorrow are replaced with utter shock.

This magic—it has destroyed buildings, dissolved men to dust. But against Drew, this incredible power didn't even draw blood.

He just—but—he can't—

I have no words. Nothing—*ever*—has survived a blast from this magic. Even the rocky cliff gave way, dissolving into nothing, and yet Drew is entirely unaffected.

He is far more powerful than I could have ever imagined, and I am royally, *totally* screwed.

"That—wow," his father says, applauding. His commanding voice echoing through the hallway. "I am truly impressed. She'll be useful, son."

"She isn't yours, Father," Drew says curtly, glaring at the weathered man. "And neither of us will be returning with you."

Deeply confused and not entirely sure what to expect, I watch Drew cautiously as a thin glimmer of hope sparks to life within me.

This could go one of three ways.

One—he's just messing with me. Again. And he'll drag me off to the Darrington Capital.

Two—he wants me for himself, and he'll just throw me over his shoulder again the moment his father leaves.

Or, three—he really is the man I've come to admire. To

adore. And he's going to defend me with his life, if he has to.

All I can do is watch and wait, and after a lifetime of being in control of almost any given situation, this is absolute agony.

For a moment, the Darrington Boss simply studies Drew's face, as if he's waiting for the punch line. After a moment or two of silence, he barks out a harsh laugh. "Are you serious?"

"Very," Drew says with a nod. Briefly, his eyes flit to me, softening ever so slightly as he scans my face. "None of this was supposed to happen," he adds quietly, only loudly enough for me to hear.

As if *that's* supposed to make any of this better.

"Drew, what are you doing?" his father asks condescendingly. "Explain yourself."

"I am protecting the dragon vessel." Drew raises his voice again, loud and clear, his confident tone carrying easily through the dark hallway.

"This isn't how you do it," Milo says, finally breaking his silence, gesturing toward me. "There's more at stake than—"

"Silence," Jett says abruptly, casting an irritated glare at Drew's brother.

I frown, glancing between the two, wondering what Milo was about to say that Jett didn't want me or Drew to know.

"I think I would like to know what's at stake, actually," Drew says with a wry smirk. "Care to continue, big brother?"

Milo frowns, adjusting his grip on the gas mask in his arm instead of answering.

"Pity," Drew muses. "Always so eager to do what you're told."

At that, Milo wrinkles his nose in loathing, glaring daggers at Drew as an old insecurity is blatantly revealed.

Huh.

He must be so easy to manipulate. To control. A few verbal jabs, and he's basically putty in Drew's hands. I narrow my eyes, studying the heir-apparent to the Darrington family line, quickly understanding why Drew is becoming the front-runner choice to replace him.

"I know what this is," Jett says suddenly, clearly disappointed. "She's spoken for, Drew. You can't have her."

"I know," Drew says quickly.

Too quickly.

"She belongs to Jace Goodwin," Jett adds in a chiding tone. "That won't ever change."

"She's the dragon vessel, for Christ sake," Drew snaps, standing a bit taller and loosening his grip on my arm. "She belongs to no one, least of all *Jace*."

Drew's touch on my arm becomes tender, and though he doesn't look at me, he leans in protectively. With that subtle motion, he makes one thing abundantly clear—if Jett or Milo want to get to me, they have to go through him first.

I'm floored.

I genuinely thought Drew was going to hand me over. Hell, I was ready to defend myself in the most horrifying way—killing him—and nothing worked. I couldn't kill Drew even if I wanted to. He's just too powerful.

And yet, when I had no control over the matter, Drew still protected me.

"You repulsive disappointment," Jett says, sneering. "You would give up your title, your wealth, everything you have—over some *girl*?"

"Gladly," Drew says without missing a beat.

The shattered pieces of my heart fuse back together with that admission, and even though we're not out of danger yet, I finally relax in Drew's grip.

I almost can't believe it—that Drew would do all that.

For me.

"This won't end well, Drew," his father warns.

Drew lifts his chin in defiance. "Care to elaborate?"

My gaze drifts between the two of them, and I wonder who would win in a fight. Drew is impressive, almost impossibly powerful, but I've heard horror stories about his father. About the entire cities he's burned to ash. About the dozens of dragons he can take on, completely solo, bringing nothing to the battle except for his own fire and fury.

The Darringtons are almost universally feared for many reasons—but Jett Darrington is the *primary* reason.

"You're running out of time," I say calmly, tilting my head ever so slightly, as if I'm bored.

For the first time, Jett looks me in the eye. His glare is chilling, but after a lifetime with Zurie, he's nothing I can't handle. I'm quickly regaining my strength after the attack on Drew, thankfully. And since I have no idea what's about to happen, I need to be prepared.

For anything.

I nod to the ceiling, vaguely gesturing toward the army of shifters above us. "How much longer do you think that gas can keep everyone knocked out? When they wake up, they'll be aching for a fight. Did you bring enough soldiers for a war? Not even you could get away with this if you get caught."

Jett scowls, his gaze shifting between me and Drew for a moment before he finally turns to his other son. "Milo, give the order to retreat."

"Yes, Father," Milo says with a nod. He pivots on his heel and charges down the corridor, off to do his father's bidding.

Slowly, Jett begins to close the distance between us as the echo of Milo's footsteps bounces off the walls.

When the patter finally begins to fade, the Darrington Boss pauses, barely ten feet away. His salt and pepper hair is easier to see now, as are the deep and weathered lines on his face.

He may still be fierce as he nears his seventies, but the ferocity won't last much longer.

"I could just take her," the Darrington Boss says haughtily. "Do you think you could win against *me*, boy?"

Drew smirks. "Easily."

It's a cocky answer, meant to intimidate more than anything, but it still wipes the smile off Jett's face. "You always did have the confidence of a king."

Drew shrugs, feigning disinterest.

"You know you're fit to rule, Drew," the Boss says quietly, with a gentle nod over his shoulder. "Not him. You."

"So you keep saying," Drew says curtly. "And yet he remains the heir-apparent."

"Because you have to *prove* yourself," Jett snaps, as though they've had this conversation before. "And now, your opportunity to do so has finally come."

Drew waits in silence, staring down his father, daring him to continue.

"You have one chance to make this right." Jett holds up his pointer finger for emphasis. "Just one."

Drew frowns. "Let me guess."

"She's your ticket back home." The Darrington Boss nods toward me. "Your redemption. Turn her over, and you will succeed in proving yourself to me. *Fail* to do so, however, and you will never set foot on Darrington property again."

With that, Jett gives me a scathing once-over and walks

down the hallway, disappearing into the shadowy section of the hallway, where the light bulbs have all burned out. Eventually, the only indication he was ever there is the echo of his footsteps.

Together, Drew and I watch the darkness, both of us breathing a little heavily as our surging adrenaline begins to fade.

I look at the fire dragon's face. "Drew—"

"Not yet," he says softly, tugging gently on my arm as he heads back the way we came.

Drew just paid the ultimate price, at least as far as a Darrington is concerned—he gave up his title, his future, and all of his wealth.

For… *me*.

CHAPTER TWENTY-THREE

As we race down the hallway, my eyes already adjusted to the darkness, my mind buzzes with questions. Theories. Concerns.

"Stop, Drew." I pause in the middle of the dark corridor, my hands on my hips as I try to process everything that just happened. "I need—back there, you—"

"I know," he says softly, stopping with his back to me.

Without his shirt, I can see the hard muscle that covers his body, right down to the alluring curve along his spine that leads into his pants.

Setting his hands on the back of his head, he sighs heavily. "Look, Rory, I'm no good with feelings. I don't —I can't—"

He groans in frustration and turns to face me, those intense brown eyes of his so like his father's.

But unlike his father, Drew watches me with desire. Affection.

Love.

He runs a hand through his thick brown hair, staring blankly down the hallway as if he wishes he could run away from this conversation. "We have to get to safety."

"We're plenty safe," I point out, gesturing back at the incredible distance we've already put between us and his father. "And I need answers."

"I care about you," he says simply, as if that's enough.

I lift one eyebrow hesitantly and gesture for him to continue.

He groans. "Are you really going to make me do this feelings thing?"

"If that's what it takes, then hell *yes*," I say with a confused laugh. "I need to understand what just happened!"

"Fine, fine," he sets one hand in the pocket of his jeans. "Look, I'm not one to wax poetic, okay? I let my actions speak for themselves." He gestures back toward the corridor where we faced off with his father. "And I hope what happened back there tells you exactly how I feel about you."

Absently, I rub the spot on my arm where he held tight. I realize now it probably wasn't to keep me rooted in place so they could abduct me. Rather, it was probably to ensure I didn't run off solo into the castle filled with a small army of Darrington soldiers. I'm good, sure, but I can still be outnumbered—and there's the very real chance I would've been caught, regardless, if I'd left Drew's side.

All of this—he did it to protect me.

Even the stupid, irritatingly dominating parts.

"I thought you were going to hand me over," I admit.

"Never," he says sharply, his chest puffing a bit at the mere thought. "Not to him, not to *anyone.*"

I smile, a bit flattered at how worked up he's getting.

"Oh, you—" Drew laughs and shakes his head. "You just said that to get under my skin, didn't you?"

"No," I say with a chuckle. "That was just a happy bonus." I briefly look at my hands, and my smile begins to fade. "Drew, you pushed me, back there." I frown, catching his eye. "You goaded me into trying to kill you."

He nods, his eyes scanning my face as he stands there, not explaining anything.

"Why?" I ask, astonished. "Why would you push me that far, to make me think I had to *kill* you—" My voice breaks.

"I'm sorry," he says gently, crossing his toned arms. "I'm not proud of that."

"Then why—"

"My father needed to see your power," Drew says firmly. "He needed to know you weren't to be messed with, needed to understand the strength you carry within you. And I…" He groans, trailing off and rubbing his face. "I needed to know that you could follow through with it. That if someone betrayed you, no matter who it was, you would act. That you would protect yourself at all costs."

I bristle with anger. "How *dare* you goad me into something so horrible!"

"I know," he says softly. "I'm not one for apologies, I'm really not, and this might be the only one I ever give you." He watches me intently. Sincerely. "I hope you forgive me someday, but it was the last thing I needed from you. To know that you could handle the difficult decisions coming your way."

His mood shifts, and he frowns deeply, his gaze becoming blazingly intense. "Because you will face impossible decisions, Rory. With your magic, with the people coming after you—that's inevitable."

I grit my teeth and pace the small hallway, shaking my head in frustration—and hating that I kind of see his point.

"That was an asshole move," I say, furious.

"I know." He nods. "I'm an asshole, sometimes."

I grimace. "Yeah, you really are."

"Are you okay?" he asks.

Truthfully?

No.

Why would I be?

As I pace in small circles, my anger boils to a breaking point. White light snakes across my skin as I silently fume, burning through my rage.

The hit on the dojo.

The false betrayal.

Thinking I had to kill a man I very much respect.

The last hour or so replays in my mind, and for a

moment, all I can do is simmer in the sizzling embers of my fury.

But, as the rage burns, I slowly run out of it.

The white light shimmering over my skin begins to recede, and the anger is quickly replaced by relief.

Tonight's outcome is definitely in my favor. Drew proved himself to me. The dojo survived. And, for once, the Darringtons didn't get their way.

"Say it again," I demand, looking at the floor, the last smoldering cinders of my anger refusing to fade.

"What?" Drew asks, clearly confused.

"Apologize," I say, gesturing for him to get on with it.

"But I just—"

"Again."

He sighs, clearly seeing where this is going. "I'm sorry."

"Again."

"I'm—" He groans. "Rory, I'm sorry."

"Again." Still looking away from him, I can no longer suppress my wicked little grin.

I wonder how many times I can get away with this.

"I'm *sorry*," he says once more, his voice strained.

I peek over my shoulder at him, trying to hide my smile, and catch his eye. It takes a moment for him to catch on, but he lets out a frustrated chuckle and shakes his head. "You're insufferable."

"You deserve it."

He laughs. "I guess I do."

As the last of my rage burns away, I sigh and slip my hands in my pockets. I don't love the way he tested me, but I can kind of understand why he did it.

I can forgive him—as long as he doesn't pull anything else like this.

Ever.

His laughter fades, and he sets a strong hand on the back of his head, closing his eyes as he tries to center himself. "We should probably—"

"Tell me why, first," I interrupt.

He looks at me with a quizzical expression. "What?"

"Why you feel so fiercely about me that you would give up your title." I set my hands on my hips, refusing to budge until I get an answer. "What attracts you to me enough to sacrifice everything."

I need to know.

Before we take another step, I *have* to know this is real and not some ploy. He tested me—and now, I'm testing him.

The *final* test.

The edge of his mouth curves downward. "You already know why."

"Say it." My voice is soft, so low and tender that it comes out more like a request, rather than a demand.

He frowns, squirming a little, looking over his shoulder as though he would rather be in a fistfight than talking about this.

It's kind of cute, actually—to see such a powerful, burly man rendered utterly uncomfortable by something as simple as his feelings.

With a frustrated growl, he crosses his arms and leans his back against the wall. "You challenge me, alright?" He sighs. "You push me and show me all the ways I can be a better man. You're my equal in a sea of the mundane. You don't want anything I have except my time and company."

He shrugs, looking away as he pauses for a moment to think.

"I'm used to gold diggers," he admits. "Women who just want to use me to climb the social ladder or spend all my money. I'm captivated with you because you're genuine." His jaw tenses, and he finally looks at me with those warm brown eyes. "You're a partner, rather than a dependent."

I smile, satisfied with that answer, and playfully wrinkle my nose. "God, you're so mushy."

He laughs and nudges my shoulder, pushing me slightly off balance with his sheer strength. "Ass."

"You like it."

"I love it," he admits, flashing me that wickedly mischievous grin of his.

That's probably the closest I'll ever hear him come to telling me he loves me, and I'm surprisingly okay with that.

Feelings aren't really my thing, either.

And just like that, we're golden. Nothing else needs to be said.

"What do we do now?" I ask, walking down the hallway toward the castle. "Jace isn't going to take the news about your dad well."

Drew shakes his head. "He can't know."

"But—"

"Rory, seriously, we can't." Drew catches my eye, his tone deadly serious. "Out of obligation and per the law, Jace would have to declare war on the Darrington line for violating a neutral zone. That is a *huge* deal. My father is powerful, and everyone in this dojo would end up dead. It would be cataclysmic, and he would be brutal to make an example of the Fairfax family for having the audacity to actually come after him." Drew frowns, his jaw tensing in dread and disgust. "Unless he does something publicly that the whole world can see and hold him accountable for, he can skate under the law and get away with literal murder."

I grimace, utterly disgusted. "That's why Garrett never got any justice."

"Exactly. No one had any proof of how Garrett died—it was all rumors and accusations." He sighs. "We really do get away with murder."

"Damn it," I mutter, rubbing my jaw as I think over our options. "I hate the idea of letting the asshole who drugged a whole dojo get away."

"And that leads me to my next concern," Drew says ominously. "I've been wondering how the soldiers got in at all, but I couldn't figure it out until I saw him in the tunnels. He hacked my phone." Drew catches my eye. "He found my codes. That's the only way this plan could have worked."

"You didn't share those with him?"

"Never," Drew says abruptly. "I knew he would try something like this if he had that info. These tunnels are supposed to be tightly secured, and I broke about forty laws getting them. But if he hacked my phone—" Drew grunts in revulsion and pulls the device out of his pocket. "I have to wipe this thing immediately and get another, one he can never access."

Drew pauses at a keypad on the wall and punches in a code. A live feed of the empty hall appears on the display, and he taps another sequence into the keypad to open the door.

As it slides open, we slip into the hallway, alert for signs of life.

Around the corner, someone moans in pain. I perk up, alert and listening for the origin of the sound.

There—the rustle of fabric. A bit of slurred muttering.

Someone's waking up.

I peek around the corner to find a Fairfax guard sprawled over the carpet, weakly trying to get on her feet. Her arms keep giving out, so I rush over to help her up.

Still groggy, the brunette mumbles incoherently when I swing her arm over my shoulder and help her to her feet. When she's finally standing, she gives me a weak nod of gratitude. "Thanks."

"Yeah, no problem."

"Did you see anything?" Drew asks the soldier.

"Give her a chance to breathe first," I mutter. "Jeez, Drew."

"Nothing," the guard says, rubbing sleep from her eyes, clearly still dazed. As relaxed as she is, I wonder if she even knows she isn't speaking to Jace. "A few hazy figures, then I blacked out. What happened?"

"We don't know yet," Drew lies.

When we're sure the guard is okay, we continue, looking for others.

After we tend to two more soldiers around the next bend, I hear the thunder of boots along the carpet from down the hall. I stand and look over my shoulder as Drew tends to the soldier at our feet.

Jace rounds the corner with about ten guards, and after the last few days of his rage, I expect fury. Commands. Anger.

All I see is dread.

It's startling—to see cold dread on such a strong man's

face. It's brief, replaced instantaneously with relief the moment our eyes meet.

But it was there.

And it makes my heart soften, a little, for this irritating hardass who has shown me so many misguided grand gestures.

Just a bit.

Harper said it best—he doesn't know how to love. He doesn't know anything but war. This connection we have, it's as foreign and strange to him as it is to me.

Maybe even more so.

He sweeps me into his arms without a word, holding me close, pressing his cheek against mine. With his hand cradling my head, he holds me tight, like he knows he nearly lost me.

It's—confusing.

Startling, at the very least.

Despite the rising surge of anger I feel for his recent attempts to control me, despite the fact that he nearly killed Tucker, despite everything he has put me through, I hug him back.

It feels oddly right.

He sighs happily as my arms slide around his waist. It's a subtle sound, barely audible, but it's unmistakable. His fingers weave into my hair, and he gently rubs his nose against mine.

"Tucker and Levi are safe," he says, gently pulling away, answering my question before I can ask it. "Levi is still unconscious and almost fully healed from his ordeal yesterday, so he won't even know anything happened. Tucker, well—" Jace laughs. "He's drooling on his pillow."

I chuckle.

"It looks like we were attacked," he says, scanning the hallway. "Did you see anything? Anyone?"

"I—" I briefly look at Drew, who frowns, watching my face and silently pleading with me to lie.

I clear my throat.

"Just silhouettes," I fib. "I couldn't make out much before I passed out. Drew dragged me to safety, I think, but it's all pretty hazy." I shake my head, trying to sell my lie. "I can't remember much."

I'll tell him the truth, someday. I'm not sure how or when, but I don't like hiding this from him.

Damn morals.

Life as a Spectre wasn't easy, but at least back then I didn't have to deal with having all these ethics. A secret was a secret—end of story.

"It's fine, don't worry about it." Jace waves his hand absently. "We're going to scan the property, but for now it's best if you get back to your room." He hesitates, fighting with his words a moment. "Uh—please."

The last word was so quiet, so mumbled, it was almost inaudible.

But he definitely said *please*.

I grin, wondering if I should give him shit for being *nice* for once, but I don't want to spoil the mood. "Okay."

His eyebrows shoot up, as if he can't believe that worked. He tries to recover, though, with a nod. "Good. Oh, and Drew—" He shifts his stormy gray eyes toward the fire dragon. "I, uh—thank you for keeping her safe."

Drew simply nods in answer.

With that, Jace gestures to his soldiers and they fan out. He and three others continue down the hallway. With only a brief backward glance toward me, he rounds the corner and continues his patrol.

"Are you really going to your room?" Drew asks, crossing his muscular arms.

"That's the plan," I admit. "After all, you and I still have a lot to discuss."

"Oh?" He lifts one brow in surprise.

I laugh. "Yeah, Drew."

I gesture for him to follow me to my room, but he takes my hand and begins to lead me in the other direction, toward the wing of the castle where he's staying.

"If you're going to make me talk about *more* feelings," he mutters with a wry grin, "I at least want to be sitting on my favorite couch for the ordeal."

CHAPTER TWENTY-FOUR

A s Drew closes the door behind him, I scan his suite. A camera sits in the corner of the living room, a familiar silver rectangle lodged in the wiring.

One of my voids.

"How the hell did you get that?" I ask, pointing to the device.

He grins. "Oh, right. Thanks for letting me borrow a few."

"*You* took them?" I raise my eyebrow incredulously. "How did you even know what they are? And how the hell did you get in my room without me noticing?"

"You were off sneaking around the castle," he says with that wry smile of his. "I figured I would pop in, see who you really are. Maybe find out what you were up to."

"Impressive," I admit. Except for a bit of my missing tech, I hadn't even noticed someone was in there. "Find anything useful?"

"Nope." He shrugs. "You're very good at covering your tracks." He grins. "I've always admired that."

I sarcastically flourish my hand and feign a regal bow.

He chuckles. "I've seen devices like that before," he says with a nod to the void. "When I saw you had some of them, I started to piece together your advanced training. I knew you were lethal, just not why."

I shake my head in mild annoyance, but I have to hand it to him. "Clever. Can you get me any more of them?"

"Maybe, but I doubt it," he admits, heading toward the short hallway that connects the living room to his office, bedroom, and bathroom. "That tech is incredible, and we still haven't figured out how to reproduce it," he adds, shouting over his shoulder.

I follow, wondering where he's disappearing to, and lean against the doorframe as he ducks into his bedroom and rifles through a duffle bag at the foot of his bed.

"Looking for something?" I ask.

"Another phone," he says absently, digging into the depths of the bag. "I have to get another one before my dad finds the conversation with my Vaer contact."

My eyebrows shoot upward. "The guy who's getting the blueprints?"

"One and the same." Drew grunts triumphantly and pulls a phone out of the bag, his thumb flying across the screen as he activates it. "He's actually a human contractor who upgraded their tech system a few years back. They scared him—bad—in an attempt to get him to lower his rates." Drew rolls his eyes.

"What did they do?"

Drew's jaw tenses. "Kidnapped his family until the work was done. Roughed them up a bit."

I groan in disgust.

"Yeah, so he's more than happy to help us out," Drew says. "And that's why I trust this guy—clear motive. He's *motivated*. I've never had a contact get me intel so fast."

"That's incredible," I admit with a hopeful smile.

"It really is," Drew adds with a chuckle, still rifling through the bag. "He's mere hours from coming through for us. I have to give Jace what I find, but don't worry—even if he tries to lock you out of this mission, you and I will go on our own." He winks roguishly. "Who needs him and his stupid army, anyway?"

I chuckle, my heart warming. "Thanks, Drew."

He grins and returns to the bag, his smile fading as he fights with whatever's in it. "Where *is* this thing, damn it…"

A second later, he finally tugs out another phone, his gaze flitting between the two as he wipes the one his dad hacked.

Jett Darrington.

I frown, silently fuming at the man's audacity.

"Darringtons really do think they're above the law," I say quietly. "Don't they?"

He sighs and lowers the phones in his hands, watching me with an intense expression. "Yeah, I guess we do."

I hesitate, not quite meaning it like that. "You're fine, Drew. But your dad…"

I don't even bother to finish the thought.

There just aren't words.

"Yeah," Drew says, tossing both phones in the duffle bag and sitting on the edge of his bed.

"He knows something." I bite my nail, lost in thought,

recalling the conversation deep in the tunnel. "About me. Something he didn't want either of us to know."

"It certainly seems that way," Drew says with a deep sigh. "Usually, Milo and I are the only ones who get that kind of intel. For him to hide it from me, well, it can't be good."

Oh, how *lovely*.

"Maybe he knew…" I start to say, but I'm not really sure where to take it. "Well, you and me…"

His eyes drift toward me, scanning my face as he waits for me to continue. When I don't, he stands, slowly closing the space between us until he's mere inches away, his powerful frame blocking out the world around me.

As he nears, still delightfully shirtless, those hard abs of his just beg me to run my fingers over them. Heat and desire simmer beneath my skin, between my legs, burning clear through to my core.

My traitorous body gets so easily distracted, lately. Though I try to focus on the conversation, to dig into what Jett could possibly know about my magic, my thoughts quickly jumble into an incoherent mess.

As Drew nears, so tantalizingly close, my thighs ache

with longing. With desire. My concern bubbles away, replaced with a deep and carnal hunger.

The things this man does to me—all without knowing it.

I'm getting tired of fighting it.

"Like I said, mushy sweet talk isn't really my thing," he admits. "But I will say this. I'm proud of you. What you did down there—all that power—you're a fighter, through and through." He smirks. "Nothing will ever stop you. I admire that."

"I hit you with a full blast of my magic," I say breathlessly. "How did you not die? How are you—"

He smiles briefly, his eyes drifting along my face, and he runs his thumb tenderly along my jaw. Without a word, he sets his hand possessively in the crook on my neck, his strong grip simultaneously possessive and reassuring. "Darringtons are fireproof. Solid. Some of us royals are, anyway." He chuckles. "Our thick skin means we can take blows that would kill other people."

"That's astonishing," I admit.

"I mean, it *hurt*," he says with a laugh, rubbing the back of his head. "Dear God, that burned worse than anything I've ever felt in my life. You pack one *hell* of a punch, woman."

I grin, glad he at least felt it. He barely acknowledged the blow at all. He has a good poker face—I'll have to keep that in mind for the future.

"I know you like giving orders, but I don't obey." He wraps his massive hands around my waist. His lips hover by mine, just out of reach and tantalizingly close. "Think you can handle giving up control for once?"

He doesn't really give me a chance to answer.

His palms are warm and soothing as he gently leads me away from the doorframe and presses me against the wall of his bedroom. He dips his fingers past the hem of my pants, teasing me with his molten touch.

He's right, of course. I do prefer giving orders to taking them, especially now that I'm free from Zurie's control. But with Drew, it's clear he's used to leading, too.

We've fought over the reins so far, battling silently to take control of any given situation, perhaps out of habit more than anything else.

"Truce?" I ask breathlessly, lifting my chin until our lips nearly touch.

In apparent answer, he lifts me by the waist and presses his hips against mine, pinning me to the wall with my feet a good foot or two off the floor.

As he leans his handsome face toward me, the bulge in

his pants rubs against my entrance. With only fabric separating us, I get a sense of just how hung he really is. It was one thing to see it, but to *feel* it...

I grin mischievously. "Is that a yes, or—"

"We're equals, Rory," he says, his voice growly and deep. "You want something, you ask for it. You don't command me, and I won't command you."

He runs his lips along my jaw, and my eyes flutter closed from the sheer joy of the sensation. "Deal."

"There is one exception," he says playfully.

"And that is?"

"My bed, my rules." He presses his warm lips against my neck, and I can't help but to melt into him. "I won't hold back—because I know you can take it."

The sensation of his kisses along my skin ignites every lingering desire within me, and any shred of resistance dissolves in an instant.

Here, now, I'm happily his.

He dips his fingers in the small gap between my pants and my waist. With a sudden, powerful twist, he rips the fabric in two.

A hole now ripped in the crotch of my pants, I gasp as cold air rushes against my inner thigh.

But he isn't done yet.

He hooks two thick fingers around my underwear and pulls, instantly ripping that to shreds as well.

"I needed those," I say playfully, even as I arch my hips toward him, egging him on.

He grins. "Oh, did you? How rude of me."

With my legs spread against him and my back against the wall, he has me pinned—I couldn't get down even if I wanted to.

And I most certainly do *not* want this to stop.

With my entrance exposed through the hole he ripped in my clothes, he doesn't give me time to even crack another joke.

After a few deft tugs, he unzips his jeans and pulls out his thick cock. He's already hard as a rock, too eager to undress.

The hunger in his touch only makes me crave him more.

Drew presses his mouth to mine and kisses me roughly. Lost in him, I weave my hands through his hair as he presses the tip of his massive cock against my entrance.

He teases me, holding it there, running it expertly up

and down the sensitive folds, sending shivers of delight through me with each pass.

"Fair disclosure," I say, gasping a little between words. "Tucker—he and I—*oh*, wow. That feels *amazing*—"

"Yeah, I guessed you're with him," Drew says, his voice rough. "But I'm not afraid of some healthy competition."

With a few light thrusts, he forces the tip of his massive cock into me, stretching me.

I squeeze my thighs against his core as I wrap my legs around him, silently begging for him to continue even as he pauses yet again, determined to tease me into oblivion.

"I'm tempted to make you beg for it," he says with a dark laugh, inching his cock a little deeper.

"Don't—" I gasp as he shoves his cock another inch inside of me, only to pause yet again. "Don't you dare—"

He clicks his tongue in mock disappointment. "We *just* agreed not to give each other orders."

I laugh, my head tilting backward in ecstasy as he begins to slowly slide in and out, working my entrance mercilessly, hinting at just what he can do what that delightful cock of his.

"Do it," he says with a wicked little grin. "Beg for it."

"You ass," I gasp, breathless as he begins to pull out of me.

The tip of his cock dips in and out, giving me only enough to imagine the rest, setting my nerves on fire with lust and need, until I can't take another second of this torture.

"Take me," I demand, setting both my hands on his face, looking deep into his eyes. My voice is thick with lust and longing, but I don't even care. "Take it all."

He grins, apparently satisfied. "If you insist."

With that, he bucks into me. He fills me to the brim, stretching me further than I even thought I could go. I gasp and arch my back, pressing my hips flat against his, somehow taking all of him in me.

He sits there for a moment, letting me adjust as he sprinkles my neck with fiery kisses.

As Drew's cock stretches me, all I can do is marvel at him. This is a man who's stronger even than me. Who can withstand my stubborn pride and survive a direct blast of the most powerful magic on Earth.

And he's *mine.*

Still fully clothed, too impatient to take off anything at

all, he slowly slides out of me. Just as his tip nears my entrance, he thrusts hard into me once more.

With one hand against the wall for balance, his other hand grips my waist tightly, holding me in place. With each plunge, he pulls my hips down toward his cock, sending a flurry of ecstasy through me with every thrust. It's like he wants me to experience every inch of him—or, perhaps he wants to experience every inch of *me.*

He nibbles my neck, heightening the sensation of his massive cock diving into me. I gasp and moan, taking him, spreading my legs wider so that he can go deeper, thrust harder, take more of me in every way.

For once, I truly am not in control.

If I wanted to pin him, I wouldn't be able to. The thought is surreal—to think this is one man I probably couldn't take on in a fair fight, and he's bucking into me as he has me pinned to a wall.

But I *love* it.

I wrap my arms around his neck as he stands upright. Quickly, both of his hands slide to my ass, keeping me rooted on his dick.

In one powerful motion, he grips my ass tightly and lifts me off his cock. He kisses me fiercely, his warm lips against mine as he explores my mouth. I ease into him, relaxing, diving into his embrace.

With absolutely no warning, he shoves my hips down and thrusts upward with his cock, ramming into me in a delightful new way. I quickly lose all track of time—and I don't care in the least.

As long as he continues to ride me, I'm happy.

I gasp against him, his hot breath rolling over me as my eyes flutter closed. Again and again, he thrusts into me, never once letting me down, never once slowing except to mercilessly tease me.

Eventually, an orgasm builds within me, starting at the tip of his cock, spreading through my core and becoming more intense as he rides me to my climax.

When it finally hits, it *explodes* within me. I cum hard, the ecstasy mind-blowing as he continues to thrust into me again and again. I moan, digging my hands into his hair, my thighs pressed tight against his waist as I finally give in.

I lose track of how long the orgasm lasts, but he rides me through the entire thing, only slowing when I finally begin to relax against him.

When he's sure I'm done, he finally releases within me

and sighs, the blissful sound both happy and content. He leans his forehead against mine, holding me tightly.

I shiver with pleasure as he empties himself deep within me, the hot rush both tantalizing and utterly delightful.

Deeply satisfied, I run my fingers through his hair, utterly spent, breathing heavily as I hold him close.

Gently, he sets me on his bed. He lays next to me grinning as he looks me over, beads of sweat pooling along his bare chest.

"You're such a bad influence on me," he says with a wry grin.

I laugh. "Wait, how am I the bad influence, here?"

"Don't act innocent." He slips his hand under my shirt and runs his fingertips along my body, tracing the curves of my waist and navel. "That was highly illegal. You're claimed by a thunderbird, after all."

I roll my eyes.

Tenderly, his hand inches upward, following the curves of my body until his fingertips brush my bra. His hand rests there, holding me, his touch soothing and strong.

"Luckily for you, however," he says mischievously, "I

have a few punishments in mind worthy of a trouble-maker like you."

With one fluid motion, he reaches behind me and roughly unhooks my bra.

I laugh, gasping a little in surprise. "Well just make yourself at home, why don't you?"

"I plan to."

"Are you really ready to go again?" I ask, impressed. "Already?"

"You have no idea what you do to me." He stands, already hard as a rock once more, and tugs off his jeans. "I hope you got enough rest last night because I have plans for how we're going to spend the next four hours."

I laugh as he hungrily tugs off what's left of my pants. "Well, let's get to it, then."

CHAPTER TWENTY-FIVE

When I wake with Drew's arm around my chest, my body buzzes with raw power. Something about riding him is unlike anything I've experienced before—the way neither of us held back, the control he had over me, the utter and complete surrender—sex with him was mind-blowing in the best possible way.

He nuzzles the nape of my neck, still sound asleep as the early morning light breaks through an opening in the curtain. His other hand reaches under me, wrapping around me until I'm completely engulfed in his embrace. He pulls me toward him, my bare skin sliding over his sheets as he holds me close and kisses my jaw.

"Mornin'," he mutters, his voice gruff and drowsy.

He adjusts his hips, pressing them against my ass, his hard cock shoving its way between my thighs. I chuckle as he eases it upward in what I can only assume is his attempt at a subtle hint.

"Think this is funny, huh?" He peppers delightfully rough kisses down my neck and onto my shoulder.

With no warning, he grabs my leg and lifts it so that his cock has free access to my body. He presses the tip against my raw entrance.

Apparently already revved and eager, he doesn't bother with any more banter.

He thrusts hungrily into me, and I gasp in surprise. I thought he was bluffing—but I suppose by now I should know better. As he roughly takes me yet again, I melt into him, unable to satiate my appetite for his rough and dominating demeanor.

As he bucks into me, I lean into him until the back of my head brushes his brow. Though he holds my leg up with one hand, his other arm tightens around me, holding my shoulder in a possessive and almost nurturing way that's utterly disarming.

I give in. Completely. For this moment, at least, I'm once more utterly and completely his.

And I freaking *love* it.

———————◆ ◆◈◆ ◆———————

I n the afterglow of my many rounds with Drew, I walk slowly through the halls of the embassy with a smile on my face. Hands in my pockets, I take in the world around me, enjoying the art on the walls for once.

Whoever decorated this place had *class.*

Gilded frames. Elegant women in medieval dresses. Kings and queens. The most gorgeous and colorful dragons I've ever seen. Every scene is a masterpiece.

As happy and satisfied as I am, I know the clock is ticking. Ian is getting impatient. Irena's life hangs in the balance, and I have two days left to make things right.

Hopefully Jace and Drew can get the blueprints finalized by noon today—because we just don't have the luxury of time, anymore.

Though I'm tempted to go straight to Jace's suite, my first stop is Tucker's room—I want to check on him and see how he's faring after the Darrington invasion last night.

I bite my lip as I knock on Tucker's door, wondering if I should tell him everything.

Yeah, probably. Tucker knows how to guard a secret.

The impulsive thought is a bit surreal. I really do trust him completely. After a lifetime with the Spectres, it's still so strange for me to open up to people. To rely on them. To let them in for good.

His door swings open, only to reveal a shirtless Tucker with a toothbrush sticking out of his mouth. He smiles, still scrubbing. "'ey, beb!"

I laugh. "You're ridiculous."

"Oo 'uv meh," he says, the garbled words barely making it past the toothbrush as he finishes up. He nods toward the bedroom, wordlessly inviting me in.

I close the door behind me as he jogs over to the bathroom to finish up his morning routine. When I finally join him and lean against the doorframe, he's dabbing a towel over his mouth, the toothbrush lying idly on the counter beside his phone.

Without a word, he plants a minty kiss on my cheek. "Do you have any idea what happened last night? Something about gas?" He laughs, shaking his head in disbelief. "I woke up with one hell of a headache."

"Yeah, about that—"

"Wait, you look different." He grins and studies my face. "You got laid, didn't you?"

"What?" I laugh, entirely caught off guard.

"Oh, you *totally* got laid." Tucker grins. "I mean, it's not a hard guess who. Jace is being an asshole and Levi, well, I don't think you're that kinky. But as soon as he's not a dragon, anymore, I figure—"

I playfully smack his shoulder.

"So now I have to share you with Drew, huh?" Tucker smirks and leans against the counter, crossing his arms. "I can handle that. A little competition never hurt."

I roll my eyes. These men are so ridiculous.

"So, last night," he says, clapping his hands together eagerly. "I assume you know what—"

His phone buzzes, vibrating against the marble countertop between us. We both look down at it, but I don't recognize the number.

"Damn it," Tucker mutters, scratching the stubble along his jaw.

His smile disappears in an instant, and he stands a little taller as the mood in the room abruptly shifts.

"What?" I cross my arms, studying his face. "Who is it?"

He holds up his hand in answer, gesturing for me to stay silent. Without a word, he takes a steadying breath and squares his shoulders as if preparing himself for a conversation he doesn't want to have.

Quickly, he taps his thumb on the screen to accept the call and puts it on speaker. "Hey, Pops."

That kills my mood. Entirely.

"Tucker," a gravely man's voice says through the speaker. "Rendezvous. Ten minutes. Usual spot."

The Knights' General is curt and to the point. No banter. No pleasantries. Just business.

No wonder he and Zurie get along.

"Can't," Tucker says, instantly mimicking his father's tone. "The giant lizards found my exit point. I've been hunting for a new one to—"

"Don't give me excuses," the retired soldier interrupts. "Just figure it out."

"What do you think I've *been* doing?" Tucker snaps. "This place is on lockdown. If I just walk out the front door, they're going to get suspicious."

The man snorts derisively. "You're a clever kid. Find an exit and get out here. Bring everything you have on the girl."

My heart sinks, and my eyes lock with Tucker's. If they want him to bring everything he has, it's because they won't be letting him come back.

This is it—the final meeting.

They've finally lost their patience.

I tense, shoulders aching with apprehension as I wonder what will happen next.

"You okay there, Pops?" Tucker asks sarcastically. "It almost sounds like you just want to see me. Did you bring a baseball and some gloves? Because if you want to make up for a childhood where I played with hand-guns like they were action figures, I'd be happy to—"

"Tucker," the General interjects. "Don't make me do this over the phone. At least be man enough to say it to my face, damn it."

Tucker's eyes nervously flit to me, but he manages to keep his tone calm and steady. "Say what, exactly?"

For a moment, the line is so quiet I wonder if it's gone dead.

I furrow my eyebrows in confusion, but Tucker shakes his head, a silent warning to be patient.

Apparently, his father just does this sometimes.

The General eventually sighs, the sound almost painfully loud after the prolonged silence. "Tucker, I had an interesting visit yesterday," the man says. "An old—well, we'll call her a friend—stopped by."

"How neighborly," Tucker says dryly.

"The Ghost isn't much of a neighbor," the General snaps. "But she is good for intel, and the dirt she has on you is truly astounding."

Cold dread shoots clear to my toes. As far as Zurie goes, this was my worst nightmare—and it just came true.

Starting now, the Spectres and the Knights are going to work together... and that does *not* bode well for me.

"Lies," the General says, scoffing. "That's all you've given us. Lie after lie after *lie*."

"Pops, I have no idea what—"

"Don't," his father interjects. "Just be a man about this. Don't try to salvage your little charade, Tucker. You can't."

Tucker frowns, standing a little taller, eyes on the screen as he speaks. "At least we can agree on that," he says, his tone shifting. "There's a lot of years you can't make up for, either."

"We've been *over* this, damn it. *So* many times." The General groans, and the muffled crunch of boots over gravel filters through the phone. "I've done everything in my power to shape you into the Commander you're supposed to be, and I'm not about to lose the best gunner in my whole damn army over some *girl*."

My magic pulses involuntarily as a surge of anger burns through me.

Yeah, sure, I don't like the way he referred to me, but I'm starting to get used to that. None of the leaders in this world see me as anything but an asset to obtain. That's nothing new.

With this asshole, I'm mostly pissed at how he refers to Tucker—like he's property, meant to serve a single role, like some mindless robot with a primary function he's currently failing to complete.

"The Ghost wants the girl," the General continues. "And I want you to come home. You're coming back to the Knights, Tucker, one way or another."

Tucker wrinkles his nose in disgust, sneering with barely contained rage. "You sure you don't want to hire a hit on me like you did for Anderson? And Emily? I can't believe you killed your own *goddaughter*," he adds, his voice breaking.

Tenderly, I set a comforting hand on his shoulder.

"Cut the sentiment," the General snaps. "He abandoned us. That was treason. I didn't *want* to kill Emily. I had to, as a warning to the others. You know the law, Tucker. A Knight doesn't join by himself—his whole family does."

"She was a *kid,* you sick—"

"But this," the General continues, ignoring Tucker's outburst. "You're just letting your dick distract you. I can *fix* that."

Tucker squeezes his free hand into a fist, pressing his knuckles against the sink counter. He grits his teeth, desperately trying to bite back what I'm sure are the scathing words that might actually earn him a death sentence.

"Besides," the General adds lazily, "Zurie's given me some tips on how to reprogram that stubborn brain of yours, and I think this time I can make it stick."

I take an involuntary step backward, my entire body tensing at the thought of either me or Tucker enduring any time at all in the caves below Zurie's home—the hallucinations, the unending darkness, the agonizing pain.

I *won't* go back, and I won't let them do that to Tucker, either.

"You get one shot, kid," his father chides, condescending and cocky. "Don't fuck it up."

With that, the line goes dead.

Tucker grunts in anger and throws his phone against the wall. The screen cracks as it tumbles to the ground, but he clearly doesn't care. He leans both hands against the sink counter, staring down at the marble, his shoulders tense.

Gently, I set a hand on his arm. He flinches at my touch, his head snapping abruptly toward me, and for a moment I see the agony on his face. The guilt. The anger. The swirling tide of disgust and concern.

The moment he looks at me, though, his expression shifts into one of relief.

He grabs me and pulls me close, cradling the back of my head as he burrows his face into my hair. We hold each other, standing there in silence as we process everything we just heard.

"You're more of a family than he ever was," Tucker says softly, holding me tight. "I've made my choice. If it gets me killed, then fuck it. At least I lived a little first."

"I won't let them touch you." My arms tighten around him, and all I can do is smile in gratitude at his bravery. His loyalty. His charming, heartfelt honesty.

He's my Tucker, and we're in this together—come hell or high water.

CHAPTER TWENTY-SIX

As the sun ticks by overhead, I lean on a balcony high in the castle and look out over the majestic ravine surrounding the dojo. Mist swirls and shimmers, dancing any time a dragon dives into the abyss.

I could get used to this.

I've been hunting for Jace all day, but I can't find him. *Anywhere.* The guards all tell me he'll find me later, that he's in meetings, discussing strategies—I'm getting a little fed up.

We're quickly running out of time to save Irena.

Maybe I should just break into his suite.

Hmm.

As I lean on the railing, enjoying the sun and debating

my options, a familiar ice dragon with brilliantly blue scales circles the forest below. He banks toward me as the wind kicks up.

I smile, letting out a grateful sigh of relief that Levi's okay.

In seconds, he soars past me, roaring in welcome. His cry cuts through the air, long and loud, and I lift my hand to brush my fingers along his scales. He growls happily as my fingertips tease along his body. Apparently satisfied that I'm okay, he dives again and flies off into the ravine to do who knows what.

With my elbow on the balcony railing, I lean my cheek on my fist and watch the world around me. It's nice to have a bit of peace after so much crazy. To relax, if only for a second.

If Drew's right, if we really have the blueprints we need, we'll soon be leaving. *Finally.* I need to get Irena out of—

Deep in my chest, the familiar tug toward Jace gets stronger. It swirls and sings, alarmingly loud, and I frown in confusion as I hold a hand to my chest. "What the—"

On instinct, I pivot on my heel, eyes darting across the double doors behind me that lead into the castle. They sit open, just as I left them.

To my surprise, Jace leans casually against the door-frame, his head resting against the elegant molding as he silently watches me.

I flinch, cursing myself for not hearing him. "How did you—"

"You're not the only one with advanced stealth skill, Rory," he says, lifting one eyebrow as he taunts me.

Touché.

I wonder if he's going to tell me about the new blue-prints Drew said are coming today, or if he'll try to hide them from me. I wonder if he'll try to lock me up and keep me here while he goes out and lives my life for me.

With that rather ominous look on his face, I can't help but wonder what fresh hell he's about to unleash on me —because that's all he's been doing lately, one after another.

Waiting for him to start the next fight, I cross my arms and lean my butt against the balcony railing as another gust of wind plays with my hair.

Casually, he strolls toward me and leans his forearms against the railing, looking out at his embassy as if he came here for the view.

We both know he didn't.

He's tantalizingly close, barely a foot away, and the connection we share burns through me like electricity. The sensation buzzes through my veins and makes me dizzy with desire.

All of which, of course, I actively ignore.

"You wonder why I'm so protective," he says casually, not looking at me. "Why I'm a little controlling."

I lift one eyebrow. "A *little*?"

He chuckles and finally tilts his head toward me, those intense eyes snaring me as he leans closer.

My treasonous body urges me to close the gap between us. My greatest impulse right now is to wrap my arms around his shoulders, to hold him close as his warm skin simmers against mine.

It's not even sexual, just impulsive longing to hold him. In that moment, I can't tell if it's me or the mate-bond. If it's really what I want, to be near him, rather than a compulsion driven by some strange thunderbird magic.

Jace's eyes drift to my lips, and he gently brushes his knuckle against my jaw.

It's tender. Intimate. Gentle and doting.

His mouth hovers a few inches from mine, but instead

of kissing me, he scans my face. "I killed three Spectres in the last two years alone, Rory."

My body stiffens on impulse. A very old, *very* primal part of me warns me to run, to put as much space between us as possible, but that's the Spectre training talking. The part of me that Zurie wants to beat into submission.

Jace pauses, studying my expression. When I don't answer, he leans in just a little more. "Do you know how many bounties there are on my head? How many people want to destroy me and everything I love?"

My jaw tenses on impulse, but I know better than to answer him. It's rhetorical, and he's trying to make a point.

"Eleven," he answers. "*Eleven* bounties, from humans and dragons alike. Revenge plots, mostly." He shrugs, like that isn't a big deal. "I face assassins at least once per month. Here's the thing, Rory—if they can't get to me, they'll start coming for you."

A bolt of icy dread shoots through me as I process what he's implying. "Because if we finalize the mate-bond," I say, piecing it together, "killing me would also destroy you."

"Even if we don't finalize it," he corrects, his grip tightening a bit on my chin. "It's not as strong, sure, but it would affect me deeply. If you died now, my dragon would go insane, and I'm not sure I could rein him in."

For a moment, I'm blindsided. I didn't realize I had that kind of influence over him already.

"You're obviously talented, Rory," he says with a proud smile. "But could you win against a dragon like me? Like Harper? Like—*ugh*—Drew?" he adds with an irritated eye roll. "The point is that, yes, I know you're a brilliant fighter. But there will always be someone out there who can take out a talented warrior like you, given the right conditions." His tone is deadly serious.

I frown, looking away.

He releases his gentle hold on my chin, and my skin goes cold as his warm touch fades.

Jace sighs, leaning his lower back against the balcony railing, staring up at the shingles high above us. "It's not even just the bounties on my head we have to worry about. The dragons who are after you have more resources, soldiers, and experience than you do. I can't simply stand back and watch you go off and risk your life without knowing for sure—beyond a shadow of a doubt—that you can take them all."

"It's not like I'm an idiot who trots off into the line of fire," I say, a bit wounded. "I know how to lie low."

"You do," he admits, nodding. "But sometimes that isn't enough. Part of the reason I'm not dead yet is because I have a team of intel officers scouring enemy communications day and night." He rubs his eyes, sighing with exhaustion. "You could have that, too, Rory, if you stay here."

"Maybe," I admit. "But I would need proof you see me as an equal, first."

He nods. "Fair enough—and I would need proof that you can fully wield your magic in any given situation." His eyes shift to mine, serious and intense. "I don't want to lock you up, Rory. I don't want you to hate me. I don't want you to feel like you're a prisoner because my dragon—because *our* dragons chose each other."

Despite the grave conversation, I smile a little at the thought of my own dragon slowly coming to life within me.

"And, so that you're aware," he adds in a grave tone. "The mate-bond goes both ways. If I die…"

Oh.

Oh, no.

"Are you saying I could go feral?" I ask, incredulous.

Jace sighs and slowly nods. "It's possible, if you're ever able to shift. Or, if you never shift, the loss might still drive you insane. No one knows, since we aren't even sure what kind of dragon you might be."

I just stand there, for a second, processing the concept. My entire mood shifts with that one realization, and suddenly I understand Jace's position a bit better.

To know that, in many ways, my survival depends on *him.* On someone I can't control, whose actions could put him in the line of fire and cost him his life.

It's... well, it's humbling. And it gives me a bit of perspective I didn't have before.

"I want you to be happy," Jace says, crossing his arms as he watches me. "Everything in me just wants to give you the world, but I have to do what will protect us both."

The comment snaps me out of my daze, and my old, familiar resentment bubbles up again. "Like nearly shooting Tucker in the face?"

Jace shrugs and looks off into the distance, biting the inside of his cheek like he's trying to keep himself from saying something that will start a fight.

"What can I say, Rory?" he eventually asks. "He's a Knight in my home, and you want me to just, what? Forgive him?"

"I want you to *apologize,*" I snap.

He hesitates, a bewildered expression on his face. "To *Tucker?*"

"To us both."

When Jace doesn't answer, all of the frustration and anger that's been brewing within me boils to the surface. I keep it at bay, trying not to let it take over.

"Yeah, *apologize*," I snap. "You can apologize for nearly killing Tucker. You can apologize for hiding things from me, for trying so hard to control virtually every moment of my life since I got here." I pace the small balcony, the energy within me buzzing as I dip into my resentment. "You have a *lot* to apologize for, Jace."

He sighs deeply and sets his hands in his pockets. I expect him to get defensive, to start yelling or point out all the ways he thinks I'm wrong. To single out all the things I've hidden from *him*. I expect him to ignore my concerns, like he has been lately, to dismiss me entirely yet again.

But he doesn't.

"You feel betrayed, Rory," he says calmly. Quietly. "But so do I."

Our eyes connect, and the intense wound is easy to read on his face.

He gestures vaguely toward the tower where Tucker

and I are staying. "You let a Knight into my home, refused to tell me, and hid a glaring security flaw from me in a place that's supposed to be a fortress. A place that's supposed to keep you safe."

I cross my arms, a bit frustrated. "Can't you see why I lied? Why I hid those things from you? Why I felt trapped?"

"Yes," he says simply, turning away from me.

Whoa.

Wait.

Did he just… *agree* with me?

"In the field, in the heat of the moment, I overreacted." He stiffens, hands in his pockets as he faces away from me. "You deserve a better man than I was back there, and for that, I'm sorry."

I squint at him in confusion, momentarily taken aback. I never actually expected him to apologize. It just doesn't seem like something Jace even does.

"Thank you," I say quietly, genuinely grateful for the dash of empathy he just showed.

He nods, looking at me expectantly over his shoulder.

Ah.

My turn.

"I, uh—" I clear my throat. "I'm sorry I hid those things from you," I admit, surprised to find it absolutely true. "I don't like doing that," I add softly.

And yet, I continue doing it.

Out of obligation—this time, ironically enough, to protect Jace.

If I told him about Drew's access to the secret hallways, I would also have to tell him about the Darrington invasion. And that would lead to war. To bloodshed. To his embassy lying in ruins.

There's so much I'm still hiding from him, and it eats away at me.

But I *have* to. At least for now.

"Thanks," he says, shoulders stiff and uncomfortable.

I guess apologies truly aren't his thing.

The thing is—I've also hidden the flip phone from him, as well as my conversations with Ian Rixer.

And, after this conversation, I think perhaps it's time to take a well-calculated risk. To heal things. To try to make this right.

"I have the flip phone," I admit, since we're clearing the air. "I've spoken to Ian a few times."

Jace groans in annoyance, but he doesn't get angry. "Yeah, I figured. That's incredibly dangerous, though, Rory."

I hesitate. "If you knew, why—"

"You want to help your sister, and I know you wouldn't give anything sensitive away." He looks at me over his shoulder again. "You're smart, Rory. Was I pissed when I found it missing? Yeah, of course. But as I was on my way to confront you, I realized that maybe this could work in our favor. I figured if anyone can get intel from him, it's you."

"Wow," I say quietly. "That's actually really impressive, Jace. All things considered," I add with a shrug.

"So?" he asks, facing me. "Did my trust in you pay off?"

I nod. "I believe his name is Ian Rixer."

"Ian *Rixer*?" Jace asks, incredulous. "That psychopath is still *alive*?"

"Oh, well your reaction is a good sign," I say dryly, wondering who the hell this Ian guy really is.

"*Gods*, this just keeps getting worse," Jace mutters, rubbing his face.

"Who is he?"

The dojo master hesitates, watching me as he debates whether or not to tell me. "Ian Rixer is Kinsley's half-brother."

Oh, this is just freaking *great.*

I'm up against the Vaer Boss's half-brother.

Absolutely *delightful.*

I rub my face and lean against the balcony railing. "So, he has access to money, resources—"

"Everything," Jace confirms. "Kinsley isn't really fond of him, but he's useful to her. He's clever. Wickedly smart. He does have one weakness, though. He doesn't like to get his hands dirty." Jace rubs the stubble on his jaw, lost in thought. "I've never seen Ian Rixer shift, and rumor is it's because he secretly disdains his dragon. Thinks it's dirty," Jace adds with a disgusted grimace. "But if that's true, it's a good sign."

"How is that a good sign?"

Jace shrugs. "If we can get to him, perhaps we can over-power him physically."

"But he'll have traps, surveillance, and all the soldiers in hell between us and him," I point out. "He doesn't seem like the kind of man who takes risks."

"True."

"Maybe it's just a ruse," I say hopefully. "Maybe this *isn't* him. Maybe it's a trick, and they're trying to trip us up by claiming this is someone a lot of people fear."

"Perhaps," Jace says, though he doesn't sound altogether convinced.

We stand in silence as the wind dances around us, watching as his soldiers patrol the grounds in all directions. I stare out at the silhouettes of dragons against the majestic mountains, dreaming of the day I can fly with them.

"We'll figure this Ian thing out," I say.

I just don't know *how*.

"We will," Jace says with a nod. He pauses, tilting his head slightly toward me, and something shifts in his expression. "Look, Rory, I hope you can at least understand where I'm coming from in being so protective."

"I think I can," I admit, a tad begrudgingly.

"I don't like..." He struggles to find the words and grunts in frustration. "I don't like *needing* people. I'm no good at it. But, Rory, I *need* you to be safe. I *need* you to stay alive."

He abruptly turns around and pulls me in to him, his

arms around my shoulders as we stand there in silence, each of us having said our piece.

In that moment, I finally get it.

I finally understand Jace.

We don't agree with each other, and we don't really see eye to eye on—well, anything.

But I can at least understand where he's coming from.

And, I guess, I can have a little heart.

I can forgive the overbearing, domineering idiot. Because, deep down, there's a good man in there.

He just needs a little push.

One way or another, Jace will see what I'm really capable of—and then, just maybe, he'll give in.

CHAPTER TWENTY-SEVEN

"I think you're going to like this," Jace says, holding open the door to the private war room in his suite.

The table inside is littered with dark blue papers. White markings and sketches cover every page, and my heart leaps with hope.

The blueprints.

Finally.

And none too soon.

I jog toward the pages, spreading out the papers one by one as a slow smile breaks across my face. "Is this—"

"All of them, yes." Jace shuts the door behind us and rifles through a few of them. "Drew's contact really came through. Even I'm impressed," he adds, a bit reluctantly.

"Wow." I page through four levels of the compound, marveling at the detail. Secured room notes. Access panels. Codes.

This is a goldmine.

All that waiting really paid off.

"I've secured the medevac chopper and a few guards to protect it," Jace adds. "Two medics will greet us and tend to Irena during the flight."

"You must have cashed in quite a few favors," I say with a glance toward him.

He shrugs.

"Thank you," I say, truly grateful.

With a modest nod, he continues to rifle through the blueprints, and I figure I already bled him dry for the day in terms of warm-fuzzy moments.

"Rory," he says, his tone serious and firm. "For this mission, I want you to stay close to me. No matter what happens."

I frown, but after everything we just discussed…

"Fine." I sigh. That complicates things a little, but I can

work with it. "But Jace, keep in mind—Ian told me he would kill anyone I bring with me. If you go in with me—"

"He won't kill me," Jace says with a confident shake of his head. "Or Drew. He knows he can negotiate for a shitload of money by holding either of us hostage."

I let out a little sigh of relief. "You're sure?"

"Very."

"And Tucker? Levi?"

"They're at risk," Jace admits. "But both of them already know the dangers, Rory. They're doing this despite the threat of death. You already know that."

True.

I sigh, mind buzzing with ideas as I debate the best way to keep each of them safe.

Jace clears his throat. "However, I don't suppose you would be willing to exclude—"

"Nope."

If Levi, Tucker, and Drew want to help, I won't stop them—besides, Levi proved he would go with me into battle, no matter how hard I try to stop him. Tucker and Drew would probably do the same.

Jace groans, shaking his head a bit in mild irritation, but I catch the barest hint of a grin on his face as he looks away.

He and I—well, it seems like it's back to business as usual, and in this case, I'm entirely okay with that.

In my pocket, Ian's flip phone vibrates. I fish it out, expecting a phone call—but the text message icon flashes instead.

Jace and I share a brief glance, and I scan through the message.

It seems we're running out of time to play our game... Let's make the final moments interesting, hmm?

I frown.

Interesting indeed.

Ian Rixer has no idea the storm that's coming for him —and that's the point. I don't want him to have even the slightest hint of what I intend to do to him.

Time to set my sister free.

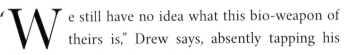

"We still have no idea what this bio-weapon of theirs is," Drew says, absently tapping his finger on one of the blueprint pages.

Drew, Jace, Tucker, and I stand around the table covered in blueprints, three hours into our planning session. Tucker chomps on a powdered donut in the corner and leans against the wall, since Jace forbade him from touching anything.

Jace scratches his jaw. "My contact in the hospital is prepared to figure out what she was infected with. There's nothing else we can do except wait, unfortunately. With his expansive lab, he'll be able to run tests on Irena's blood once he gets her in there. He's prepared to do so at a moment's notice."

"And the antidote?" I ask.

"He'll examine it first, of course," Jace says casually. "Just in case it's a fake. But with a bit of analysis and some blood samples, they'll determine if the antidote will work or not."

I tense, not liking the risk in this plan, but it's all we have.

As I rifle through the papers, a plan begins to form in the back of my mind. "Where's the page with the tunnel access? The one that—"

"Here," Drew says with a wry smile, pulling out one of the papers from the rest and setting it in the middle of the table.

I grin in thanks, unable to mask a flirty sidelong glance at the fire dragon.

In my periphery, Jace tenses, glancing jealously back and forth between me and Drew.

Eager to diffuse the situation before either of them can start anything, I clear my throat and tap the page. "We don't have much time left, so we have to act tonight. It looks like there are four main entrances we can take that have minimal security."

"Minimal is being a tad generous, don't you think?" Drew says with a laugh. "There's at least four men at each post, plus an access panel and cameras."

"Yeah, well, I never said it would be easy." I shrug and point to one of the tunnels. "Drew, I think you should go in here. You can overwhelm the guards before they sound the alarm, and I'll give you some of my remaining voids and my modified handgun to take out any cameras you encounter. How's your aim?"

"Impeccable," Drew says with a cocky grin.

"Voids?" Jace interrupts, confused.

"Yeah, uh—hmm," I hesitate, wondering if he'll make the connection to his command center. "They're little square devices that can—"

"Put a camera on loop?" the dojo master finishes with a

weary sigh. He sets his face in his palm and shakes his head in frustration. "Rory, seriously? The person breaking into my command center—that was you?"

"Exonerated!" Tucker shouts from the corner, pumping his fist in the air.

Jace shoots the former Knight an irritated glare and just gestures for me to continue, like he can't deal with this right now.

"Right." I clear my throat. "Tucker enters here—"

"No, no, not there," Drew says with a frown. "Too much surveillance."

I hold the paper up, tilting it a little. Quirking an eyebrow, I wonder what he's seeing that I'm not.

"Here is better." Drew taps another tunnel, not far from the one I originally chose. "Trust me. With the limited angle of the corners here—" He taps the page. "—and here, Tucker can get in without being seen. Provided he can take out the guards."

"Bet I can get more than you," Tucker says with a smirk.

Drew leans his palms on the table, surveying the weapons expert with a wry grin. "I'll take that bet."

"Alright, gents, focus." I shake my head, trying to

suppress a laugh. "Levi distracts them here," I say, pointing to another spot on the map of the fortress exterior. "Ian is smarter than Mason, so he'll be expecting a decoy attack and will quickly mobilize against Levi, but Levi is stealthy and lightning fast. He can handle it."

"Yeah, no kidding." Tucker polishes off the last of his donut. "His body count at Mason's place was almost a hundred. Eighty-three, I think?"

"Really? Jesus," I mutter. "Well, he'll be able to draw military power away from the main compound. Drew, you're our security guy. I would like for you to get to the command center and cut off surveillance and power. Uh, please," I add with a brief glance, trying to comply with the no-bossing-each-other-around rule. "Tucker, you're going to get us out of there in one piece."

In my peripheral vision, Jace tenses, glaring daggers at the former Knight standing across the room. "Are you sure it's smart to leave *him* in charge of our only way out?"

"Dude, I'm *right* here," Tucker snaps, clearly annoyed.

"We have to do this as a team, Jace," I say curtly. "Together, or not at all."

The dojo master shrugs in answer, and I get the

distinct impression he's coming up with another plan in case my trust in Tucker falls through.

Trying to bite back my annoyance, I press on. "At this point, just about everyone knows about Jace's connection to me, so they'll be expecting him to be there. They might know about Drew and Tucker from Mason's security footage, but I doubt they've been able to identify everyone. They likely have no idea who Tucker or Levi even are, and we can use that to our advantage. Given Drew's strength as a dragon, I figure they won't expect him to infiltrate their compound in human form, and that gives us a leg up. They'll be looking at the skies, waiting for him to attack from another direction. All of that gives us a distinct advantage." I look around the table at each man, pausing for a moment. "Any questions?"

"Yeah," Drew says with a slightly sarcastic tone. "What are you and Jace going to do? Sit back and drink cocktails?"

I grin, leaning my palms on the piles of paper littered across the desk. "Since they know for sure both Jace and I are coming—" My grin widens at my mischievous little plan. "—he and I are going to get caught."

CHAPTER TWENTY-EIGHT

J ace and I crouch behind a thick mountain bolder overlooking the Vaer compound where they're holding Irena.

This is it.

I stretch my fingers in anticipation, knowing full well there will be a lot of bloodshed before the night is over.

Careful to keep my head low, I feign an attempt to hide. Beside me, Jace does the same, his body temptingly close. His attention focused on the compound below us, he absently slides his hand across the boulder near mine, and I can practically feel sparks as our bodies ache for each other.

I scan the compound beneath us, trying to ignore the way my heart calls for him.

Their advanced thermal tech has probably already picked up our heat signatures, but that's kind of the point.

"Twenty soldiers on patrol," Jace says quietly, squinting as he surveys the scene below. "Wait, twenty-four."

"Every bit as bad as we thought," I say with a shrug.

The tension builds in my shoulders as I wait for the signal. We can't move until Tucker and Drew are in position—they'll only get one chance each to tear through the weakened defenses once Levi, Jace, and I act as decoys.

This is a risky plan. It's built on precision, timing, and trust—trust that Drew can get to the command center. Trust that Tucker can get us all out. Trust that Ian is cocky enough to gloat and show me where Irena is.

I grit my teeth, a little nervous, wishing I had more control over the situation. The intel we got was good, but there's always risks at a facility this advanced—and well-guarded.

"Hey," Jace says quietly, his voice a little gruff. It's a soothing tone, soft and tender, and it catches me off-guard.

Though the rest of me remains utterly still, my eyes flit toward him. He's watching me with a concerned expression, and as our eyes meet, he leans slightly toward me.

"This is going to work," he admits. "Yeah, sure, I would rather you were safely back at the dojo, but this is our best option. You came up with a solid plan."

I smile. "Did that hurt for you to admit?"

"Maybe a little." He chuckles, turning his attention back to the facility below us. "I'm used to coming up with the logistics by myself. It's not usually a team effort."

With a small chuckle, I shrug playfully, trying my best to diffuse the tension in my shoulders.

Without a word, Jace slips his hand over mine, and a small white spark pops in the air between us as we touch. It fizzles, like static electricity. Heat courses up my arm, radiating from him, and I feel a bit calmer with his touch. He squeezes my hand lightly, weaving his fingers through mine.

It's intimate. Kind. Gentle. Everything I've come to think Jace can't be.

He gives me a brief smile and returns his attention to the facility.

In true Jace form, that one little moment said so much, and he did it all without saying a word.

We can do this, it said.

Together, we're unstoppable.

And, perhaps most notably—*Don't give up on me.*

My smile fading, I try not to think too much about the quiet little moment. As difficult as he can be, as much as he pushes my buttons and drives me wild, I just can't dwell on any of it right now.

The facility—Irena—needs my full attention.

Despite the tension in my shoulders, I try to relax. So much of this plan hinges on me playing coy. I have to appear relaxed and confident—even when my gut is twisting with anticipation.

For the fight.

For my family.

For *revenge.*

A roar splits through the night, piercing and violent. Instantly, it's met with a dozen more, and a colorful assortment of dragons take to the skies.

Levi's signal—and the beginning of our little attack on one of the most secure buildings I've ever seen.

I square my shoulders. No turning back now.

Time to get caught.

CHAPTER TWENTY-NINE

With a sharp punch to the back of a soldier's head, I take him out.

He falls to the ground, his black uniform identical to the other four guards we just took down.

A red light beeps on the control pad by the door that leads into the fortress, and Jace quickly tugs an access card out of one of the soldiers' pockets and slaps it on the scanner.

He holds his breath, eyes shifting between the still-red access panel and the door. I fidget, eager to get in, eager to get on with this.

Two angled half-walls arch out from the door, offering a small enclave for us to hide in. I lean my back against one of them, trying to stay out of sight of the camera in the concrete yard between us and the wire fence.

It should be turning toward us at any moment, and we absolutely *have* to get inside before it does.

We can't get caught out here.

It's too early.

On the ground, the soldiers should be out of frame on the camera. Sure, security might notice the sudden and suspicious absence of guards by this entrance, but all that matters is we get inside.

We have a bit of hunting to do.

The access panel flashes green, and the door buzzes as it opens. Jace holds the door and ushers me inside, his eyes fixated on the camera as it slowly turns toward us.

We race through the empty hall toward the laundry room—our ticket into the fortress. A boring entrance, sure, but we ideally need to explore a bit first.

It's good to have a backup plan, and we need to know what we're up against in terms of military forces.

Jace and I sneak through the halls, and I wish I had a com in my ear so I could talk to the others. However, we can't give Ian access to a secure communications line, and he'll definitely check for one when he catches us.

Too bad. I want to know how Levi is faring, fighting all those soldiers. I want to know if Tucker made it through into the tunnels. I want to know if Drew is heading to the command center, or if he's been caught.

The success of my plan hinges on everyone else's success just as much as mine, and it makes me nervous to have so many moving parts. At any moment, the tide could turn, and we would be royally screwed.

Every instinct I have warns me to take out the cameras as we pass them, but I can't waste the voids. Not when the point is to eventually get captured.

Ahead of me, Jace pauses at a corner, peeking carefully around. My ears strain for the clatter of footsteps, but it's quiet.

Too quiet.

One of the flaws in my plan is that we have no idea where Irena is. Even Drew's guy didn't know, so part of my job in all this is to goad Ian into taking me to her.

An arrogant guy like that—once he sees me in chains, he'll want to gloat. Show me how close I came to saving her. Maybe force me to watch as he injects a poison, trying to get me to agree to things in an effort to save her.

Men like Ian—they like having power. Over others. Over life.

True, he could just throw me in a cell and kill Irena out of spite, but the man put a dining table in the middle of a field, just to throw me off.

He likes his theatrics.

In a way, I suspect they're his only source of fun, and he's not about to let a prime opportunity to display his power pass him by.

I'm taking a risk, true, but it's my only option.

Jace looks back at me and nods his head toward the corridor, a silent gesture to follow him as we continue our hunt through the fortress.

I nod.

"No, not that way," a familiar man's voice says over the loudspeaker.

Ian's voice is like nails on a chalkboard after all the silence, and I grit my teeth, wondering how long he's been watching.

Jace and I hesitate, making eye contact, but ultimately

we can't give ourselves away. He could be bluffing, or this could be a recording—we have no evidence he actually knows we're in here yet.

We continue as we were, ignoring the voice, though the thin hairs on the back of my neck stand on end.

Through the muffled loudspeaker, Ian clicks his tongue in disappointment. "Rory dear, I offered you quite a fair deal. And this is how you repay me? Taking out my men?"

We pause at another corner, trying to ignore the voice. It cuts through the air, affecting my ability to listen for signs of soldiers around us, but I strain to do it anyway.

As far as I can tell, it's clear.

As we turn the corner, Jace stiffens, setting one arm out to shield me.

A man stands in the hallway, standing perfectly still. He's dressed in an immaculate suit, his hair perfectly combed and tidy. With one hand in his pocket, the other holds a cell phone near his mouth.

He grins knowingly at us. "Hi there, Rory dear."

His voice booms through the speakers in the ceiling, probably for added theatrics.

I lift my chin defiantly, wondering where his armies

are. This hallway is a long, empty stretch without doors—the only access points for a military are around the various corners about fifty feet on either end of us, and I would have heard them lying in wait.

Then again, I didn't hear Ian. Between his eerie ability to stand utterly still and the painfully loud speakers, he screwed with my ability to detect the enemy.

This has to be a trap. Otherwise, it would be too easy to kill him.

"Looking for the trick?" Ian says into the phone so that his voice booms again over the speakers.

"Cut that out," I demand, annoyed.

"No, I think I like it." He grins obnoxiously. "It makes me sound like God, don't you think?"

Jace briefly looks over his shoulder, and a sudden look of panic crosses his face.

"Move!" Jace shouts, shoving me out of the way. I hit the wall hard, my head banging against it as a massive pulse of energy shoots down the hallway at us. Jace tries to swerve out of the way, but it hits him hard in the chest. He rolls, a hole burned in his shirt, steam rising from his body as he lies unconscious on the floor.

"Jace!" Though my head aches, I push myself to my feet, ready to race toward him.

"Stay where you are, princess," a familiar man's voice says from behind me. He looks at Jace and whistles in delight. "Man, I can't tell you how long I've wanted to do *that*!"

I grit my teeth, looking over my shoulder to find Guy Durand with a massive handheld cannon, smoke billowing from the strange mechanical fixture attached to its barrel. He aims it toward me, sneering, and the end begins to spark to life.

"Stop, idiot," Ian snaps.

Guy's smile falters, and he lowers the cannon like a wounded dog who just got yelled at by its master.

With a disgusted sneer, Ian taps something on his phone and shoves the device in his pocket. "Well, Rory dear, I apologize for the *help's* behavior," he nods toward Guy like the man is an insect. "He's new."

I frown, not sure what to do.

There has to be a bit of a fight—I can't let Ian think he got me too easily.

But with Jace hurt, there's suddenly a very large wrench in my plan.

My eyes flit down to the thunderbird. Thankfully, his chest slowly rises and falls, but it looks like he's hurt pretty bad. Though I want to run to him, to check on him, I don't want to get a pulse from that cannon, too. It won't do any good if we're both unconscious.

"Cuff them, moron." Ian snaps his fingers at Guy.

The former Fairfax dragon grumbles and sets down the cannon far away from me. Strange metal domes hang from his belt by chains, their barrels large enough for hands to fit through, and I suddenly see where this is going.

It's cute that he put the cannon down, though. He must have thought this would be easy.

I tense, looking inward and tapping into my magic as I prepare to take him out.

The click of a gun cocking snaps through the air.

I tilt my head slightly to see Ian with a pistol aimed at Jace's head. The Vaer Lord watches me with one eyebrow raised, as if seeing what I'm going to make him do.

Damn it.

Begrudgingly, I lift my hands in surrender.

Guy roughly slides the heavy cuffs over my fingers like mittens, the metal domes engulfing my hands completely.

The moment the iron touches my skin, my body feels weaker. My knees buckle slightly as the device seems to drain the magic from me.

Ian shoves his gun in a holster hidden beneath his suit coat and walks toward me, roughly tapping the metal cuffs with a thick finger. "A little measure for added protection, since you so enjoy punching people."

As Guy locks the second pair of cuffs on Jace's hands, the dojo master groggily comes to. He glares up at Guy, still groggy, but clear-headed enough to know who he's looking at.

His nose wrinkled in disgust. "I should've killed you when I had the chance."

"Guess so," the former Fairfax dragon says with a sneer. "Get up." He kicks Jace roughly in the side. The dojo master grits his teeth, hissing briefly in pain, but manages to hide most of the agony.

The thunder of boots hitting the ground echoes down the hallway, and two dozen soldiers round the far corner. Each wears the black uniform of the Vaer and carries a rifle. They approach in fluid fashion, perfectly in step, no doubt a show of force from Ian.

I glare at him over my shoulder, and he grins back.

Jace gets to his feet, teetering slightly and wincing in pain. Though my hands are cuffed in front of me, I lean my shoulder into him, trying to help him up.

"I'm fine," he says quietly, glaring at the men around us. "Stay focused."

"Want to see your sister?" Ian asks smugly. "Before I kill her, of course, since you broke the terms of our agreement."

"We never had an agreement," I snap back. "And if you kill her, Ian, nothing in this world can save you from what I'm going to do to you." I nod toward the soldiers. "Not even them."

He grins, giving me a once over. "You've been fun prey, Rory," he says with a chuckle. "Truthfully, I expected a better rescue attempt, but it will still be sad to see this end."

With that, he snaps his fingers and walks down the hallway. Guy roughly shoves me after the Vaer Lord, and I shoot the traitor an evil glare as I follow.

So far, it seems like Ian hasn't picked up on the nuances of my plan. Good, because it's all finally starting to come together.

Now, to see if all the pieces of the puzzle fit as I

thought they would—or if everything is about to fall apart at the worst possible time.

With stakes this high, there's no middle ground.

CHAPTER THIRTY

A metal door in the wall slides open, and Guy roughly shoves me and Jace through the doorway.

The spacious room inside is mostly empty, except for a familiar metal hospital bed similar to the one Zurie was strapped to. And, laying on it—

Irena.

My throat tightens, and it takes everything in me to not run to her. Finally, after all this time, I've found her.

And she does *not* look good.

Her skin is ghostly white, so pale I almost expect to see clear through it. Her hair is dry and frizzy, a few strands clinging to her cheek. Four monitors arranged above her head display various vitals, and I anxiously look for the pulse.

It's weak. Her heart's barely beating.

My training kicks in, and I scan the room for weaknesses and exit points. Unfortunately, there's no green goo in sight. No antidote. Damn, I was really counting on it being in here.

I grit my teeth in frustration, trying not to let my emotions get the best of me, and continue my scan. Metal panels line the room, but one panel on the wall opposite me is not like the others. The color is slightly off, as if it's made of different material than the rest.

A secret door.

Based on the blueprints, this is probably one that leads to the tunnels. That's a good sign because, aside from that one option, we're screwed—no windows, no other doors, not even a vent big enough to crawl through.

Jace leans into me, and despite the danger, my skin blisters with warmth and longing at his touch. My body instinctively leans toward him as we each scan the room, formulating backup plans.

"She doesn't have long," Jace mutters to me with a small nod toward Irena.

"I know."

Ian walks in behind us and takes a deep breath, like he's outside enjoying the fresh air. Hands in his suit pockets, he casually strolls around the small room with a grin on his face.

"I'm a little disappointed," he admits, running his palm along his red silk tie to flatten it. "I expected more of a firefight. A bit of foreplay, maybe." He chuckles, his gaze drifting to my chest and along the curves of my thighs.

I wrinkle my nose in disgust. "Pass."

He shrugs, like it's my loss, and snaps his fingers. "Squad one, line the walls. Two through four, the hallway."

Six soldiers enter the room and stand at attention along the walls of the sparse medic ward, surrounding us. Their guns held tight to their chests, they stare blankly ahead, with all the personality of mannequins.

But I suspect Ian prefers it that way. He seems like the sort who enjoys personality and fire only long enough to snuff it out.

The remaining soldiers snap to attention in the corridor outside as the only other exit slides shut, sealing me and Jace in the room.

"And you, well," Ian adjusts his suit coat as he looks at

Jace with disappointment. "I did warn Rory that I would kill any of you that she brought with her, but I guess she called my bluff." He smirks at me briefly, but quickly returns his attention to Jace. "You might be useful. I wonder what we can get out of Harper in exchange for you? And my, my, what *will* she think? I suspect she'll be quite disappointed. The mighty Jace Goodwin, breaking laws? Costing the family millions, maybe *billions*?" Ian chuckles. "And so easily taken captive, no less."

Jace tenses his jaw in anger, wrestling with the cuffs like he wants to snap them off and wring Ian's skinny neck.

Subtly, I elbow him in the side, trying to get him to chill.

We can't let pride screw everything up at the last moment.

Because everything we've done, everything we've pulled together, all comes down to this.

To Drew.

Once Drew's in the security center, he can guide Tucker to our location. Once he's in command of the facility's inner workings, he can give us the distraction we need to break free.

But we're here—in Irena's room—and the tides have yet to turn in our favor.

Ian's still in control. The guards still have access to the room—and we have no way out.

I tense, adjusting my weight as the strange metal cuffs continue to drain my energy. I try to flex my fingers, but I can barely move them.

Deep down, I hope these cuffs aren't draining my power for good. Harper mentioned magic-draining technology exists—technology that can steal my gifts away forever—but all I can do is hope Ian isn't currently using it on me.

I *really* don't like relying on hope.

"You," Ian says disdainfully with a nod toward Guy. "The adults are talking. Go wait in the hall."

Guy grumbles under his breath, casting a brief glare toward Jace. I figure he wanted to be part of the ridiculing, wanted a part in causing Jace as much pain as possible.

Without a word, he obeys, shoving roughly past Jace on the way out. The two share a brief and intense glare, and it's clear that one of them is going to die the next time they meet.

Looking for something to get Ian talking, I nod after

Guy Durand as the door slides shut behind him. "If you hate him so much, why let him live?"

"He's useful," Ian says with a lazy shrug. "Ish."

"And me?" I prod. "What's useful about me? I'm just a girl who fell in a hole."

"Oh, you." Ian laughs, waggling a finger at me like I've been naughty. "Quite the understatement, don't you think?"

"Not really." I shrug, trying to goad him into saying something he shouldn't.

Ian's smart, sure, but he still has his weaknesses, and my guess is his biggest weakness is the desire to show off. To have a grand event.

And I very *purposefully* denied him one.

Our capture was easy. He barely had to lift a finger. He barely got to play. And now, he's going to make up for all the fun he missed out on in capturing me.

I try not to grin as my plan comes together. I don't want to get cocky, since so many pieces are still missing.

Absently, I scan the speakers embedded along the ceiling, wondering if Drew's close to the security center yet.

Or if he got caught, too.

I tense, trying to rein in my concerns, trying to focus.

"Do you know what your limits are?" Ian asks me, tilting his head in curiosity as he begins to slowly pace the room. "By now, I assume you know you're the dragon vessel. Power of the gods and all that." He mockingly shakes his hands, like he's feigning excitement. "To think, all that power in that little body of yours."

His eyes once more rove over my curves, and his gaze lingers a little too long on the space between my thighs.

Jace angles himself possessively between us, momentarily blocking my view of the Vaer.

"Oh, Jace," Ian says mockingly. "Enough of that."

Something buzzes, and Jace groans in agony. He falls to the ground as Ian continues to pace around us. He holds his thumb to a small black remote, grinning calmly as he watches Jace writhe in agony.

Jace grits his teeth, his body arching in pain.

I kneel, wishing I could hold him, comfort him, do *anything*.

"What did you do?" I snap, glaring at Ian.

Ian releases his hold on the button, and instantly, Jace

relaxes. The dojo master gasps for air, curled over himself, his muscles giving out on him as he tries to stand.

"These cuffs are special," Ian says with a nod toward our bound hands. "Designed for thunderbirds like our friend Jace here. After all, we have to keep creatures of magic and lightning in line somehow, am I right?" He grins and waves the remote in the air. "Who would have thought some high voltage electricity is enough to take down a thunderbird?"

"Fuck you," Jace says through gritted teeth, the veins in his neck bulging.

"Such language," Ian says, clicking his tongue in disappointment.

Jace manages to sit upright, and I lean my shoulder against his to help him stay up this time. He nods weakly to me in gratitude, and I can't help but wonder if the cuffs would have the same effect on me.

After all, I'm not a thunderbird.

I'm something more.

"Rory dear," Ian says absently, tapping the remote against his chin as he looks off into space. "I've been debating what to do with you."

"Oh?" I ask sarcastically.

"Quite. Kinsley wants to bleed you dry, of course," he laughs lightheartedly, like it's a joke they share.

"Of course," I say dryly, as if that's not horrifying.

"I rather enjoy your fire, though." He begins to pace toward us, angling between me and Irena, making a point to step between me and the only reason I'm even here. "However, I think we can make you behave with the right—well, let's call it *leverage.*"

His thumb hovers over the button on his remote, and he looks briefly toward Jace again.

"Don't," I say instinctively, trying to give Jace at least a little time to recover.

"I'm fine," Jace says in a painfully terrible attempt to lie. He coughs and tries to stand, teetering as he finally gets on his feet.

"Ah, there we go." Ian grins. "See? All we need is something to bargain with. Like Jace's life, for instance."

"Or Irena?" I ask, finishing his thought for him.

"Quite. Yes." He lazily gestures toward her limp body. "That one worked brilliantly, don't you think?"

"She's barely alive," I snap. "Give her the antidote."

"I'll consider it," he says with a lazy shrug. "But given all the ways you've—"

The lights abruptly shut off, and I anxiously look at Irena's vitals system. The monitors continue to beep and drone, likely running on a backup generator.

Thank goodness.

"What—" Ian hesitates, looking up at the ceiling as a few backup lights pop on.

His eyes flit briefly toward me, and I allow just one wry smirk through my stoic mask.

It would seem Drew has made it to the security console after all.

Thank freaking *goodness.*

"What are you up to, Rory dear?" Ian asks, tilting his head in mild curiosity.

"Just playing our game," I say with a shrug. "Don't you like having fun?"

"Absolutely." He snaps his fingers, and the six guards along the wall instantly point their guns at Irena. "But will your brand of fun get your sister killed?"

I square my shoulders, calling his bluff. "That would kind of defeat the point of this whole rescue, wouldn't it?"

"It most certainly would." Ian sets his thumb on the button, just waiting for any reason to press it.

It's surprising to me for a shifter like Ian to focus so much on influence and control, rather than physical might. He hasn't shifted, hasn't thrown a single punch, nothing. He just introduces consequences and enjoys watching his prey dance for him.

But I won't dance, and I'm done playing.

Even though my muscles ache from the draining effects of the iron cuffs, I shift my weight to my heels and silently reach for the magic in my chest. It burns and sputters, growing stronger as I reach for it.

My hands warm, the magic already itching to break free.

Ian shakes the remote. "Rory," he says with a disappointed tone. "Are you truly going to make me do this?"

I don't answer. Not now, not when I need to focus. I continue to keep my hold on my magic, waiting for it to build. Waiting for it to fill every vein.

With the heavy iron cuffs, the magic moves slowly. It drips and meanders, barely able to stir, but it's there.

It's growing.

I just need more time.

Ian sighs in disappointment. "Fine, have it your way."

He presses his thumb against the button, and a searing blast of agony burns through me. It rips through my muscles, through my veins, through every inch of my body.

My hands reflexively tighten into fists, straining against the metal domes keeping me in line, holding me back, reining in the power that no one but me should ever control.

It's agony.

My knees wobble, and my body desperately wants to give out. It wants to fall. It wants to writhe in pain and curl into a ball until this is all over.

But I don't give up that easy.

I open my eyes, glaring at Ian through the pain. The electrical current is relentless, burning through me like lightning, but I fight it with everything I have. I channel all of my adrenaline, all of my anger, all of my *pain* into my hate-filled glare.

For the first time, I see Ian's smug little smile falter. Slowly, he steps backward, putting Irena between us, like she's a shield that can save him.

He's wrong.

My magic pulses. It ignites, desperate to protect me, desperate to end whatever threat is attacking us.

Us.

Me and this magic within me—my growing dragon— we're a team.

And Ian Rixer is going to *die* for what he's done to us.

The six guards cock their guns, still aiming at Irena and waiting for the command to fire. But as I watch them, their resolve is starting to shift. They nervously glance at me, likely wondering how I'm still standing.

White light skitters over my arms. My torso. My legs. It races across my skin as my magic builds.

Ian taps a few other buttons on the remote, and the electric pulse somehow gets stronger.

I groan in pain, swallowing the whimpers of agony as the horrible pain builds. With no other choice but to go forward, I push through it.

I always push through.

I never give in.

I can't. I don't know how.

Several men bang on the door to the hallway, their urgent shouts muffled by the metal door.

"Rory dear," Ian says condescendingly. "Don't make me kill you, now. It would be such a waste."

The iron around my wrists cracks. White light streams through, like there's a blistering sun in each of my palms, and I glare at him.

Given how Ian's face contorts into an expression of utter horror, I can only imagine what I look like.

The guards all hesitate, eyes wide as they realize their time has come.

With a small boom, the metal around my hands shatters. The pieces fly in every direction like shrapnel, and Jace barely ducks out of the way. A piece crashes into one of Irena's monitors, but with seven armed men about to kill us, I just can't worry about that now.

A few more chunks of metal hit two of the guards square in the face, knocking them out cold. Their guns fire as they hit the ground, and the deafening thunder of gunfire booms through the small space. A dozen bullets hit the wall harmlessly, but one lucky bullet does some of my work for me. One of the remaining four guards goes down, holding his stomach as blood seeps from a bullet wound.

Three down. Three to go.

I lift my hands and fire, the pulses of my magic taking out the remaining guards with effortless precision. They dissolve into dust, just like the Knights who attacked me at the middle school.

Ian frantically turns up a dial on the black remote in his hand and points it at Jace. "I can kill him, Rory. Instantly. If you move, if you so much as raise a hand toward me, he will die."

With Irena's body between me and Ian, I square my shoulders, studying this man who has harassed me for so long, dangled my sister's life in front of me like a carrot on a stick.

My magic burns within me, brighter than it ever has, closer to the surface than ever before. Ian tried to break me, tried to kick me to my knees, tried to cripple me entirely—but he only made me stronger.

And now, the fool would *dare* threaten to kill Jace, too?

"Do you still want to know what my *limits* are, Ian?" I ask with a wry smile as white light blurs across my skin. "How about you and I have a little fun and figure that *out*."

CHAPTER THIRTY-ONE

I think Ian Rixer finally understands the trouble he's in, and the poor fool doesn't look like much of a fighter.

White light sparks along my skin, and I revel in the sheer power that burns through me. It fills me, as warm and doting as an old friend, spurring me on to test my limits.

"Rory," Jace says quietly.

His voice is so distant.

Like muffled words through water.

I turn to face him, the world around me bright and muted. He leans against the wall, a concerned expression on his face as he watches me intently.

He opens his mouth, speaking again, but I can't hear him.

My magic—my power—it's overwhelming. I can't waste energy trying to figure out what he's saying. Right now, my magic propels me forward, fueling me with a singular mission.

Murder.

Everything in me aches to kill Ian. To rip him to shreds. To watch as this brutal asshole turns to dust.

But I can't.

Not yet.

And it takes everything in my soul to hold back.

"Give me the antidote," I demand, my voice chilling and dark.

"If you kill me, you'll never find it." Ian lifts the remote, his thumb hovering over the button in warning of what he's about to do to Jace.

Briefly, I think about destroying that damn remote—it's the only thing holding me back from throwing Ian around a bit to try to loosen his tongue. I absolutely believe he would be willing to kill Jace, and right now, that's the only card he has to play.

Reactively, a bolt of white light shoots from me, like a

bullet. It hits the remote with brilliant accuracy, shattering it to pieces.

Behind me, Jace's cuffs fall off with a heavy thud, and he groans in relief. I quickly tilt my head to check on him. He stands, joining me, rubbing his wrists as he tries to get the blood flow back to normal.

Honestly—that was luck, and I don't like relying on luck. Destroying the remote could just have easily set of an electric shock that killed him, and I didn't even have time to debate my options.

For a moment there, my magic had a life of its own.

There's a quiet blip of worry in the back of my mind at how instinctive that was. My magic acted on the barest thought, fulfilling a silent wish without me so much as lifting a finger.

Gritting my teeth, I try to rein the power in a little, but it pushes back. It's starting to taste its true potential—it doesn't want me to stop *now.*

"You were saying?" I ask Ian condescendingly, masking my concern with a cocky smirk.

"Don't do this, Rory dear." Ian slowly backs up, toward the secret door on the far wall, and I wonder if he's foolish enough to think it will really work when Drew has this place on lockdown.

Maybe he's just desperate enough to try.

Too bad for him, but I'm done playing. I take a step toward him, and he runs.

The coward *runs.*

He reaches the door and smacks his thumb on a hidden scanner, no doubt trying to open it, but I dart toward him and grab his collar before he has a chance.

My magic fuels me, giving me strength I shouldn't have. Lifting him off his feet, I let his Oxfords dangle over the floor as I glare into his eyes. "The antidote, Ian!"

Fast as lightning, he draws a gun from his waist and aims at Irena. As Jace begins to shout a warning, Ian fires, not bothering to negotiate, knowing full well that his only chance to survive is to keep me distracted.

I, however, am just a *hair* faster.

Instinctively, I tighten my grip on his collar and tilt my body, trying to throw off his aim. His elbow curves, and the bullet digs into the ceiling as the gunshot echoes through the enclosed space.

But he doesn't miss a beat.

He's ready to fire again.

This time, he aims at my chest.

A gunshot thunders through the room.

He misses my heart, but only barely. The bullet digs into my chest, tunneling through me, ripping me apart from within.

"Rory!" Jace yells, his voice ripping through the quiet space, laden with panic and fear.

I drop Ian, and for a moment, he seems to think he's won. The thunder of Jace's footsteps stop abruptly when Ian holds his gun toward my head. He looks at the thunderbird, grinning in victory.

The pain blistering through my chest is agonizing, but I can't let myself stop. Not now. Not when we're so close to victory.

The magic eggs me on, numbing the pain, urging me to finish this.

As white light continues to shimmer over my skin, barely contained, I grab his neck with one hand and the barrel of his gun with the other. His eyes go wide, and it's clear he thought I was down for the count.

That mistake will cost him his life.

"Give. Me. The. Antidote. You. Fucking. Asshole," I say between agonizingly painful breaths.

My hand tightens around his neck, my fingers

pinching his veins and windpipe, ready to end this in whatever way I can.

"You won't get anything from me," he says, grabbing my wrist, his manicured nails digging into my skin. He draws blood, but I don't care.

"Last chance," I warn.

"Go to hell," he says, the whites of his eyes starting to slowly turn red as I cut off his air supply. He laughs manically, the last shreds of his composure dissolving as he realizes he's going to die. "I'll save you a seat when I get there."

"Have it your way."

If he won't give me the information I need, I'll find it myself. His entire compound belongs to me, now— with Drew in the security center, I have free reign.

I pour my magic into my palm, letting it seep from me into the man who has tormented me just for the hell of it.

He'll get my magic... just not in the way he wanted.

Ribbons of white light burn beneath his skin. His eyes go wide, his mouth opening as if he wants to scream, but nothing comes out. He just watches me, astonished, as my magic surges within him.

So close to having my power to himself—and yet so far. To taste it, but never wield it.

Seems like a fitting end.

The ribbons of white light begin to multiply until they cover his entire body. With a quiet little sigh, he stops fighting. The magic finally consumes him completely. He goes limp in my hand and dissolves into light, the weight from his body in my grip slowly dissolving into nothing.

As the last of him fades, I can't help but feel a bit disappointed. What a shame.

Ian Rixer was brutal, cruel, sadistic, and manipulative. He tried so hard to kill my sister. To kill Jace. To kill me. He burned and abused everyone around him until there was nothing left for him to take, and then he discarded them. It was just his way—to him, every living thing existed merely to serve him in some fashion.

It feels almost wasteful to give such a beautiful ending to such an ugly soul.

CHAPTER THIRTY-TWO

"Rory," a man says, his voice echoing. Strange.

I know that voice.

I squeeze my eyes shut, the world around me spinning and bright. Something pulses within me, radiant and overwhelming, stunning and marvelous.

And *powerful.*

"Rory," the voice says again, a little clearer this time.

I feel the soothing touch of warm hands, and though the world around me is startlingly bright, I squint until I see the dim outline of a face. Strong jaw. Blond hair. Stormy gray eyes.

As his fingers brush against my palms, my pulse slowly begins to settle. His touch soothes the blistering white light within me, calming it until I can see again. Think again.

I feel my feet touch the floor before I even realize I was hovering in the air. Instantly, I'm thrown off balance, and I fall into him. He wraps his arms around me, holding me tight and letting me rest against his hard body as I groggily come to.

The last few ribbons of white light fizzle away like water in a desert, and I'm left with an overwhelming exhaustion and a sharp pain in my chest. I want to sleep, for days if possible, and it's a struggle to even keep my eyes open.

"Can you hear me?" Jace asks quietly.

I weakly lift my chin and nod. "What—did I go somewhere?"

He chuckles. "You were floating a bit, but nothing crazy."

I laugh. I can't help it. Rubbing my face, I look around the room, trying to get my bearings. Irena still lays on the metal bed in the center of the room, one of the monitors shattered above her. Several soldiers lay dead on the floor. And Ian—

Beside me, a small pile of white dust is all that remains of the brutal asshole.

The thud of fists on the door to the hallway catches my attention, and very quickly, I remember everything still at stake.

A sharp and agonizing bolt of pain shoots through my chest, and I grimace as I hold a hand over the bullet wound. "Damn it."

"You're okay," Jace says quickly, as if he's trying to convince himself as well as me. He sets his hands on either side of my head, intently scanning my eyes for signs of shock, probably. "You're holding up great."

"Was that a compliment?" I ask weakly, grinning at my stupid joke. "Isn't that three in the same day? Do I have to start paying for these?"

He laughs. "Hang in there. We're almost out of the woods."

"Or the compound, rather," I say, slurring a little and still rather woozy.

Apparently, I tell terrible jokes when exhausted. Note to self—try not to talk when I get this way.

There's a sharp thud on the other side of the hidden door in the wall, and I instinctively lift my fists, ready to fight whatever comes through.

More soldiers, maybe. Guns. Hell, maybe a dragon or two.

When fighting the Vaer, any horrible thing I can imagine coming through that door is probably possible.

The jolt of adrenaline clears my head a little, helping me prepare for the fight. However, I don't know if I can access my magic again—not after an episode like that.

With another rough thud, the door swings open, and Tucker stands in the hallway in a full military stealth suit, covered head to toe in guns. A few of the holsters are missing their weapons, and I imagine he's had to use quite a few of them to get this far.

"That thing is heavy as *hell*," he snaps, gesturing over his shoulder at the portable medic tube Jace secured for Irena. "It's like pushing a food truck uphill."

I squint at him in confusion, a little caught off guard. "That's... oddly specific."

"Happy, Jace?" Tucker says, spreading his arms as if he just finished a magic trick. "I didn't leave you high and dry. Guess not all Knights are assholes, huh?"

"Come on, you two," Jace snaps, ignoring Tucker's jibe and grabbing the handle at the front of the advanced medical gurney. He lugs it toward Irena's bed and begins studying the various IVs hooked up to her.

As he examines her, I anxiously scan the gurney while Tucker keeps watch at the secret entrance. It reminds me of a glass coffin with a few blue screens slapped on the front of it, and goosebumps cover my arms at the thought.

"Good. We can do this." Jace pulls three of the IVs out of her, leaving only the saline solution. "Lift the lid, Rory."

I oblige him and unlock the top of the advanced gurney. It hisses and slowly lifts open, giving us plenty of space to slide my sister inside.

Together, Jace and I lift Irena and get her situated, hooking the saline solution to the inside of the lid. As we close the lid to seal her inside, a massively heavy thud rails against the door to the hallway, and I suspect we're about out of time.

"Can you guys get *on* with it?" Drew snaps over the loudspeaker.

"It's kind of a delicate process," Jace snaps back, his voice loud and irritated. "But by all means, keep distracting me!"

Tucker whistles urgently, ushering us into the tunnels.

"They're about two minutes from breaking down that door. We have to go."

"Did you bring the coms?" I ask Tucker as the gurney finally seals itself. A small blue screen at the foot of the wheeled table pops to life, and I get a glimpse of a heart rate monitor as it beeps in steady rhythm.

"Here," he says, tossing me two of them.

Jace and I each grab one and place it in our ears as we wheel Irena toward the tunnel.

"...and this place is *swarming*," Drew says into the comm.

"Rory, take point on the gurney," Jace says, snatching a rifle from Tucker's back.

"Hey!" Tucker says, annoyed. "I'm not a walking weapons rack! *Ask* first, man!"

Ignoring their banter, I grab the handles at the back of Irena's gurney and push her down the hall, her eerily pale face haunting me as we descend into the dark tunnels below the Vaer compound.

"Engaging lock," Drew says in my ear.

Behind me, the door to the sparse medic ward slams shut on its own, and a massive deadbolt slides across the door, sealing it.

I smirk. Good luck getting through *that*.

"Drew, we still need the antidote," I say, following Jace and Tucker as they lead the way through the tunnels.

"I've been looking," Drew says absently, like he's managing twenty things at once. "There's a research lab not far from you that might have a few vials. I'll guide you there."

For the next few minutes, we race through the tunnels to the sound of Drew cussing under his breath and guiding us through the halls.

"There," he snaps. "I see you on the cameras. That's the door."

I wheel the medic gurney to a stop and lean against the door, listening for signs of movement. Several machines whir to life, and the muffled conversation of a few people debating something filters through.

"Drew, how many people are in there?" I ask.

"Four. All scientists. Eight soldiers stand out in the hall, probably guarding it from you, but I can lock them out."

Good.

I can work with that.

"Here's the plan," Jace says quietly. "Tucker, stay here with the gurney. Rory—"

With all the remaining fury still left in my chest, I grab a handgun from Tucker's waist and kick open the door.

It bangs violently against the wall, and I lift the gun toward the first face I see as I enter. "You're going to hand me my sister's antidote, and you're going to do it *now*."

Drew sighs through the comm. "Engaging lock on the research lab's door..."

Four wide-eyed scientists in white lab coats stare at me like deer stuck in headlights.

"Now!" I snap, trying to shake them from their dazes.

They know *damn* well who I am and what I'm talking about.

"Okay!" a blonde woman says, lifting her hands in the air. "Okay, yes, it's—it's over here..."

"Get it," I snap, gesturing for her to get on with it.

She fumbles with a key ring in her pocket. Hands shaking, she finally manages to find the one she's looking for and slides it into the lock on a small cabinet in the wall. As she opens it, steam rolls out, hitting the floor like dry ice.

Carefully, she lifts a vial of green liquid. "This is what you want, right?"

"Hand it over," I demand.

She obliges me, and as her fingers brush my open hand, she trembles harder.

"This will cure her?" I ask, lifting the vial.

"Yes," the woman insists, shaking violently in fear.

"If it doesn't, you know I'm going to hunt you down, right?"

It's a lie. I just want to know it's real.

She nods, eyes wide, quivering and unable to speak. Unless she's the most brilliant actress in the world, this truly is some random scientist in the wrong place at the wrong time.

"All right, back to work," I say, gesturing with my gun to the vials and steaming beakers around us. "And thanks for your help."

I step into the hall and slip the vial in my pocket as the door closes behind me. The emergency deadbolt engages behind us, locking out anyone who might try to force their way into the tunnels after us.

Jace pinches the brim of his nose, eyes squeezed shut in frustration.

"What?" I ask, handing the gun back to Tucker. "It worked, didn't it?"

"Let's just go," Jace says, gesturing down the hallway.

"That was hot," Tucker says quietly, nudging me with his elbow as he races ahead of me to scout the corridors with Jace.

I grin. At least Tucker gets me.

We race through the halls toward our exit point. Every step brings us closer to freedom. Every second brings us ever closer to healing Irena and putting this whole mess behind us.

Very soon, the Vaer won't have any leverage on me anymore—and that's going to be so incredibly liberating.

But it all hinges on this—the exit.

Possibly the hardest part.

Getting away from a military compound without being noticed—it feels next to impossible.

But if anyone can do it, it's us.

We round the bend, and a rush of fresh air rolls over us as the massive double doors at the far end slowly open.

"I just opened all of the exits in the tunnels," Drew says

through the com in my ear. "Just to throw them off. That should leave them scrambling *just* long enough for us to get away."

"You're the best," I chime into the comm.

"Yeah," he says, and I can hear that cocky smirk in his voice.

All of us pick up the pace, running a little faster, excited to be done.

"Guys!" Drew says through the comm. "Lookout—"

"Jace, wait!" Tucker grabs the shifter's shirt and yanks him backward just as a hail of gunfire rips through the dark tunnel from another corridor.

As the storm of bullets slashes through the tunnel, the three of us take cover along the wall. Jace sets his hand against his abdomen, clearly unsettled, and looks at Tucker in astonishment.

"You—you saved my life," he says, as if utterly shocked by the concept.

"Well, yeah," Tucker says, shrugging as he cocks his rifle. "You're a jackass sometimes, but that doesn't mean I want you dead. Plus, she kind of likes you," he adds with a nod toward me. "So, you get extra Tucker-saves-the-day points, I guess."

With that, he aims his rifle down the adjacent corridor and opens fire. The grunt of men taking bullets fills the air, and several thuds hit the concrete floor.

After only a moment's pause, Jace joins the gunfight, and together the two of them make short work of the opposing forces.

As I guard Irena's gurney, one hand on my bleeding chest, I'm kind of jealous. I'm used to being in on the fun.

Injuries *suck*.

But as I look down at my sister's unconscious body, I'm filled with too much gratitude to care if I miss out on a firefight. At least she's safe.

Ish.

"Looks clear," Drew says through the comm. "I'm going to bail. Meet you guys back at the embassy. Keep me posted on your locations."

"Roger," Jace says, his tone crisp and militant again. "Tucker, take us out."

"Oh, so you like me now?" Tucker says with a grin.

"For the moment." Jace laughs. "Don't push your luck."

As we run into the night, the chop of helicopter blades

slicing through the air captures my attention. A short distance away, two helicopters wait for us.

"Wait, why are there two of them?" I ask, brow pinched in confusion.

"I called the second one," Jace says with a shrug. "It's good to have a decoy, so they don't know which one has Irena."

"Bullshit," Tucker says with a curt laugh. "You have the second one in case I failed to come through."

"Yeah," Jace says, grinning, his lie exposed.

Through the com in my ear, Drew chuckles.

Two women I've never seen before jump out of the first helicopter, hunching to avoid the whirring chopper blade as they race toward the gurney. They slide it out of my hands, easing it toward the helicopter with practiced grace.

I don't want to let go.

If I wasn't so weak from the bullet wound, I might not have.

One of the women scans my shoulder and frowns. Without a word, she yanks a small flashlight from her pocket and flashes it in front of my eyes, as if she's checking for something.

I wince in the sudden light. "Hey, what—"

"Sir, she needs medical attention!" the woman shouts at him over the loud whir of the helicopter. "The gunshot—"

"I know!" he shouts back. "We're heading back to my medical bay. Focus on the girl!" He nods toward Irena's gurney as the first woman locks it in place for the flight.

"Get her help immediately, then!" the woman warns, wagging her finger at him.

He nods, and she jogs back toward the chopper.

My heart twists, and a possessive impulse warns me to rip the gurney from their hands.

I just got my sister back—and now I already have to give her up?

My hands flex and stretch as I try to steel myself. This is the way it's supposed to go. They're professionals. They can help her.

I can't.

"Wait! Here," I say to the woman who just checked me, handing her the green vial from my pocket. "Do *not* lose this."

She nods and smiles reassuringly at me.

With that, they slide the doors closed, and the helicopters slowly begin to lift into the air. I hurry backward to give them space as they take off in unison.

And there goes my sister.

I hope we can get her the help she needs before it's too late.

And there it is again—hope. I've done all I can do. Now, yet again, I have to wait. I have to trust. I have to relinquish control.

It's more agonizing than any bullet wound.

"I'm out of the facility," Drew says through the com. "Are you guys clear, yet?"

"Almost," I reply.

"Wait, where's our ride?" Tucker asks as the helicopters speed off in different directions.

Ah, right. There's a reason I didn't tell Tucker this part.

At that, Jace smirks. His body shimmers, and I quickly step back as he begins to shift.

"Oh, hell no." Tucker says, shaking his head as he joins me. "You don't seriously expect me to let him carry me off like some damsel from a tower!"

As Jace's form grows, he stretches his massive wings,

his beautiful black scales shimmering in the moonlight. He opens his glowing blue eyes, digging his claws into the dirt, ready to fly.

With a few huffing breaths—dragon laughter—he grabs me and Tucker and bolts into the night, as silent and undetectable as a shadow.

"You're an *asshooooole*!" Tucker shouts up at the dragon carrying us off.

As the final shreds of adrenaline start to dissolve within me, I laugh. All I can feel is grateful—that we're out, that Irena's safe, and that I have such wonderful, ridiculous men in my life.

Even with a bullet in my chest, I'm pretty damn lucky.

CHAPTER THIRTY-THREE

"You're sure?" I say, leaning forward in my seat as I rest my elbows on my knees. "You're absolutely sure?"

Jace and I sit together in a hospital ward. Across from us, Irena lays in her new hospital bed—one that actually looks comfortable, thank goodness. A half dozen monitors beep and buzz around her, reporting just about every known vital sign.

As I move, however, the wound in my chest stings. I grimace, holding my hand over the bandages beneath my shirt. Jace sets a hand on my shoulder, watching me with a concerned expression, but I smile reassuringly at him.

I'm fine, really. I just need to move a little slower for a few days, that's all.

Thanks to the magic in my core, I'm already healing far faster than I would be without it—give me a few days, and all I'll have is a scar.

"The vial you, uh, *procured*," he says with an eye roll, "is responding well in the experiments they're running on her blood samples. So far, so good."

Wow.

We actually did it.

The real antidote.

I sigh with relief, setting my head in my hands as I let that sink in. Part of me was terrified that it was all a trick, that there wasn't even an antidote to begin with, that it was yet another lie the Vaer tried to stuff down my throat.

But it's real. And Irena's going to get better.

"How long?" I stand and walk to her side, leaning on the thin railing of her new gurney as I watch her face. She already looks better. Her skin has some color to it, now, and her pulse is normal.

Jace stands and slips his hands in his pockets. "How

long until she wakes up? We think we have about a week or two."

I frown. "A week?"

"Or two," he says again, no doubt trying to help me manage my expectations. "This antidote is designed for dragons, Rory. Not humans."

Ah, damn it. I knew there was a catch.

"It's okay," he says. "Because the tests are positive, it looks like she'll be able to take it. We just have to give it to her in smaller doses. That's why it'll take so long."

I nod, understanding the doctor's caution even though I wish he would hurry the hell up.

We stand together in silence for a moment, watching Irena breathe. After so long without her, I almost can't believe she's really here.

"Back in the compound," Jace says suddenly, jarring me from my thoughts. "When you killed Ian…"

I lift my gaze to meet his, wondering where he's taking this.

"I've never seen your magic react like that," Jace eventually says. "It was greater than any dragon I've ever seen, and to your credit, you kept fairly decent control."

"I guess I can handle being 'fairly decent,'" I say with a chuckle. "Thanks, I guess."

I smirk, wondering why compliments are so hard for this guy.

"Your magic is getting stronger, Rory," he says firmly. "And that means it's going to fight to control you. This will only get more difficult."

"I can handle it."

He smirks. "I know."

We let the conversation fade again, and I cross my arms as my thoughts race back to the Vaer facility, back to the near-death experiences, back to burning away Ian into white dust.

"Thank you," I say softly, taking a deep breath as I smile warmly at him. "You really came through."

He nods. "In the end, I would do just about anything for you, Rory." The corners of his mouth tilt upward, and he watches my face with guarded affection. "You know that."

As I sit on the edge of a cliff overlooking the

embassy, I sigh a happy sigh and lean back on my palms. My feet kick over the abyss as I watch Levi soar through the air, spinning, making the mists dance for me.

He pauses, grinning at me, and dives back into the white fog.

I smile. Goofball.

"Hey, babe," Tucker says, planting a kiss on my cheek as he sits beside me.

"You look chipper," I say with a grin.

"Jace doesn't want to kill me anymore," he says with a lazy shrug. "It puts a spring in your step, I won't lie."

I chuckle.

"Are we brooding?" Drew asks from behind us.

The massive shifter joins us and sits beside me, hugging one knee to his chest as he lets the other dangle over the cliff.

"I think we're watching Levi show off," Tucker says with a grin. "But yeah, she might be brooding."

"Hey." I lightly smack him in the arm.

Drew wraps an arm around my shoulder and playfully

kisses the side of my head. We stare out at the mists, letting our minds wander in the silence.

The Vaer still have one last piece of leverage over me—they know I'm a Spectre. They could reveal this to the world at any point, and it could ruin everything. So far, however, they've chosen not to—and I wonder if that's because they want me *alive.*

To make matters worse, Zurie is after me and desperate enough to make alliances with the Knights. So even if the Vaer don't reveal my secret, there's a good chance the Knights will.

How fun.

None of that matters, though—I have bigger fish to fry. The bosses want to meet with me, and I need to figure out a way to bring Levi back from the brink—before I lose him forever.

But I'm not alone anymore.

My magic gets stronger every day, and there's no telling what my limits really are. With Tucker, Jace, and Drew at my side, I can do anything.

And if I can truly get my sister back, I'll be utterly unstoppable—as long as she isn't the one who betrayed me to the Vaer in the first place.

I frown, unwilling to believe it. But soon—very soon—
I'll be able to ask her myself.

Ready for more? Here's what to do next...

1. Join the **FB group**

2. Sign up for the **email list**

3. Go **preorder the next book**

YOU'RE MISSING OUT...

Join the exclusive group where all the cool kids hang out… Olivia's secret club for cool ladies! Consider this your formal invitation to a world of hot guys, fun people, and your fellow book lovers. Olivia hangs out in this group all the time. She made the group specifically for readers like you to come together and share their lives and interests, especially regarding the hot guys from her novels.

Check it out! Everyone in there is amazing, and you'll fit right in.

https://www.facebook.com/groups/LilaJeanOliviaAsh/

Sign up for email alerts of new releases AND exclusive

access to bonus content, book recommendations, and more!

https://wispvine.com/newsletter/dragon-dojo-brother-hood-signup/

Enjoying the series? Awesome! Help others discover the Dragon Dojo Brotherhood by leaving a review at Amazon.

http://mybook.to/DDB1

ABOUT THE AUTHOR

OLIVIA ASH

Olivia Ash spends her time dreaming up the perfect men to challenge, love, and protect her strong heroines (who actually don't need protecting at all). Her stories are meant to take you on a journey into the world of the characters and make you want to stay there.

Reviews are the best way to show Olivia that you care about her stories and want other people discover them. If you enjoyed this novel, please consider leaving a review at Amazon. Every review helps the author and she appreciates the time you take to write them.